How They Spent

the Money

How They Spent the Money

SJ Alawine

LONGSHORE
REBEL

PRESS

For all the women in my family, young and old, here still and passed on

GENEALOGY

Granny Kate (Katherine **White**) →

1.Everett, m Pauline	2.Baby, died	3.Prentiss	4.Thomas	5.Baby, died	6.Willis	7.Janie, (m Daniel **Williams**)	8.Liza, (m Calvin **Tanner**)
Anne		James ("Preacher")	Jimmy		Alex Guy	Sandra	Jean Ann
Larry		June	Dobber			Jerry	(m Bob **Clark**)
Marcus		Rhonda	Linda			Maggie	1.Sue
Porter			Richard				Berry (Calvin Asberry)

How They Spent the Money

"SO SHE GOT the DNA results back, and she's just your average white chick?"

"No Native American at all," he affirmed.

"Not second cousin to Sacagawea, once removed?"

"Not even four times removed. Just a plain old white girl. She was very disappointed. Of course she didn't tell *me*, but she did tell Mama, and I found out from her."

I had to keep my eyes on the road, but I could laugh with Berry, and did.

"I told you, DNA always trumps genealogy sheets," he said when we stopped laughing.

I concentrated on the mudholes and washes and didn't argue, because I sometimes did agree with him, and it was rendering me obsolete.

Not a great thought to have at the beginning of this little journey of ours; but with hindsight later I'd end up considering it rather minor after all, compared to a dead body washing up in the creek.

LEAVING TOWN, I'D merged from four good lanes of highway into two at a place where the civil engineers decided there wasn't enough traffic to justify a big road anymore. Things got rougher from there, small patches of bitterweed crowding the edge, pines lurking overhead, untrimmed, inexorably creeping inward to reclaim the land, uproot the asphalt, recycle it back into the rock and petroleum it came from. I'd told Berry that, when we left his mother's; and he said, "Not our problem. Maybe in 50 million years."

"Won't be *our* problem then, either."

He made a noise that could've been agreement, or scoffing. I was used to his stretches of silence; he was one of those types you might call "introverted", or maybe "antisocial", depending on how favorably you felt about them in the moment.

"Your car's gonna be muddy," he remarked when we left. Liza's house was right at the turnoff from the two-lane highway, right where the open places holding woods at bay got fewer and farther between and were ringed with barbed wire. On some days dust churned up behind you, hiding where you'd come from; sometimes, like today, mud oozed up around your wheels like slow-hardening lava, hindering your journey back; but in any sort of circumstance or weather, you always felt uprooted, transplanted from the clean and modern into another part of the world, a place you'd seen in dreams or, sometimes, nightmares.

"Can't help the mud. It must've poured buckets out here last night."

He sipped from the big mug of coffee he'd brought along, slurping because it was still too hot—I guessed: I didn't take my eyes off the ruts and heaps of gravelly slush we were easing through.

"I thought maybe we'd be the first people back here this morning, but looks like there's already been traffic, and it's played hell with the road."

He made the mocking sound again. "Lot of bother for you, having to drive out here today, gotta be *today*, to get this stuff."

I explained to him that I'd told her I'd come this morning, had promised a week ago; how would any of us have known then it would storm the night before?

"Could've put it off till things dried up."

I slapped sideways at him, prompting him to gesture emphatically at the road. "Both hands, please. I know you: You just didn't wanna go by yourself."

"Look, your mother's house is on the way, you know, and if I had to do it, well, there you were. So why not bring you, too." I'd felt mildly guilty for showing up unannounced, uninvited. Things were very quiet at Liza's when I'd knocked on her screen door—not even a TV going with game shows or the morning news, and he'd approached with her to see who'd be at her house that time of day. I'd told the explanation while he fixed the mug:

"I'm running up to Granny Kate's to get those things she said she wanted me to have. I saw Berry was here, and thought he'd like to go along." Liza'd nodded, as if she understood it all just from those words alone.

He'd shrugged: "I'll go, sure."

"I hope you got some breakfast," I added now; then—because I wanted to know, and he was antisocial: "So, you here to visit a few days?"

"Just till this afternoon. She's old."

Did that mean he was visiting Liza because she was old, or his visit would be short because she was old? I puzzled over it. Either way was true: She *was* old. So was the woman we were going to see—Liza's mother, his grandmother, my grandmother, and if he'd just let me know he intended to be here today, so I hadn't found it out by seeing his car parked by Liza's front porch, I might *have* put off the errand for another day, just spent the morning there with him and Liza, a quiet, cozy chat.

But I was glad he'd agreed to ride along, fixed that coffee, and was in my car, introvert though he was.

We passed Irene Posey's little brick house, with a carport where she parked her ancient Ford LTD. Then trees shouldered in again and the ground was marshy at the swamp where Conjure Creek slashed through.

The creek had flowed deep last night, you could tell, deep and fast enough to pile rocks and pieces of trees against the crumbling supports of the ancient bridge: "Weight Limit 2 Tons," the sign said. A road crew toiled lazily, shoving bits of debris around as we crossed the still-swirling water. There were eight of them, eight workers: five on the bridge deck, standing in one spot trying to look busy, and the other three leaning against the old pilings almost underneath. Berry snorted a short laugh. "Eight fat guys in one place. Trying to look busy."

I looked in the rearview mirror, saw Edwin Bonner, the county constable Granny Kate depended on for routine patrols, behind me, pulling over at the bridge. The crew leaped away from the pilings, got to work then, waving their hands for him to come here, look— They gathered together and pointed toward the eroded bank.

"What's she giving you?" he asked.

"A boxful or two of old letters, a few pictures, I think some family records—cards, mementos; you know."

"You being the one of us all that keeps that genealogy crap. The designated library. Watch that hole there."

I hit brakes; slid. " 'Genealogy crap'? Don't sneer at me. One day you'll wanna know something and you'll have to ask *me* for it. Be prepared to beg, if you don't start respecting me."

He laughed, reached over to pat my face, a little hard, actually—such small things we could do, and did, to invoke the days long gone. "You better modernize. Scan the pictures, put all that stuff in your computer. Need any help?"

"I'm capable, smartass. All of it'll still have to be stored, somewhere. Those words and pictures in my hard drive are just things you read. The actual stuff—*that*, you touch; that's your real connection to the past."

He snickered, and it was then that he told me his middle-aged sister Jean Ann had done that DNA test, a new thing she'd found out about just recently, to prove we were all part Indian.

AND THEN ONCE more barbed wire guarded an open spot where Granny Kate's cypress-plank home, early 1900's, and a few small outbuildings huddled. It looked like a living history exhibit somewhere; you'd expect reenactors in long dresses and bonnets milling around, stirring molasses over fires.

I parked in the shade of an ancient oak, well away from the house.

We could see the side and back yards were layered with soft patterns of sandy-colored, sinuous mud over the sparse grass, and on top of all that, pebbles and bits of trash, a Styrofoam cup or two from God knew where, an empty potato chip bag. Standing above a quarter-inch of silt now in the garish sunlight was the faucet where Berry and I had long ago washed our hands too many times to count after helping with garden chores, and the faucet wove itself into that memory, and even an image of the two of us standing there, washing, splashing each other in the heat.

"Water got up pretty high," he murmured pensively.

Then we sat without saying anything else for a minute or two.

One storm after another had blown up this summer, thunder at first almost as gentle as the high school tubas and drums playing at football games five miles away, then hail crashing down here and there, falling like a hissing white curtain. Wind knocked down big old trees sometimes and flung unripe walnuts around like little green golf balls. From my living room I'd wonder how I'd ended up in town, me, a country girl raised on a dirt road like this one, listening for gritty, gravelly noises as rare traffic carefully eased past in the rain. These days I stood at a window, hearing instead the regular *ssshhhhisss* of tires on asphalt...me, used to moonlight illuminating sodden fields of overgrown Johnsongrass instead of gleaming onyx on expanses of wet street. Street lights dimmed in sync right after the next flash of lightning, a driver stepped on brakes, startled, maybe, skidding on the wet street. In a town you felt safer, people close at hand, and if it happened to you, it happened to them, too, but out on the country roads you felt alone, separated from neighbors by the sheets of driving rain and hail and the acres of trees flailing about in the tempest. It was a stormy summer; and I wondered—my insides tightening the way they do when you're in a waiting room outside intensive care—how Granny Kate fared in this old house as the wind had tossed rain-heavy branches this way and that and rain filled the ditch and then her yard and then Conjure Creek, and eroded supports under that old bridge you had to cross if you went to see her. And what we would do if the bridge one day was just gone and we couldn't go back there.

Berry, silent and brooding in the passenger seat next to me, probably had the same things going through his mind.

The TV weatherman this morning had called it a locally heavy downpour, for in town we'd had rain but nothing like what the north part of the county had; and the cloud that brought lightning scaring the drivers on my street moved on in ten minutes. But, said the weatherman, fifteen miles up the highway it was a different matter, trees down, roads washed, some damage, and so on and so on, with pictures flashed onscreen to make you nervous, to make you feel as if you had shared that experience.

"Lots of trash out back," Berry muttered. "Gonna have to get somebody to clean it up."

There was movement behind the screen door of the house; we could tell someone had walked around inside, maybe wondering why we were parked in the yard.

"She probably couldn't see it was us, might not know your car, might be wondering what we're up to. I hope Porter's there," he added. "Maybe I'll help him start picking up that trash out back before we leave."

I didn't answer that one. I hoped Porter wasn't there, and I felt guilt about that, as I always did, but I couldn't help it. So, yes, I'd been relieved to see Berry's car, to have him along, so I wouldn't have to be here, just me, by myself, with them today.

2

THE HOUSE SEEMED quite silent; but as we approached the steps, we heard her TV through the screen door, and the rustle of upholstery, or maybe paper, or maybe shoes shuffling on the floor—it was hard to tell...a soft noise as of old dry leaves moving around in a breeze. Berry knocked briskly and called out, "Granny Kate! Don't bother—we'll let ourselves in."

But of course she wouldn't have that, and, anyway, he nearly tore the handle off the screen door trying to open it.

"Sonofabitch."

She tottered nearer, the corner of her mouth twitching as if she considered laughing at his sotto voce curse, and she unhooked the latch.

"Well, that's nice."

"Sorry." He shook his hand.

I leaned in to hug her.

"At least you started fastening that screen door," he remarked.

"It'd just slow somebody down long enough to let me see who's about to knock me in the head," she told him. "Let me get you a bandaid." And she turned her back to us and fetched him one from a box on the table near her armchair. Which made me consider that she needed a box of bandaids at hand all the time.

It was steamy inside. I always felt like a peeping-Tom or worse when I so much as glanced around in here; did it seem I was making an inventory? So I said we ought to move outside to the porch where it was shady and not too hot yet. And it was there we sat, not wanting to meet her eyes, glancing down instead at the blue- and green-printed fabric of the cotton dress that fell across her knees.

"How was it last night?" Berry said.

She gazed at us, a querulous sort of irritated expression furrowing her brows. "'Bout what you'd expect. We stayed in. I'm not scared of weather. You've seen it all when you're my age."

"I'll get us somethin' to drink," Berry offered, but she shooed him off and eased up from her rocking chair and accepted assistance only with the door.

"Long's I can have company, I'll do the servin'."

My imagination and past experience brought up a vision of Mother, or Berry's mother, worming details out of us about this visit: How'd she look? She get around all right today? ...Well, yes, she stirred around pretty well, in fact, got up and fetched us some drinks—and then the accusation: *You let her wait on you?*

"Get in there and help her," I hissed.

"Said she didn't want any help."

We heard the rustling again, the whisper of shuffling shoes and of well-worn clothing swishing around, and in a moment she returned with a pitcher of lemonade in one hand and four small plastic vessels stacked together, probably stuck together in the summer humidity of the drying-up puddles, four glasses, not three. She took her seat again, groaning just a little in response to the creak in her left knee. She'd outlived those knee replacements some years back, those metal appliances. Like so many other things and people in her life, they wore out before she did. She did let Berry pull the cups apart and fill all of them, hand them around with a little flourish. I sipped and waited and tried not to look at the fourth one which she set down beside her, her gentle rocking accompanied by the tapping of her gnarled fingers on the chair-arm. She still kept a few chickens which pecked the ground of the side yard inside a little fenced-in area. One, loose, roamed around toward the front now, and she glared at it, and her rocking became more agitated, but I didn't particularly want to put the bird back up, and I noticed Berry didn't offer, either.

We sat in expectant silence, sipping the lemonade. One of her grandsons had nailed some fake Victorian gingerbread to the porch some years back and then painted it pink, since faded and peeled. I noticed that once in a while Berry's gaze turned briefly there in a kind of skeptical glance.

"What do you know that's new?" she asked.

"Not much. We just came to visit, and get those old records," I offered. "The ones you told Mother to have me come get. Like I said I would, the other day," I reminded her, trying to sound dutiful.

Guilt affects posture, Berry had told me one time. He had used that bit of knowledge when he talked with teenagers; you had to be something of a psychologist to be superintendent of an alternative school. I realized I was slouching as if I carried a heavy backpack, and stared ever lower, now at her feet instead of just her knees, waiting for her to speak, this woman who, through my mother had eventually produced me, who'd given me a fair share of the genes that made me, to whom I had nothing really to say. The hen squawked. She scowled at it.

"Porter fixes us somethin' to keep cool with every morning, after he stirs and gets dressed," she said. "He's always worryin' about us drinkin' enough water."

"You ought to run that air conditioner in this heat," Berry said solicitously.

"You hot?" There was that odd little twitch on her lips again: "Y'all wanted to be outside." Which was true, of course. "Too early in the day to turn it on now."

"I hope you do use it, though."

She flapped her hand toward him. "When that sister of yours and her old man brought that thing in, I told 'em they dry you out, that's what they do. They take the water out of you. You use 'em, you can't ever quit. They got you hooked."

"You could be right, there," and he laughed a little. "But, really, was it bad out this way last night?"

She shrugged. "Just a lot of lightnin' and rain. Porter took a walk after it got cool, but he come home about nine, right after it started. Saw the chicken house was all shut up, chickens all in it." She glared again at the errant hen. Berry or I ought to get up and do something about it, I guessed, since it was worrying her.

"Well, tell me where those boxes are, and I'll take 'em to the car," he said all of a sudden, a non sequitur if ever there was one.

"Sit down and just visit," she ordered. "Porter can bring 'em after a while. He knows where I put 'em. They aren't heavy. Besides," she went on, "I want to hear about this music thing."

His back straightened, and he pinched at the flesh under his chin. So she knew about James's Civil War club and the awkward prank the two of us had played a couple of months ago. Berry glanced at me, and I at him, like two guilty children caught licking our fingers and then dredging them through the sugar bowl, which she had in fact caught us doing years ago here in this very house. It was faster than using a spoon, and sneakier.

"Music?" I said.

"Aren't you two a little old to be playin' jokes on James Preacher?"

"We are," Berry agreed with a laugh. "And we won't do it again."

"I hope not. Caused enough trouble for a while. You ought to be ashamed." Then, her face crinkling up at the corners of her eyes: "So tell me what you did. I heard some of it, but Liza wouldn't tell all of it."

So he did, a summarized version, anyway: "I slipped a CD to James by Maggie, since he trusts her."

"Or did," I said.

"I got tired of everything he's been saying about me. Don't *I* count?" he said plaintively, and guffawed, and she laughed with him, a little. "So he played it at his club meeting."

"Did you put bad music on it?"

"Well, to me it wasn't bad," he mumbled. "Probably surprised him. Should've listened to it ahead of time."

She shook her head.

We were all silent for a few minutes again, as if straining to hear that water, the tea-colored creek flowing onward underneath the old bridge, but it was too far down the road; we couldn't hear it from her house. I followed her eyes to the side yard, and that chicken, saw the new thin layer of silt where the water'd got up during the night; had that made noise like the creek, had she had fearful thoughts as it washed around the house?

It had always been easy to come here for the family get-togethers—more people talking, reminiscing, remembering things through filters of their own, all different, and nobody had to engage in actual conversation with her, but only to ask how she was, or if she wanted somethin' out of the kitchen; because, what would you say, otherwise? She was our Parvati, our ancestral mother enthroned on her rocking chair; we offered her food and drink but couldn't talk to her.

"Would you just put that old biddy up for me, Berry?"

He twitched as if she'd thrown water at him. "I never was any good with hens, you know that."

"I would *love* to hear a story you haven't ever told us before," I said hesitantly. "Something maybe none of us ever asked you."

She gazed past me into the yard for so long that I didn't know if she'd heard me, then brought her eyes back to mine. "Don't ever ask an old lady to start talking. We will do it. But now"—she pointed a spectral, gnarled finger at him—"I bet you got somethin' to ask. You always do. Always gettin' things out of me to write your own stories about."

"Maybe not, this time," he said. "I just rode up today with Maggie, to visit. And, God, it *is* quiet. I always forget. There hasn't been a car go past since we got here. Makes me wonder if the crew's closed off the bridge to inspect it, after the storm...." He looked up the road, but we couldn't see that bridge from here.

"I doubt it. It's held many a year. It's fine. Not too many folks live back here anymore. You're just not used to not havin' people come and go all the time."

"Was it lonely after people moved out?"

She answered me but kept staring toward the bridge she couldn't see. "I had Marcus and Anne and Larry. And Porter."

"Yes, you had to raise your own grandchildren"—I wanted to say it; it was there in my mouth to say, and as if she knew that, she went on: "You do what needs doin'. Somebody has to do it." She glanced back at me, and now for a moment the cloudy eyes seemed piercing and clear, the brown-black color of the water in the cypress swamp spanned by that bridge we had crossed on the way in. She owned that cypress swamp and about eight hundred acres of mostly good land besides, none of it farm land anymore, although her older children had picked cotton off it long years ago.

"Really, nothin' much's ever happened to me. I grew up and I got married and had eight babies, popped 'em out fast, too fast. That was what it was, in my day. And all but two of 'em's gone. I'm an old lady that's buried her children. There is nothing good or encouraging about that. They tell me I'm still sharp and I should be grateful. So I guess I am. You wanna hear interesting things, you probably need to talk to somebody else. Porter!" she yelled all of a sudden. "Where are you?"

He appeared unexpectedly from around the corner of the porch, where he'd probably been all along, with a half-full garbage bag in one hand, the other holding two beat-up shoeboxes balanced on his hip.

"You need to put that biddy up."

"I'll put it up, directly. Here are your boxes, Maggie. They have a lot of old things in them."

"How are you, Porter," I said.

"Lettin' that bird have its freedom just a while longer," he told her. Then he turned toward me, though he didn't exactly meet my eyes. "Your tires, they don't look like the tread's all that good. Don't think I'd wait till the rain started before I left. The gravel's washed off the road, and your tires aren't new."

"I'll watch," I said and glanced up at the sky where only a few clouds passed overhead.

He climbed the steps to set the boxes and the sack of garbage on the porch and reached for the fourth glass, draining it fast, gulping the lemonade noisily, and put it down, playing with it, rolling it around on the circle of its base. I was almost mesmerized, watching the tumbler pick up glints of light and reflect them on the battered boards, so I looked away, and at him, instead.

"Every time I see you, I always think you are the very image of your mama," he told me gently. He smiled at the chair I sat in, then turned his eyes toward the chicken in the yard and made a cackling sound, which startled the hen, so it flapped its wings and sought the haven of the fenced-in area, skittering back and forth against the fence, gabbling, while the birds on the other side of the enclosure edged away, clucking in sympathy.

"Quit tormentin' it and put it up," Granny Kate ordered, but her lips smiled.

Porter laughed, inched silently down the steps again and approached the hen. When he was a little boy trying to escape the everlasting teasing of his cousins, he would hang out with the chickens, squatting low on the ground next to them, cooing and clucking as if he felt as one with them, figuring out things about their behavior and watching their jittery little movements. That was in the days when more people than just Granny Kate kept chickens. Now it seemed to be mostly his job, instead of hers.

He captured the escaped bird and took it to the opening in the enclosure and tossed it gently inside before checking, with excruciating slowness, to see that the gate was latched. "Don't know how it got out. Maybe it wanted its freedom so much it defied its biology and flew over the fence."

"Or maybe it had already got out and you just missed seeing

it," she contradicted sharply.

He didn't seem to take offense: "Maybe." He came back to the porch. "How're you, Berry? I've always wondered something: Did you hate it when they made fun of your name? I would; I'd hate it. They made fun of mine before, too. Asked me when my train had left."

"You see what I mean, Maggie—now, there's a story behind that, and I could tell it, if you want," Granny Kate said suddenly.

"No, please do not tell that one," Porter said, not quite smiling.

"Or *you* could put it in one of your things you write. That's why *you're* here, find some other things to write about, isn't it?"

Berry stared at her. "I came with her because the road was a mess, she didn't want to do it by herself—"

"I know you well," she interrupted, shook her finger at him. "But I'm out of stories. I'm ninety-nine. I already gave you all I had, all my stories. I have no more stories. I'm finished with it." She leaned near him, clutched his knee in a grip that looked tight and not altogether affectionate, but which a casual observer might just think was her way of supporting herself as she leaned over.

"Everybody loves a good story," he said gently, cautiously.

"They aren't all good. Past gets messy dug up. Like that chicken yard. Best let it fill in so you don't have to smell it," and she let go of his leg.

"Archeologists that dug up your back yard a hundred years from now would still find that chicken shit," he said very softly. "No matter how much stuff was on top of it. It'd still be there."

"And it'd still be chicken shit, too, wouldn't it. Wouldn't've changed into gold." She did not laugh, but her lips wore a frozen, grim smile. She sat quite still for a moment, staring at that empty road.

Then he said a strange thing that made me hate him for that moment: "I don't mind not having the gold. The shit will work just as well."

"Let it pass! Bible says to forgive and forget," she countered, and they'd started talking about something I didn't follow; but it seemed Porter understood, a secret little smile pulling at his mouth.

Berry raised his brows. "Oh, does it? I don't remember that 'forget' part."

"Didn't Liza ever make you read your Bible?"

"Oh, I read it," he told her grimly. "I read it enough. Don't go quoting it to me, please. Depends on if it's Old Testament or New Testament justice."

"Well, Maggie's getting those boxes, so I tell you what: I'm gonna send you home with something, too. I'll give you the old family Bible right now, today. It's got that tiny little print I can't read anymore anyway. And I will ask you next time I see you if you've read any of it, and you'll have to tell me." She began to raise herself slowly from the rocker.

Berry sat gently pinching the flesh of his upper throat under his chin, worrying it nervously, a flat, unemotional expression on his face. Tension release, he told me later. He wanted to decline that gift but didn't dare, wanted to tell her not to preach at him but at James Preacher who needed it more.

Granny Kate paused at the door. "What's Edwin Bonner doin' here? Ain't that him drivin' up?"

Edwin, a tall, overweight man with surprisingly black hair, who wore large belt buckles because someone once told him he looked like Elvis, came to the edge of the porch and parked one shoe on the bottom step. "Maggie, Miss Kate, Porter, how you all? I see you made it okay last night." I noticed he didn't speak to Berry; still mad about that "Elvis" piece, it seemed.

"Little lightnin', some rain, that was all," she said scornfully. "Got into the back yard, but we'd already put up the chickens, so it didn't do nothin' but clean out the droppin's, you know. Buried 'em under some more mud," she added, pointedly glancing at Berry.

Edwin laughed softly with her, and his face got serious. "Miss Kate, there any old cemetery maybe on the back of your land somewhere, maybe some old unmarked family cemetery?"

I noticed her back got stiff and straight and her brows lowered over her sometimes bright, sometimes cloudy eyes. "None I ever knew of."

"Well, it did rain an awful lot, lotta water runnin' last night…it could've come from up higher, I reckon…" He glanced up the road toward Conjure Hill and scratched absently on his chin, and like people standing next to one person who looks into the sky we were all, even Porter, compelled to turn.

Conjure Hill looked fantastically, cartoonishly steep from here—an optical illusion heightened by the presence of a cluster of tall pines on one side of the road at the top. You got up there, anticipating a picturesque view to reward your climb, an idyllic pastoral scene spread out beneath you; and, after gazing downward for a time, the stillness and utter quiet that had at first struck you as so peaceful brought instead a terrible melancholy, for there below was just an old dirt road bounded by beggar's lice and blackberry thickets, an old tumbledown house in the poorest state in the country, and nothing romantic about any of it at all. The hill, a ridge that marked the east edge of Granny Kate's property, was next to impassable in bad weather, going up or even descending, because the road was not only steep but also curved in a half-C midway down. From the high spot the land tumbled into a cypress slough, the creek bisecting it; Granny Kate's house was halfway between the hill and the swamp. Behind her henhouses the land began to rise again and leveled off into acres of mostly gently rolling timbered land that was the second-best possible playground for us grandchildren and great-grandchildren when we'd visited her.

—Second-best after the hill which, with its name, was too awesome for any but the biggest fools of us to attempt on our bicycles. Some people claimed it was one of the last straggling hills in the Appalachians. We could walk up it, puffing harder and harder as we neared the top and saying, "Fuckin' hill!" once we were out of the adults' hearing—though many of them would and did say that, themselves, we weren't supposed to, being sinless infants. We'd stand at the apex and admire from there the view of Granny Kate's weathered gray cypress house and the yard giving way to the forest behind—but we didn't actually play there. All our lives we'd heard about how the car came down the hill too fast to make the curve and ran over our cousin Dobber's foot, which—after a few days' neglect because his parents put off going to a doctor—eventually required the amputation of about half of it. It being an authentic and not just a boogerman story—Dobber had a block in one of his boots to show us—we chose to ease down the hill through the trees, a good distance away from the road, when we got tired of just looking at the view.

"What you talkin' about, Edwin?"

"Miss Kate, nothin' for you to worry about. The men yonder"—he motioned toward the creek and the swamp—"they was a box washed up under them limbs they been clearing out, a fair-sized good stout box, good thick cypress box"—he measured two feet or so between his hands—"and the men they didn't much think anything about it, but you know people, so they opened it, and it was, well, I guess somebody used it for a coffin sometime or other, because it was the remains of a baby."

"A baby, Edwin? Good Lord."

"Yes, ma'am. Been dead many years, looked like. Box tryin' to come apart on us, but it was fixed up sometime or other with a gown of some kind—not much left of it, but it was fixed up once, a little lace left now, and we have to take it in, you know. So I came to ask if you knew about some old family graveyard on your land."

She shook her head, her eyes fixed on the distance where the bridge would be if she could see it from here. "My Lord. I have no idea why it would be there."

"Maggie." He jerked his head toward his car. I scrambled down the porch, Berry tumbling after me. Edwin addressed his remarks backwards.

"Miss Kate, now don't let it worry you much; people's lived in these parts a long time, and likely it's something from long ago. I just wanted you to know we was takin' it in to the coroner. I'll check back on you and Porter later today. You don't worry now.

"Maggie," he went on, "I guess I shouldn't've told her, but it was her property it was on."

"She'd've found out, Edwin, she keeps up. People talk."

"That's true. Now, I don't know I can keep it out of the news. It's not typical for an old lady like her to still be livin' by herself, well, even with Porter around to help."

"Porter? He's probably more a hindrance than a help."

"Y'all like to believe that, don't you? Whatever he does, here she still is, living here, at her age. Anyway, it's just my advice, if either of you got connections down there at the paper—"

Berry started to say something, but Edwin went on, ignoring him: "You ought to tell them not to say much about it—tell them not to be specific about where it happened, so nobody comes up here to bother her, you know? They don't have to tell every single detail, do they?"

"No."

"And in the meantime the coroner'll try to figger out how old it is and whatever else he can."

I shivered, remembering all the times as a child I had played in those woods near the creek, all the times I had stumbled and skidded down the bluff. And all those times maybe right past a baby in a stout cypress box.

"I'll see to it they leave out her name," Berry said.

"Relic hunters don't have no respect. Conspiracy folks'll be up here tryin' to find something else," he added.

"I'll see to it it's handled," Berry repeated. "Can we take a look?"

"Why on God's earth would you want to do that?"

"I've seen worse."

Edwin gave him a calculating, studying look and jerked his head slightly toward the porch. "Ought not to upset her by openin' it right here."

"We'll follow you back down the road a ways, how about that?" Berry offered, and with another look and at last a shrug, Edwin waved to Granny Kate and left.

I whispered to Berry over my shoulder. "We ought to stay with her long enough to see she's all right, people might know already, those guys down there at the bridge...they could've already taken pictures, called people." I glared backwards at his soft laugh.

"I'm going to look."

"You won't if I don't stop. My car."

"Oh, you're gonna stop, because you'll be behind Elvis there, everybody stops to see Elvis."

"I hope it gives you nightmares. I hope you can't sleep tonight or tomorrow neither."

We sidled back to the porch, not wanting to give too much information out. She was still staring at that distant point, an annoyed and somehow puzzled expression on her face.

"People ought to've seen to it their loved ones was properly took care of," she commented.

"Maybe that was 'properly took care of' for those days," Berry said.

"Well, I guess *this'll* be bringin' more traffic," she said resentfully.

"Edwin and I're gonna ask for the media not to say where it was found."

"Yeah, I guess you could do that." Her eyes came back to him and now they were bright, crinkled in the corners with that smile that forced up the loose flaps of her face. "You know, I do read, or I get Hazel or Porter to read to me sometimes—you tell 'em all that; I know they think I ain't got good sense anymore." She paused: "But I do keep up, and I did 'specially like that thing you wrote about Jean Ann."

"Jean Ann? I don't use people's names, not in my humor pieces, I could get sued for that, you know—what made you think I ever wrote anything about Jean Ann?" He winked at her.

She chuckled softly.

Porter sat on the edge of the porch, his legs dangling over, his shoes swishing against the damp ground. I watched the fretful, anxious tapping of Granny Kate's fingers on her rocker, and she noticed I was staring. "I will be fine," she told me briskly. "Things like this don't bother me; I've seen it all. I'm a tough old woman. Y'all go on and do what you need to. And come back and visit again, but don't wait long."

"We'll see you soon."

She nodded slightly, and I knew she knew we probably wouldn't. Porter slid off the porch to walk around my car, inspecting it, and when he kicked each one of the tires and twice said, "It's gonna rain!", I just had to go, even if it meant meeting Edwin to look in that stout cypress box.

"Somebody needs to teach me how to drive better so I can take us to get groceries," Porter said. "I have tried to get somebody to do it for a long time." I looked at Granny Kate to see how I should respond to that. "I drive out here, but not on the big roads," he went on. "I need to get my license, so we don't have to depend on ever'body else."

"I'll ask around who can do that," I said.

"It would keep us more independent. Now if it starts rainin', you oughta slow down," and he swung himself back onto the porch with surprising agility and headed into the house.

Granny Kate just sat and watched with that far-off bridge not in her sight, the bridge at which, as we neared it, I saw the patrol car parked. I stopped just behind Edwin. A cold, suspicious look on his face, he watched Berry open his door.

"Come take just a peek," Berry whispered.

"Go to hell."

He laughed at me and conveniently left the door open so I could hear whatever he and Edwin might have to say to each other, but I turned the radio on to drown it all out. Edwin opened the trunk of the patrol car and wrestled with something out of my sight, then delicately, gently even, lifted a wooden lid up to chest level. Berry leaned over and gazed for a moment. The *shisshissing* of the water under the bridge, which I could just barely hear over the jangling of the rock music, the respectful silence of the workers who stood at the other side of the road, even the steady rise and fall of Berry's shirt as he breathed—it all seemed to last many minutes.

Liza would've said it was a bad sign. Things happened neatly, predictably in town, the way they were supposed to. But nothing out here had ever been civilized enough to surprise you when something like this turned up. It was maybe even appropriate for it to wash up from the ground here, a long-dead, failed and forgotten thing.

Edwin eased the lid down and wrestled with whatever he had, before—a fastener, maybe, a rope or something—and shut the trunk lid. I saw Berry's mouth move; they nodded at each other coldly, and we drove off to our own particular destinations.

"Did you hear what Porter said?"

"Which one of the things?" I asked.

"About the chicken wanting its freedom enough to make it defy its biology. I did not expect that out of him."

"He spent a lot of time talking to 'em; he would know. Guess you'll have to put that into one of those things you write."

That was mean; so he was quiet for the space of a mile. "You should've looked," he said at last.

I waited at the stop sign for two cars to go past. "I wonder why Edwin took it into the patrol car. Why he didn't wait for the coroner to come out and get it, look around to see if he could find anything else to show where it came from."

"I actually asked him that. He said it was all of one piece, and he saw no need in making a production, getting too many people out, causing too much publicity. That's what he said." The second car went by, and I looked and noticed he was frowning a little. Puzzled-looking. I pulled through the stop sign.

"Aren't you even a little curious about it?" he asked.

"I've seen dead babies before. Or did you forget. Bad enough when they're something more than just bones."

That shut him up. And it was also mean, and I was ashamed and glad we were at his mother's house by then. I went inside, to be respectful, made small talk as he called someone. Liza and I eavesdropped as he identified himself—his name was fairly well known by now, and he used that. Somebody passed him on to the editor whom he asked to be considerate: "If you have to post something about it, please leave out her name and address and all that. She's an old woman more or less by herself far out in the country." Then he whirled around, snapped his finger and said, "Shit!", his eyes wide; Liza sighed at this disrespect. All of a sudden he was in a hurry and grabbed his duffel bag and walked out the door with me; and as we got into our cars, he glanced up and swore—softly, this time—as drops of rain hit his face. Then he laughed. And so did I, after a moment's thought. I headed to town, but he drove on up the old highway.

I waited for two weeks for something to show up in the paper about the box, but the only story I ever saw was a tiny one in the second section, saying just that the coroner believed the body of a baby found in a local creek had washed out of an unmarked grave dating from sometime maybe even a century ago. Somebody in town that asked to be anonymous had paid to have it interred in the First Baptist Church cemetery. The obscure little news item brought it all back to me—the four of us at her house, the hen scrabbling around anxiously, Edwin approaching with his question—and it was only then I remembered we'd left those two shoeboxes sitting on the porch next to Porter's garbage bag. I made a guilty mental promise to drive back up and get them, sometime or other. Maybe when somebody else could come along.

Mother said Granny Kate shrugged her shoulders when she read the article. "At least Berry got it settled without bringin' every Tom Dick and Harry out here trying to dig up my back yard," she said.

3

GRANNY KATE LOVED Porter the way some old people love prodigal grandsons who race up the road in hot-rodded pickups or always seem to be sporting black eyes; but with Porter, Berry said, the attachment wasn't hardcore nostalgia for youth—not a longing to be able to do those things again—but determination to protect a vulnerable: "She's always been worried somebody's gonna take him away from her, come and put him into a mental hospital." He hesitated: "Don't know why she thinks that, because then one of the others'll have to hire somebody to stay with her, take care of those chickens, fix the leaks in that old roof. And, anyway, he makes plenty of sense. You just have to kind of be patient and listen."

Every time he said that, I rolled my eyes.

Maybe modern psychologists would've labeled him "mildly autistic," or say he had Asperger's or something; but when he was growing up, all we knew was there were just things in him that didn't work the way they did in other people. Talking to him, all of a sudden you'd realize the conversation had strayed and somehow you were discussing the Plains Indians' ecological practices, though you yourself knew nothing about that. But he did, and he was telling you how they used all the parts of the buffalo they took, and so people really should do more recycling, use all the parts of a chicken, which was our staple, our modern equivalent of a buffalo. Maybe we could even learn to eat it skin, bones, and all, ground up into a powder and mixed in with our vegetables, like gumbo. You'd get all the protein out of it and it was good ecology. Ecology and recycling—those were his obsessions, what every conversation eventually came back around to. And you stared at him, not sure if he was putting you on or serious, and he met your stare with a calm, maybe even mocking one of his own, but not really looking straight at you, but sort of behind you.

My older cousin Richard, knowing as bullies always do that when people feared him, recommended I should find a way to be at the stop sign down the road from Granny Kate's house sometimes, because, he said, Porter hung out there: "He'll wave at you, and if you wave back, he'll turn around and drop his pants and moon you, it's just another little greetin' of his for special people he likes. I bet you already gone down there to see it, haven't you?" Richard was one of the more unspeakably horrible relatives I feared as a kid and later just despised. And later still I learned you couldn't believe much he ever said; he could look you in the face and lie. So, in the same way I entered dates into my family records, I put those stories of his into a mental file specially marked "Lies."

But everybody did know Porter sometimes wandered up and down the road at night, with a billy club for protection. Maybe it was a paranoid episode. Or maybe he *was* actually looking out for Granny Kate, as Edwin believed. But as she got older, and his eccentricity by contrast with our own stolid lives seemed more unforgiveable, the grandchildren talked about him, about "doing something" with him. She was firm that she wouldn't have that and worked out an arrangement with the sheriff's department: So long as he didn't actually assault anybody with his billy club, came home when he was supposed to, didn't pick up anything valuable from somebody's actual yard, they should leave him alone. After all, she reminded the deputies, he was only doing the same things the teenagers did when they could get by with it.

And she was a still a sharp old lady, and they were mildly scared of her. She pointed out she was land-poor; it was all tied up for the heirs, she wouldn't sell an inch or a tree off it now for herself. And Porter had no real workplace skills; even Walmart might not hire him, and he'd have to go on welfare and be a burden to the community if she didn't look out for him herself, because he'd never lived alone and might not be able to figure out how to, at his age. And if the deputies were after him all the time for every little thing, some judge would eventually decide he was a menace and put him somewhere; and taxpayers, of which number they could count themselves, would be supporting him.

As when we'd sneaked sugar, she was still good at that kind of thing. The last time she had to go to the courthouse because Porter'd been hauled in for trespassing or some such thing, the new young deputy who'd brought him in actually apologized to both of them. And after that, they left her alone and waved at Porter as they patrolled. From then on, Edwin saw to it any new guy understood the arrangement.

She found out her old neighbor Irene Posey was the one who'd called the deputy. Irene had been watching a "Most Wanted" crime show on TV, and her imagination got the best of her. Irene felt bad when she found out it was just Porter's footprints beside her mailbox, and not those of an escaped chainsaw murderer from the great state of Texas; and as expiation she took a coconut pie to Granny Kate for Porter to enjoy. I knew all this because Berry was there that afternoon with Liza, and he told me Porter eyed the pie with apprehension and said he guessed he wouldn't be eating Irene Posey's food anytime soon. And it wasn't from holding a grudge against her, neither, he told Liza: He just knew things.

IF BERRY'D REALLY put any thought into it, he'd have wondered that day why I was even available to go up into the country, drive past his mother's house at the edge of civilization, notice his car was there in her yard. Maybe, having been in education most of his life, he'd just defaulted to "summer vacation"—without remembering I'd never been a teacher, myself, and so why should I be roaming around anywhere in the middle of the week. But, then, in a way I was glad he didn't think to ask, because I'd quit my job that year—just quit, without having another one in hand, and I was inexplicably ashamed of that, as if I didn't have the right at my age to be irresponsible. I'd given George the half-assed excuse of wanting to think about things I could do when I actually got old, and he'd said, "Sure, take some time. Go back to college if you want." But I wouldn't do that. I just wanted to find out whether, with every hour of the day free now, that was enough time to calculate the value of my life.

A rainy spell at the end of August, several days of it, of wandering around through the empty rooms of my house in claustrophobic desperation, made Mother's caustic voice a welcome diversion one day: "Liza went to check on Mama and Porter this mornin' and brought back those boxes you were given." A silence heavy with accusation weighted down the next words, so they came out slowly: "I thought you and Berry went up there a while back to *get* 'em."

It was a neat trick she employed to discover an error in something I'd done that I'd otherwise felt good about. "There was a lot going on that day, you know. We got involved with Edwin Bonner. It slipped my mind."

Another silence expressed her skepticism about that, a silence just long enough to make me want to fill it but not long enough to let me. "Well, why don't you come up and get them. I'll make some sandwiches and we can visit."

I hesitated.

"What else you gonna do in this rain?"

Which was true, and she also had that knack for knowing when I was struggling; and maybe she was, too, that day. So we ate, and Mother quilted while Dad peered into the shoeboxes as I rummaged. In a while his interest waned: "Those things ought to go to one of Liza's kids; they're all about Cal's family—" Cal being Berry's father. I wondered if Liza'd even looked at them, why she'd send them on to me, not saved them for Berry or Jean

Ann. Maybe, passive-aggressively, she was repudiating Cal; everybody knew the two of them had nearly divorced long ago. Or maybe it was because Granny Kate told her I was to have them, and even at her age she wouldn't defy her mother. Whichever, there they were: Some old, old photos of people I couldn't identify, folders with family-tree sheets neatly labeled, old letters arranged by date and rubber-banded together. Whoever'd kept it all was a little OCD. I put the ancient pictures aside; there was just something unutterably sad about those nameless faces staring solemnly at me from a hundred years ago. *I can't help you; go away…* Same with the genealogy pages. The names meant nothing to me, and I wondered how Granny Kate had ended up with the stuff when it clearly had nothing to do with her own relations. The letters had been addressed to her nephew who, before he died ten or so years ago, had been another holder of the facts. So that was probably why she was giving everything to *me*, the next library, as Berry'd said, the person who'd keep things that had meant so much to someone, one time, which meant nothing to anyone, now. I opened a few of them, pulled out missives hand-written on old notebook paper getting crispy and yellow with time, the blue lines turning greenish…it was no use: It was all meaningless.

Rain fell steadily against the roof. Mother quilted away, Dad watched her, glanced at me once in a while. I laid the genealogy sheets in a U shape like a valley in one of the shoeboxes and put the letters on top to hold everything down; the photos went into the other box. I'd take them home and scan them, as per Berry's advice, email them out, see if anybody else knew who those long-dead people were.

I picked up the pictures and prepared to leave, hugging Dad, patting Mother's back. I left the first box on her coffee table. "Whenever you think of it, ask Liza if anybody in her family wants these things. Dad's right, they *are* mostly about Cal's side."

"Mama gave them to *you*," she told me, fairly sparking with disapproval.

SOMETIME AROUND THE end of October, a couple of families who lived near Conjure Hill reported that on two or three nights their penned hunting dogs barked wildly and then settled down as fast as they had started up. Calls were placed to Edwin and he sent his patrols out at different hours; but nothing turned up until one evening a deputy went by Granny Kate's about seven and found her and Porter out in the yard, muddy and exhausted, Porter hauling a backpack with several water bottles and a compass as he half-carried her with his other arm. The deputy called Edwin. Granny Kate was right sharp with him, Edwin said, and give him to know wasn't nothing wrong and she was just fine. He detoured up the highway to stop at Liza's and discuss this new development. Next morning she got Mother involved.

"What on earth were they doin'?" Mother demanded.

Liza fluttered her hands in the peculiar, helpless way she had. "Couldn't tell you. Edwin said she was pretty short with him, and Porter just gave him a look. And all I got out of *him* was, she told him she wanted to take a walk, she'd do it on her own if he didn't go with her. Jean Ann's goin' on again 'bout puttin' her in a nursing home before she just turns up dead on the road somewhere."

Some cousins said she must be looking for a cemetery, the cemetery the stout little box had come from, and this confirmed everybody's opinion that it was all up now, time for the family to do something about her. Jean Ann called a few of the cousins to meet her at Liza's house. It was an ambush by her on her own mother, Berry told me, though she claimed she just wanted Liza to hear their thoughts and try to be objective. But Liza got Berry involved, as defense, which thwarted Jean Ann's scheme. He told me later he didn't understand what Jean Ann could've had in mind, getting any of the others to come—other than just making trouble, which she'd always been good at. Liza, being the youngest remaining child, made decisions on Granny Kate's behalf by herself, thank you. Mother had always abdicated that role. I'd often wondered why, when she had the same right Liza did.

I asked Berry if Granny Kate, then, had turned over power of attorney to Liza, and he laughed: "You kidding me? Not on your life. You think Mama would've tried pushing that through court?"

Jean Ann, he said, acted stern, almost belligerent that day: "She is *ninety-nine*, Mama. Out there with just Porter, they should both be fixed up someplace good for 'em where they could be took care of. The government would do it, and it wouldn't come out of her estate. And you ain't so young yourself, and you can't keep on takin' care of her and him, too." A cold glance from Liza. "Her mind—well, it happens to us all. And his—his has always..." She stopped there.

Berry said Richard enthusiastically agreed with all of that, and his eyes gleamed, as happens with all bullies who've grown too old to actually do the horrible things in their minds but take delight from other people suggesting them. Berry just watched, and he kept quiet. After a while it seemed to him they forgot he was there at all.

After a while Liza seemed beaten. "We could hire Hazel Rowell to stay part-time," she suggested; but Jean Ann hissed at that. "Not her. Just make everything worse."

"They *have* been friends all their lives, and they're both old—it would help 'em both."

"Two old ladies, stuck together, nothin' but old times to talk about. Both of 'em about half-crippled."

Berry said he just couldn't help it, he kind of made some sort of noise then—"Probably gagged a little," he said—and Jean Ann stopped and gave him a look, then turned away. "And who'd pay for that? Anyway, she's obsessed, just obsessed, you have got to face it she's losin' her abilities now, finally—"

But then Liza turned on her: "I won't hear you sayin' that, cause you know it ain't true. She's probably frettin' over something, but no doctor'd ever say she's crazy, and no daughter of mine's goin' to say it, either. I've had enough of this, and if you feel like somethin' should be done, any of you, get up here and do it, like I've been doin' all this time."

And Berry said Jean Ann shut up, and so did the others.

And four days after that, Mother called and told me Granny Kate had died.

4

THE IS PROTOCOL for Southern funerals, rules about where you stand and what you wear and what you're expected to say, even which memorial flowers are displayed in the most prominent places, depending on the relationship of the person who sent them to the deceased—this one next to the casket, that one a little further away. There are women who carefully pull the little cards out to see who sent which, and tactfully move a gladiolus spray closer to the casket, or ease it away a bit, as if the corpse can appreciate how much time and money an arrangement's had put into it. They never call them the "dead person," but, the "corpse," as in, "She lay there, a corpse." Funerals are choreographed like weddings. So Mother had placed me and Sandra and Jerry on the right side of the room, where the carnations and chrysanthemums sent by children of old friends were thickest, those people not being as important as nieces, nephews, children; and, the three of us mere grandchildren, our positions were sort of parallel to those floral arrangements. Jerry, though our brother and just as kin, escaped rather soon, being a man. Sandra and I, and most of the other women there, accepted that: The protocol required more of women. We wouldn't have to stay there the whole evening, but at least for a while, until the crowd of respect-payers who'd flocked in early to get this required task done left for a good, warm supper. I didn't hold that against them: I did the same thing at wakes—went early, left, picked up something in town to eat at home.

Sandra had called that afternoon on lunch break from her job in Memphis; she said she'd arrive in the early evening with Amy. I asked why she didn't just take the whole day off, and she reminded me of the rules: Our grandmother didn't rank quite as high as, say, an aunt or an uncle would, and so there was no reason for her to miss those extra hours of work. I shouldn't have asked at all. I could tell right away it pissed her off; we tended to do that to each other.

"I *am* planning to stay tomorrow, since they're doing the funeral then. That way Amy and I can take our time and go back on Saturday."

"You're bringing her?"

She was surprised I'd ask; I could hear it in her voice. "She ought to be at that funeral. Not many people can say they remember, they actually remember, a great-grandma." As if in my silence she heard a criticism of that, she went on, "It may not mean much to her now, but when she's older, it will."

What *will* it mean to her, I wondered; but I held that back. "If you say so."

"I do say so. If they'd just set that time for later in the day tomorrow, I might've waited and come down early in the morning. But I'm not getting up at five to drive there, and so we gotta do it tonight."

I could tell why Amy seemed resentful all the time. "How does she feel about missing school tomorrow for this?"

"She'll do just fine!" Now her voice was getting sharp. "I'm not in a mood to drive by myself, anyway, getting there at dark, those shitty little beat-up roads y'all have." Scorn, thick enough to make me feel responsible for the roads myself. "So we'll see you later at the wake." Then she told me to go to Mother and Dad's and bring them to the funeral home, and that hit the limit of orders I'd take from an older sister.

"They can go on their own."

"But they won't have to navigate the streets by themselves if you bring them."

"But they go to the doctor's office in town all the time."

"But not at night. And it's her mother! Look, I've done my share of it before I left that area," she finished, her voice louder, "and you can just do it, too. You don't have a job or kids to hinder you, like I do." And there it was again, that whole thing about the kids. It always stopped me cold, and she used it for that.

Chrysanthemums and ferns and other greenery...the aroma was nauseating. I stayed as far away from the bank of flowers as I could while Granny Kate's family and acquaintances strolled by remarking on my clothing, glancing quickly, cursorily at Granny Kate—not for long; that took too much out of you.

"You were all so fortunate," "What a full life," "You had her a long time," and so on.

It was required of me only to smile and nod. After their mandatory but brief time in the parlor was finished, the men always went into the lounge to talk football, or outside to smoke, looking relieved, leaving their women wandering around in the parlor, holding cousins and friends about the waists and standing near the casket to comment on Granny Kate's burial clothes and flowers. More distant relatives, who weren't going to be there long anyway, and some of the older gentlemen, who had kinder sensibilities, hung around.

Porter stood across the room glancing our way, his face stolid and frozen; after a while Amy began to crumble. "I *hate* this. I'm going to the lounge."

Sandra sighed deeply in exasperation. "Not everybody can say they remember a great-grandma," she scolded. "You can stand being here a while longer."

Amy glanced sideways at her mother, rebellion thinning out her lips into a long, clenched line, and backed away. Mother had told me Amy was turning into a regular pain in the butt. More than once this summer, Amy had called her and Dad, bawling about what a witch Sandra was, wanting to live with them. They weren't aware she'd called me a few times, too. And, if they didn't, *I* knew what it was all about: She was getting close to that age where she had to figure out how she fit in with the rest of us, or if she did; and whether eventually she'd shudder and go off far away, someplace else to live, or stick around where her roots were.

ONE OF THOSE times Granny Kate'd been sick during the last few years, we were in her room at the hospital, several of us: Mother, Dad; Jean Ann's girl Susie, and Susie's husband; and Liza, of course, being Granny Kate's youngest and, by then, only other living child besides Mother. And George. George wanted to go out to the hall; it wasn't his place, he said, he wasn't real blood family. He was certain it was a death watch that assembled us there, for Granny Kate was ninety-one then and had pneumonia, and it would surely finish her off this time.

But, really, George just didn't want to see "IT"—that was the word I used. I kept my eyes glued to her chest to make certain each struggling breath was followed by another, *willing* it to be, because I didn't want to see "IT" either. And if I had to stay there to keep her alive, damned if I'd do it by myself; my husband could just be there, too. So he'd fidgeted and sweated by the window, as far away as he could get from the bed, other than stationing himself by the door, and that would be in the way of the nurses who came in from time to time. And after a while a rather cheerful conversation had begun, because of course in the midst of what was the dying, the living just rolled along, and we talked about who was getting married, and who'd had a baby, and who'd been jailed for DUI. George glared at all of us. "Maybe it'd be better if we went outside."

Susie was casual: "Oh, it's okay, she can't hear too well anymore, and, besides, she's the next thing to blind."

I leaned in to look at the half-open eyes hooded with translucent yellow lids, and I swear to God she winked at me.

And the pneumonia didn't kill her. After it was obvious she wouldn't go on and die just yet, her two puzzled doctors shook their heads and talked to Liza, saying she ought to go to a nursing home or at the least a retirement apartment when they dismissed her, not even glancing at the shriveled-up old woman lying six feet away. So all of them—doctors, Liza, Liza's daughter Jean Ann, Berry, all of them whirled around and gasped at the sound of the motor rasping like a growl to emphasize her words, as she held down the button to raise her head and told them she wouldn't go. She'd live where she wanted. She and Porter'd managed pretty well these years by themselves and they'd durn well go home and manage some more.

Then she hung on to get past ninety-nine; and, now, looking at that face here surrounded by creamy satin, I felt as if she might pop open those shiny black-brown eyes and wink at me again.

GEORGE WORKED AT the refuge and had been setting up deer decoys at the edge of the roads that day to catch trigger-happy hunters. Federal money was tighter, so he also patrolled the lake. But that wasn't a big deal these days, he'd said absently that morning before he left; not too many anglers because the Corps of Engineers was drawing down the water to kill off lotus plants. I left him a note when Mother'd called about Granny Kate. We left each other lots of notes these days: *Gone to the library*, I'd write on a scrap of paper. Or I'd come in and find a message from him: *Be back on Tuesday, working overtime, staying at the primitive campground*. Days sometimes passed without either of us seeing each other in the house. "God, when are you going to put up some paintings, do a little decor?" Berry would ask when he visited, shuddering, and I'd remind him it was my house and suited me just fine, the nice clean white countertops and creamy walls. Perfect blank slate to lay a bright-colored note on. Tonight there was no way to get in touch with George, as he might or might not have a cell phone along with him; so I had put the green note on the kitchen counter to tell him about Granny Kate.

PEOPLE CAME AND went, some I knew, some I'd never seen. We dragged up stools for Mother and Liza; it was too much for them to stay on their feet all evening, and they kept me informed about who was who: Smith, Granny Kate's lawyer, who was carefully quiet and said nothing of any significance; grandchildren of some men who'd worked with her husband in the far distant past; and eventually her longtime Black friend Hazel Rowell, whose daughter Sally and grandsons escorted her in, never letting more than a foot of space open up between them and her. I hadn't seen Sally in years. She didn't live in the state anymore, and I'd never heard anybody say where she'd moved. Then I felt Mother's fingers on my forearm. I was a middle-aged woman; would she ever quit pinching on me? I remembered Granny Kate clutching Berry's knee—not affectionately, but as if in a kind of warning. Liza glanced at Richard, who'd edged back into that parlor a while earlier, reeking of cigarette smoke, and approached Miss Hazel now himself, a grin on his face that seemed to me just too genuine. She let him hug her—that was what it was: She *let* him, did not participate herself, and I didn't blame her, and Sally and her grown sons flanked her and stared right back at Richard. It was all strange and unnatural, and I was relieved when he stood back a little, keeping that grin on his face.

There was a slow-moving sort of wave of cousins then—Jean Ann and James Preacher, Rhonda and Anne—coming at Hazel, two of them hanging onto her arms, the other two kind of hugging her on either side, all crying a little, except for James Preacher, who only wiped the edges of his eyes with a crushed tissue that he stuffed back into a pants pocket after he got the job done. Eventually it was just her and Liza and Mother together by the casket, talking softly about how we'd been so fortunate to have Granny Kate for so long, and she'd been ready to go, how she'd been *prayin'* to go—a statement James Preacher, hanging around nearby, seconded heartily—and Amy said loudly, "That's it, I'm out of here." She dashed for the closer exit.

The three of them hung over the casket for some minutes, maybe even ten minutes, at last merely standing in reverential silence. In a while others approached again, leading Hazel toward a chair, and she sat down flanked by her protective grandsons who nodded in an overly grownup way that was actually kind of funny as different relatives of mine eased up and spoke to them all. Sally talked distractedly to Mother, saying things I couldn't hear, things which made Mother's lips get that straight line to them that she had when I let slip a damn or hell. All of a sudden I realized Hazel was rising with the help of Sally's sons and said she had to leave, and Sally sought me out; and a quick hug had to suffice for years of absence between us, long years that made us look away from each other's eyes, for there was no way to bridge the gap anymore.

"I need to get her home. I don't like being out in that part of the country late at night." Our eyes met; she tilted her head slightly at me. The sons' posture grew straight and dangerous again. "It's good to see you. You okay, these days?"

"Fine," I told her.

"You look good," she said, and then she laughed a little. "You remember me showing you and Sandra how to braid hair my way?" She gave me a different kind of look and turned away. "We have to go now."

"Will we see you tomorrow?" I asked Hazel.

"I don't know," Sally interjected smoothly before her mother could answer. "She's not been well just lately, and this hit her hard. If she doesn't come, y'all don't hold it against her, will you?"

There followed a chorus of denials: "Absolutely not—" "You know we wouldn't—" and the little group eased out, speaking to someone here or there as they left. June, caught in a surreptitious glance at them, smiled brightly and eyed Hazel's stooped back as she left. The room turned itself back on, the mumbling resumed, men reappeared at the far doorway with paper cups of coffee in hand, glanced in, took their cups back toward the lounge.

And then Porter came up behind me breathing funny. I smiled at him.

"She really looks lovely, doesn't she." He patted Granny Kate's hair. "They fixed her up so pretty." He began to weep loudly like a child. Richard, still roaming around in that parlor to enjoy all the misery he could, smiled, his eyes shining with delight.

"The pore thing," Liza murmured in my ear. "He found her, you know. She'd not got up the usual time they ate their breakfast, and he realized right away somethin' was wrong. Said he'd had a feeling about it. He found her. She'd already been passed on some hours. When he tried to shake her awake, she rolled off onto the floor. For a while he thought *he'd* killed her. Took Bob and Larry both to convince him he didn't."

Porter wiped his eyes on his sleeve at last and turned to catch us staring at him. "I have to get my license now," he said. "Somebody's got to take me to do it. She never wanted me to. She figgered I'd try to drive in town. How will I manage on my own without one now?"

I glanced at Liza for help answering that question, and another one that popped up in my mind concerning him.

"I always took all the groceries and stuff to them," Liza admitted.

I told him we'd see, and then I went to Mother and said I had to leave right then, or go out into the cold damp, because I was allergic to flowers and was getting sick. I coughed a couple of times for evidence.

"And Amy's sneaking smokes," Sandra announced, coming back into that parlor. "I'm going to ream her out for it."

Outside, I shivered in the muggy cool air, and Sandra stood by the bland funeral-home doors and blessed Amy out for smoking; and in front of a small group of amused cousins Amy swore she hadn't been and stormed into Mother's car and slammed the door in Sandra's face. Every time she turned her sulky head to her window, I could smell the cigarette. If she hadn't been smoking herself, she surely had hung around with somebody who did. Mother rattled on and on, casually, unemotionally, about the lovely flowers around her mama's corpse, interrupting herself at some point to say over her shoulder that she guessed Amy'd be spending the night with them. "So instead of going home by yourself, why don't you plan on staying with us, too? You two can just sleep together in your old room, all right?" Mother said.

Amy gave me a look and sighed. "Sure. I guess."

I went by my house to pick up some decent clothes for the funeral tomorrow, leaving the three of them in the car while I turned lights on and off in search of nice shoes, a pair of pantyhose without runs, some underwear and pajamas. I added a line or two to the note on the kitchen counter, in case George should come home, and locked the doors behind me. The deep, cloudy darkness—not even a glimmer of moonlight—loomed around us when we arrived at last, and Mother wanted to know if I needed some medicine; she could have left sooner if she'd known my allergies were acting up. But then, "You know, Liza looked old tonight, I'm worried about her," she went on immediately, and I saw she didn't really expect an answer, which meant she knew my excuse had been convenient and false.

5

THE THING WAS, both Richard and James's sister June were old-fashioned and unrepentant racists from way back. They claimed not to be, said nobody should get any special rights anymore for anything, and if that offended you, well, it was your problem. Berry told me it was just another way to shove people around without actually using your body to do it.

Everybody had tried to forget the sixties, but I'd heard people say—quietly, and not in his presence—that if Richard had been around when the three boys were buried in that pond dam, he was the sort who would've been driving the backhoe, smiling as the dirt mounded up over their graves. The way he'd been tonight, standing aside, eyes gleaming and fixed on Hazel, took me back a long time to afternoons spent up country, a poorly-maintained dusty road traversing a bridge over a creek, people hanging around outside an old cypress house, not really wanting to be there, not really liking each other, just trying to find someone to single out to receive the self-loathing they couldn't contain inside anymore. It was either pick on some kid, or leave, and for a while none of them could do that, because they didn't have their own cars, had come along with relatives and were stranded now, milling around like people who'd missed a bus that they'd had dreams of taking them to a new place.

Last night at the funeral home Hazel and her family had left before the others, and nobody was stranded there anymore; but it wasn't really much different, those same people wandering from one spot to another but still in a place designated for the dead.

AND I'D LEFT last night, too, and everybody who'd left with me had been glad to get away.

WHEN WE ALL outgrew running up and down Conjure Hill, Berry used to climb the old wooden swinging gate at the edge of Granny Kate's garden, staying away from the wilder, older cousins, and gaze at the road, watching as if he thought any minute something remarkable, some miracle of salvation, would show up in clouds of pink dust, like God taking Elijah up in a whirlwind. — As Granny Kate's own children had doubtlessly watched through their lives.

Sometimes Porter's three older siblings would hang around the fence, being almost-orphans, the castoff children their grandmother was having to bring up. Not really fitting in with all the rowdy cousins, but not having settled families like the ones who formed a third group, they wavered back and forth between the fence and the house, vaguely ashamed of Porter but not really comfortable around the others, either, wanting to give the impression they weren't tied there, weren't obligated to stay with Granny Kate when everybody else escaped. Porter hung around, sometimes climbing up beside Berry, saying odd things, never really talking to anybody but at them, and ultimately settling into the same kind of introspectful, mournful silence that held Berry in thrall. The two of them never budged from the fence, once they were on it. Inexplicably—at least to me, in those days—Granny Kate had told them to stay put there, and at first I didn't understand why; the two of them weren't the ones who got into trouble, it was the older boys. Nonetheless, they did stay put.

Sometimes they were left alone—the family outcasts, just on the edge of the activities—and sometimes they were harassed. Somebody like Richard or Dobber with the little secret objects they showed off to each other, or Alex with his flask of whiskey and hand-rolled cigarettes, or even James before he got religion and started preaching—one of them would notice the two boys, perched on the fence, Porter talking towards nothing, Berry ignoring him, his face blank, and you knew when it was about to happen: Whichever one of the rowdies felt particularly wicked that day would call out something in a suspiciously casual voice— "Porter, whatcha been up to lately..." And all of a sudden, Liza or even Granny Kate herself would intervene: "Let 'em be! They ain't doin' nothin' to you, you heathens"—and everybody would grin. She never worried about any others, but she wouldn't tolerate anything done to Berry or Porter. At those times I understood how she'd ruled all her kids, and kept on with those grandchildren, for she bellowed angrily and took a few steps off the porch with the large walking stick she kept handy, and they cleared out, backed away from her with nervous little laughs.

Berry read a lot and brought books along, sitting there on the gate with some worn-out copy of something in his hands. Porter joined him on the uncomfortable perch, hunched over, rocking a little back and forth, and Berry often read the book aloud. They were like two peculiar birds clinging to a phone line, and perhaps that was why the others tormented them just as, without even thinking about it, they would've used BB shot to scare off cowbirds. I wanted him to read some of the books to me, too, told him so, demanded it, actually, and scrambled up one day beside him. He'd stopped, given me a speculative, measuring glance, and stuck a scrap of paper in to mark where he had been, and started over at the first, and his voice and accent changed, and he became a different boy.

" 'You don't know about me without you have read a book by the name of "The Adventures of Tom Sawyer," but that ain't no matter. That book was made by Mr. Mark Twain, and he told the truth, mainly. There was things which he stretched, but mainly he told the truth. That is nothing. I never seen anybody but lied, one time or another—' "

"Why're you talking like that?" I interrupted.

"It's the book. I'm reading what it says. That's what you told me to do."

"You already did this part," Porter complained.

Ignoring him, I said, "That's not the right way to talk."

"People talked like that. It's *dialect…*"

I eyed the book. Berry did not object when I looked at the *dialect*.

"It's hard to read things like that."

"You oughta try; it might make you smarter."

I shoved him down, and he yelled above the hoots and laughs of the rowdies at the other side of the yard, and he stood up and pulled on my leg till I fell and busted my knee, and so we were even, and I had earned the right to sit up there with the other two misfits. And it was a long time before I knew why he read aloud.

And the years passed. Mother grumbled regularly that Granny Kate was dwindling, "going down", reminded us she wouldn't be around forever. So we gathered and ate, left the tables and separated outside whenever the weather permitted, Richard's group going to the edge of the yard nearer the cypress swamp, Berry and Porter and his siblings and I staking out the fence on which we no longer sat but now used as a lounging spot, and a third group of slightly older, teenaged cousins hanging out near the house. The grown women drew cleanup inside and discussed their women stuff, and the men sat around in the living room and shared hunting tales. Sometimes Hazel Rowell's children or Joe Miles, the son of Hazel's brother Joseph, wandered down the road and spoke to everybody as he passed by. He was a rambler, walking or, later, driving all over the county; he liked to ramble as much as my cousins liked sitting and watching for something, and probably for the same reason they did sit and watch. They all shouted "Heys" back and forth across the yard to the road, and he walked on.

And the years passed. Mother dragged me and Jerry and Sandra on missions to Granny Kate's; and likely as not, there Miss Hazel would be, helping Granny Kate can pears, or green beans— something or other that one of them had harvested too much of and wanted not to waste; so they'd share the work as well as the produce. One or two of Hazel's own kids might be along, maybe Ben sitting on the floor playing checkers with Porter, who always won. Upon some sudden whim the two would leap up and dash outside to stand at the big gate and resume their watch; and if one of the girls was along, she and Sandra and I would take turns braiding each other's hair. Sally showed us how to cornrow, and I'd try it out on Sandra, or Sandra on me, while Sally watched and gave advice. In the kitchen Miss Hazel and Mother obeyed Granny Kate's brusque orders regarding Mason jars and lids. On the way home—after leaving a nice shiny, clean row of canned tomatoes or green beans on the kitchen table—Mother would give Sandra and me a look and tell us to take our hair down. And we'd pull out the neat braids we'd plaited earlier, pull them out *carefully*, remembering that Sally'd told us not to tug too hard or it would break off short.

And the years passed. At some time Sally and her sister and Ben stopped coming along with Hazel. Maybe they just got older and it wasn't cool anymore, which was an excuse I'd have appreciated for myself; or maybe there just wasn't so much food that had to be preserved after everybody grew up and left home. Or maybe it was all the trials and the mistrials and the retrials, the appeals of those men who'd killed the boys. Liza and Mother'd tried to keep us in the dark about it, but we found out, of course, and somehow Berry became obsessed and talked about it a lot. He wanted to dissect the psychology of people who would do awful things and still walk around like the rest of us, go to church, mingle with normal folks who didn't carry terrible secrets inside them. He wanted to know if there was a way you could look into their eyes and see into their souls, sort them out like that. I wondered if we *all* had terrible secrets inside us, but he didn't want to think about it.

If Mother overheard him ruminating over these subjects, demanding my attention to his questions, she informed him he was talkin' about things he had no business even thinkin' about, we were too young for all that, and we were to hush up. "Like it never happened," he'd mumble after she went on about her business; I heard that frequently from him through the years. He said he figured the adults all knew people who'd done the murders and just didn't want us children finding out they were folks we'd visited. And then he started getting into people's faces about it in a kind of passive-aggressive way, asking Sally if she'd ever known anything, and she'd give him a sideways, apprehensive glance, because even if she had, would she tell *him*? That was before she absolutely quit coming with Hazel. I told him maybe it was *why* she quit coming, told him it was maybe his fault, and why hadn't he left her alone; *she* didn't do anything.

There was a bumper crop of corn, unexpected, more than anybody'd hoped for, and as it was a sin to waste food and too much for one family to handle, it would be shared. Liza dragged Berry to Granny Kate's to help when it got ripe. We all toiled in the corn field, pulling the ears, and Hazel brought her kids, too. Her family would take home half the bags later, when they'd been packed. Two or three hundred or so ears of fresh corn to be cut off the cobs, cooked and spooned into freezer bags, the smell sweet and yeasty, the hot juice splashing out on your hands and fingers sometimes, making you yelp—"and don't let air get into the bags," Granny Kate ordered, "you get in there and mash 'em down so there's no air on top…." Hot, sticky work.

Being the youngest of the kids, barely teenagers, Berry and Sally and I were ordered to fasten the bulging sacs of light-yellow corn with wire ties and push them neatly into little boxes so they'd eventually freeze as square bricks, easily stacked. We worked noisily, arguing, resenting. We hated the job, and, finished, we dashed outside to lie on the porch and talk, with Berry the uncharacteristically silent one today, brooding, plotting. Hazel emerged from the house and collected Sally to go home. Berry sighed deeply and said we all were owed going to the movies. All of us, and Sally, if she wanted to come along, because she'd worked hard, too. That was him for you, saying it in a way that made a denial unjust, knowing it wasn't going to happen. Hazel glared at him, and Sally fidgeted nervously. Liza emerged from the old house, wondering about the sudden quiet on the porch, and Mother followed behind her, and he said it again, louder now, defying all of them, and the rest of us looked at the porch planks. Liza drew a slow breath in—not of surprise, because this was Berry, after all, and nothing he said surprised her. Mother's mouth curled. "Get your lazy selfs up off that porch, all of you, and hope we don't find somethin' else for you to do when we get you home. Movies. And you all think you worked enough to earn *that*. And you and Sandra, the very idea; y'all just go clean up that sink. I want to hear no more out of you."

I WONDERED WHAT I'd said, or done, to get her that mad. At thirteen you still sometimes want your mama to be pleased with you.

Berry told me later that she wasn't mad, she was scared. "All those things in the news. My mama and Miss Hazel didn't want Sally to go with us. Because Sally's Black, and all the others"—I knew who he meant: not Marcus, Anne, Porter, or Larry, but all the rowdy cousins—"they'd have something to say about it if they found out."

"Then why'd you ask?" I wondered. "If you already knew."

He scoffed at the question.

IT WAS SOMETIME later that fall that Richard sat on the fender of his old beat-up truck one afternoon, talking about what he was about to install next on it, glass packs, maybe, or he might lift it; he'd worked overtime and got some extra pocket money. As he held forth about these improvements, his small reverent crowd turned to watch Joe Miles skid down Conjure Hill in the souped-up '59 Chevy *he'd* just bought somewhere; they turned and Richard's monologue halted. And he said, "He don't know his place anymore." That one sentence sticking in my mind through the years as a marker for the end of a certain era and the starting of another, the separation of the sheep from the goats.

We were at Granny Kate's again, not the usual whole bunch but a slim representation discussing Alex White and how the day before, he'd taken off with the Mason jar his papa kept for loose change. It was a big pickle jar, with even some bills in it, and Alex sneaked out in the middle of the night in Willis' car, a tan Buick, taking the jar along with him; for Willis was saving money to get another vehicle for Alex.

Willis had married a younger woman—"*had* to marry her," they said, but quietly, because in those days you didn't say it too loud—and then didn't know what to do with the son that arrived a few months later. In a proud way he kind of expected him to be wild when he was older, got after him with a belt when he *was*, because it was all he knew; and then his wife ran off with another man when the kid was just thirteen, left him with Willis, saying she felt bad about it, but he'd be better off around his family. And *she* wouldn't.

Richard's truck had actually been Willis' gift to Alex—titled to him, even—but then suddenly it was Richard driving it around, and Alex riding shotgun. The story was that Alex owed Richard money for something, some escapade they'd pulled off, had no way to pay it, and just turned the truck over to him to settle that debt. At least that was what they told relatives; but Alex always seemed unhappy about it, and Richard looked altogether too pleased, as if, as if, Berry wondered, maybe he had something on Alex, and that was a convenient blackmail. Everybody knew Alex was responsible for certain mischief in the neighborhood, small stuff missing from Irene Posey's utility room and the like, packs of cigarettes taken from people's cars while they were in church. Berry wondered if Richard was putting him up to some of it, keeping himself at a distance: They were about the same age, but Richard was smarter than Alex and would do that. When people talked about it and he was around, Alex'd shift his eyes. It was predictable and kind of fun, goading him into betraying himself. You couldn't help but enjoy it, even if it did make you ashamed; you recalled how they'd agitated Porter on the fence, so were you doing the same thing?

That day we ate an abbreviated meal in respect for Willis, who sat in Granny Kate's armchair picking on his food as if after a funeral. Then we went outside into our little groups and whispered, some with oddly sad expressions that looked like envy that Alex'd got away. And Joe Miles happened by in that Chevy, showing out just like all the rowdies did themselves, spewing gravel to the left and right like little hardened waves flying up beside an overloaded ski boat. Taking away Richard's audience. He managed to skid to a sudden stop in the yard and started climbing out, proud of his accomplishment. James's face split into a wide grin, and he walked out toward Joe.

"Comin' by here, showin' his ass," Dobber affirmed Richard's assessment, sotto voce. "He don't know his place no more."

"Dobber, you just jealous of that car," James snickered.

Granny Kate's ears—deaf though she truly was at other times—always heard Dobber or Richard. She bustled off the porch as soon as the sudden hush fell. "Joe, how're you today," she called; but this time it didn't stop Dobber from following Richard, hobbling purposefully to the edge of the yard as Richard made a soft remark to Joe, something that froze the other cousins in their tracks; and Joe looked shocked for a moment and stuck out his chin, flung his hand out towards the road before he threw himself inside the car and slammed the door, gunning the accelerator and tearing up the road in a pebble-punctuated frenzy.

Then for some time that afternoon, he drove up and down in front of the house, slowly, and Dobber and Richard and the others bunched up under the big old sycamore tree and stared as he passed.

Granny Kate watched it all from inside now; you could see her face through the screen door. But she didn't threaten them with her walking stick because somehow her time had passed that afternoon, and it wouldn't do any good anymore.

JOE DIDN'T COME home a few days later. But he was the rambler, his rambles getting longer both in distance and time. Stopping by Granny Kate's one day with Hazel and Henry Rowell along, Joseph shook his head: It was nothin' he hadn't figgered'd happen sooner or later. The boy'd up and left, probably to his Northern relatives where he might get a better job. If he run out of money or gas, somebody'd hear from him. And sure enough, they found his car locked up, the fuel tank empty, in a parking lot in town. The sheriff came around to ask questions concerning that earlier afternoon; looked to him like the tank could've been siphoned off, but the car *was* locked and nothing suspicious, really, and *yet*. Granny Kate repeated what Joseph'd told her: Joe'd gone to Chicago maybe, caught a bus possibly, and left that junky old car that wouldn't have taken him very far. Hazel confirmed that as her opinion, too, and as for his other relations, they also agreed.

Edwin Bonner, some years older than Richard, and newly designated a deputy, wondered a little about the Chicago story and hung around Richard a while, prodding about that deal with Alex's truck. The rowdies said they thought Joe'd done well to leave where he'd become unwelcome. Edwin didn't like that attitude much and told them so; then, just to be sure, he kept at Joseph Miles until he got a Milwaukee address on Joe, promising Joseph first he wouldn't tell anybody else, so Richard wouldn't find out.

Mother hoped their consciences ate at 'em all their lives, "Like Herod gettin' eat up by worms," she quoted from Matthew. "Runnin' off their own neighbors," and her mouth was grim.

By the time Joe left, Richard's group had permanently segregated itself from the rest of us, their hushed conversation stopping if anybody else got near, as if there were things just too important, too secret, for others to comprehend. Berry had already started analyzing; gazing at them as they cussed and smoked underneath the trees. "They know there ain't really any difference between people, they know they ain't any better—but they just gotta *be*, somehow, and they'll put anybody they can below them. When you're on the bottom, you gotta be an awful good person not to try to put somebody, anybody, down lower than you are, just to *have* somebody lower."

If there was a gathering at Granny Kate's house then, and if Dobber or Richard was outside, one of them stared belligerently at any of Hazel's relatives as they passed by until they were out of sight, challenging them to remember they didn't own that road, or threatening, or reminding, or something. By then James had got religion, and he remonstrated with them, but not too much; they'd turn away and tell him to go off and pray with the other sissies out there by the fence.

And the years passed.

6

MOTHER HAD MADE chicken salad in the late afternoon before we left for the funeral home, so we ate sandwiches now, Amy recovering from her hissy fit and looking sad the way teenagers do when they imagine themselves abused or feel guilty or both. Mother said she wanted some coffee to warm her up, even if it made her lie awake half the night and pee the rest, so we took cups back to the living room and offered one to Amy, a gesture which, with its implicit recognition of her getting older, perked her up.

A long, rather pleasant silence ensued. Amy'd realized already I wasn't going to let Mother pick a fight with me in front of her. She sighed now with disappointment or something else and said she thought she'd go to bed. Mother went with her to fix the one in my old room for the two of us, and returned.

With Amy more or less settled, we three went to the living room.

"Everybody's comin' here after the service tomorrow," Mother said abruptly. "At least try not to cause a fuss with anybody."

"I never start the fights."

"I don't care who does it, I don't want 'em."

I changed the subject. "It's hard going to bed after being at a funeral home."

"Oh, the old way was probably best. Where they kept the corpse at home and just sat up all night, taking spells."

A long thrilling shiver went up my back. I glanced through the propped-open swinging door that separated the living room from the dark kitchen. But we might as well have been doing an in-home wake right now, with the quiet night sifting in on us and the house dimly lit and us talking about Granny Kate. I gently pushed the door so that it swung shut.

"Why's everybody coming here? Why don't they go to Liza's? She's younger than you. She could have them."

"Because I told 'em to. She's the baby of the family; the youngest always take it harder. She looked after Mama a long time." And why didn't you take more of it yourself, I thought, but didn't say. "It's just hard. Even when they die that age. And folks couldn't go up to the old house, now, could they? Too cold."

"She lived in it. Was it too cold for her?"

"And the roads are bad right now, and muddy..." she hedged.

"And people would walk around slipping stuff into their purses and pockets all day, too, wouldn't they." I said what it was about, really, and she didn't respond to that.

The dampness had got into everything. My coffee cup warmed my fingers like the hot old bricks Granny Kate had once talked about using in bed to warm her cold feet, back when. It had been a cool November that day, too, and even the rowdies had eventually crowded into her old house to get warm, talking about what hunters used in their socks; and she'd laughed scornfully and explained the old-timey way to do it.

It seemed right to think of such things, and so I told the story and sat with the warming stone in my hands.

"A night like this reminds me of somethin' that happened a long time ago. I was just a boy," Dad began, and at that moment Mother stomped out to the kitchen, shoving against the swinging door, hitting it so hard that it stayed open as if huddling fearfully against the wall, and I saw her march to the window over the sink and stare out back into the dark yard. I watched her for a moment or two. Something must have *told* her she was being watched; she turned to see me and gave the swinging door a nudge that sent it back into its proper position, where it shivered on its hinges.

WE WERE ALL storytellers.

It was why the dry column Berry'd done for years in a Tennessee educational magazine, writing as Dr. Asberry Tanner, eventually and inevitably metamorphosed into the tales about his own family, the identities of those he eviscerated on paper barely disguised, so that even a Granny Kate could figure out who they were. He'd started with a scholarly, poignant case history everybody knew was Porter; but from there he just couldn't help it and went on to the other stories, the ones we'd all heard, the ones they hoped he wouldn't tell. Or hoped he *would*, in the next installment.

I tried to ferret out the narratives hidden in my collections of dates and census records and land deeds.

All the older generation who grew up in the backwoods, who'd clawed out a living at the garment factory, like Liza and Cal, or at the creosote plant, like Liza's father, brought the measly dollars home and sat around clay-backed gas heaters in the fall and winter and told stories. The money paid the taxes, a set of tires for the car, groceries; not much left for what we later called "entertainment." When we gathered at Granny Kate's and some callow grandchild or great-grandchild asked her what she'd done for fun back then, she gave them short shrift: "Made our own."

I'd heard Dad's story before, but I listened politely.

There I was, he said softly, starting in media res, of course, like any good Mississippi Homer, barefoot at the edge of that dirt road, totin' two squirrels I'd shot earlier, and there it was, that panther: I could see it a little through the leaves, and I knew that if I ran it might come for me, so I made myself, made myself walk slow and quiet all the way to the front yard, following the light in the distance that they'd left on for me, but all along, as I walked towards that light, I could hear that panther padding next to me through the woods—pat, pat, pat...

He walked his fists softly across the coffee table, because any good storyteller used sound effects.

...and when I turned, it had gone off into the woods; but the next morning we found tracks in the soft mud in the driveway, and the tracks measured five inches across.

"Don't see 'em anymore this part of the country; they're extinct here," he ended the tale. "It's a shame."

His dollars, Mother's dollars were adequate for us; we had televisions, movies, skating nights; but the storyteller never went away, and once in a while he'd see the three of us, children, playing catch in the yard after supper, chasing fireflies, and he'd sit on the edge of the steps and start a story, and we'd straggle up and listen.

Sometimes the hunting trips had had different endings. We huddled in the dark on the porch, bumps prickling our skin, and waited for the panther to leap or scream—"They sound like a woman cryin' when they holler," he would tell us, and then demonstrated as we shivered—as we waited, he would whisper: So I walked on, and the moon went behind those clouds, and I couldn't hardly see the road home anymore, and suddenly I heard somethin' go whooff, and two big paws landed on my chest right here—We froze.

And it barked, and it was my big old collie dog coming to lick my face. And we would laugh in relief.

"You ought to write some of this down while you still remember; it would make a good story someday," he'd tell me, because even then I was accepting my family-appointed job as record-keeper: Wasn't I Janie's quiet, literate child who'd rather eat a book than a plate of barbecue?

"You don't see things you used to see roaming the woods in the old days." He'd sigh gently at the end of the hunting stories and, rubbing his hand across the night bristle on his face, would stare out into the darkness at the edge of the porch.

He never wrote many words consecutively on paper, but we kids sat on the front porch with him on summer evenings, feeding mosquitoes, and he put stories together the way Mother pieced quilts, until there was a complete picture you could stand back and look at and admire.

Mother would clatter things, for she was there, inside, in the background; or sometimes she'd come to the screen door to say, "Time to start baths so we all have some hot water." And so we would leave the eerie magical semi-darkness of the porch for the brightness of inside.

She was always somewhere in the house, watching TV or merely near the window as she quilted—her one hobby which she indulged in at night or when the weather was not too hot, stabbing tiny needles into fabric and batting, grimly completing one section of the pattern, moving on to the next. She did it not necessarily with pleasure but because it must be completed, finally writing in permanent ink on one corner the name of the family member or acquaintance for whom that quilt was intended. That would be somebody who'd accomplished some noteworthy thing—they got married, or they had a baby, or graduated from high school; something or other.

Once in a while, and especially, it felt like, when Dad told stories about my cousins Richard or Dobber or some long-dead relative of hers, she'd join us, in the summer, at least, listening to the bugs murdering themselves trying to break the screens to get to the lights inside. It was as if she was there to fact-check him, to make sure he got the details right, as they were *her* family's secrets he was spilling with relish. There was something about her being there that changed the mood in the humid dusk, and it was less fantastical and more like a newspaper column, and Dad employed fewer sound effects, fewer adjectives, trying not to offend her. I felt guilty that as a girl I hadn't liked her as much as I did Dad.

I already had *my* quilt; she'd given it to me when George and I ran off to Alabama one weekend when I was halfway through college, ran off and got married there, because they didn't require a waiting period for a license. She'd given it to me with reluctance, because I didn't have a regular church wedding, and, she told me, the whole family was going to think I was pregnant—this with a sharp, questioning look at me—but she'd given it to me nevertheless. And then she started another one for somebody else, sitting in the living room and working with stern diligence, but by then there was nobody for Dad to sit on the steps with; we were all grown, so grudgingly he learned to quilt with her so he would have an audience.

It took a while later for me to realize I was jealous of Berry because he was earning some money and some renown by doing what Dad used to do, what he'd told me I should do, what I'd quit doing a while back.

"COME HELP ME with these few dishes," Mother commanded from the kitchen.

I chose to rinse, the better to see that they were clean, holding the chipped plates down in clear hot water as she gave them to me swathed in bubbles and sometimes little pieces of chicken salad and bread crumbs. For some time she'd refused to buy a dishwasher—"No dishwasher'll help my hands now," was what she always said—and her fingers were like light-colored sausages fried until the skin was papery, and shiny, ugly hands, hands that had worked hard. I drowned the dishes in the sink one by one and examined my own hands. Well, they weren't pretty, either.

"I'm glad you quit working," she said suddenly.

I held a reluctant platter down until the air gave out under it and it sank.

Berry'd preached his tale about posture to me too many times: I read in hers now an expectation of some kind of remark from me agreeing with her. "Oh, yes, I love my free days," I could say, maybe. But those days had nothing in them, just too much coffee and staring out the windows, and I'd grab my notebooks to work at the library, leaving the house in desperation at the hugeness of the silence around me. And there I'd be till night, composing posts for a blog I emailed to the relatives who claimed they wanted all the family history, but quit reading once they figured out there weren't any revelations that would change their own lives now, in a modern place in time. As Berry said: They were all just plain old regular chicks, like everybody else in the world.

As if she knew the things I wasn't answering, she said, "You ought to find something different to do with yourself. Quit doin' that stuff, writin' down dates and tryin' to find old records and all. You're usin' up your life livin' somebody else's that's long gone."

There are times it's best not to say a thing, and I figured this was one of them. I dried the dishes in silence, and then we made our way back to the living room, bringing refilled cups with us, shuffling our feet on the rugs she had bought last year. I kicked off my low heels. "Your feet will be cold," she said. "Here. I'm wearing socks. You put on my houseshoes." But that was really too much even for me, so I told her I'd get into pajamas and my own socks, instead, and I went to my old bedroom.

I yanked off the dress as fast as I could in the cool air, Amy's soft snoring sounds betraying the crying she'd probably indulged in a while ago in the privacy of the bed. Pulling on my pajamas, my back to Amy, I felt uncomfortably certain something had changed in the room since I came in. I glanced sideways to find her sleepily watching me.

"Thought you'd zoned out."

"I had. Oh, you didn't wake me up, don't worry." Her steady observation was unsettling. "You and Mama slept in this room together." A statement, not a question, and she knew that, already.

"A long time ago."

"I guess she was different then."

"Probably. It's hard to remember."

She was almost mumbling by now: "They're mad at each other a lot these days. Calling each other crazy, being mean. Somebody'd think they can't stand each other."

I considered this a moment and realized who she meant.

"I've stayed with 'em a few times. You didn't know I was visiting. Last summer." She shook her head very slowly. "So they been doin' it a while. I heard 'em other times besides tonight."

"You hadn't told me."

"It's kind of scary. I didn't want to get you scared."

This made me smile. "They aren't really mad...I think *they're* getting scared. For each other. Because they're old."

"They think they're not so sharp anymore," she agreed, "their minds, you know. They're scared of that. I'd be." She'd closed her eyes again. "I'm so sleepy, Aunt Maggie. Can we can talk about it tomorrow?"

"I doubt it, not likely tomorrow. Tomorrow night, after the funeral, maybe. We'll see." She shrugged under the piles of quilts Mother had laid on her, and I left my old room.

And then the smoke alarm screeched.

Mother dashed into the kitchen, from where the malodorous clouds issued, and came out brandishing a cookie sheet with two black, round things reeking. They looked a little like hockey pucks. Amy stood bug-eyed in the living room, shoes and backpack in hand, prepared to evacuate.

"Why'd you heat up biscuits anyway? You just ate!"

Dad glanced away, apologetic and embarrassed. "I'm sorry, Janie. I saw 'em and thought jelly on one would taste good for a dessert...."

"Oh, it's just burned biscuits, whew," Amy said. "I've done that. I microwaved some noodles last week, forgot the water. You don't want to know how bad it was. It was just an accident," she added pleasantly, a quick glance at Mother.

"Just shows you not to turn the oven on and walk off! Go back to bed, honey, and would you text your mama and remind her I expect her to be here tomorrow after the funeral."

Amy's scowl wasn't promising, as she retreated silently. "I'll do it later myself," I said.

Mother rattled pans around and slammed the cookie sheet down on top of the stove. That was to make us feel guilty for not helping her, and worked well: "Maggie and I'll do that," Dad told her, and we busied ourselves rinsing our coffee cups, which we hadn't even touched that time, and putting away the dishes from earlier. The light glared over the sink as I stowed away the coffeepot. Cool, damp night air flowed through the window Mother had opened to dispel the stinking aroma of burnt bread. There were still crickets chirping on humid evenings. Or maybe they were rain frogs.

I had lived in town too long.

We went back to the living room where Mother was placidly looking through an old picture album now.

"This's the only one I have of Mama, young," she said.

"It's weird even thinking about being ninety-nine. I guess I could've gone to visit her a little more," I told her.

"Yes, you should've."

When I couldn't sleep at night, when George snored peacefully somewhere over on the other side of the bed, a presence in the room, but not, somebody I had known intimately, but not, I was awake with my guilt. As now. So why hadn't I visited Granny Kate more? For the same reasons every kid had: Because she was old.

Because she just sat. —Or, worse, slowly, painfully lumbered around. And the other thing, that feeling Berry often goaded me about: "You need for her to be the same, and it's easier to keep somebody the same in your mind if you don't see 'em. They're frozen in time for you."

"Some of them are still sayin' her mind went bad." Mother looked challengingly at me.

"I don't think so," I said. "She didn't seem vague when Berry and I were there a few months ago, when they found that coffin down at the creek. We were up there that day, remember."

"That was a real strange thing," Dad put in. "I wonder sometimes what it was all about."

"Just a pore youngun buried by somebody long ago," Mother said caustically. "I never understood why folks were so interested in all that. It was disrespectful of Mama. Why bother her about it?"

"Did they bother her about it?" I asked.

"They talked some," she said darkly.

Dad recoiled at the belligerence in her voice, shot her a glance and changed the subject. "Well, Granny Kate she did have a hard time with Porter for a while. With *all* those kids."

"We can talk tomorrow," Mother said suddenly, like a person who had just made up her mind about something really important. "There'll be folks here to talk to, and ten to one they'll be talkin' too much. So, when they all leave, maybe we'll talk. You go to bed, and I'll get you up in time to get a bath in the morning."

As directed, I crawled into bed beside Amy.

THE DAMPNESS GOT to me, I guess, and Mother's house had no central heat. Not that she'd've probably used it, anyway, any more than Granny Kate used that air conditioner Jean Ann bought her. But I dreamed I was in a fire; and in the immobilizing fear of those kinds of dreams I could not get away quite fast enough and the flames engulfed me, and then Mother took a quilt, or her long dress was a quilt or something, and she wrapped it and herself around me to put the fire out and save me.

I woke up, throwing back the covers I'd cocooned myself into. Amy stirred, but I said, "Shh, it's okay," and she slept on.

7

THERE WAS A barred owl hanging out on the lowest limb of the sweetgum tree, sitting there in a kind of stupor almost at eye level in the broad light of morning, like a drunk unsure how to find his way home.

Amy was still asleep when I'd got up quietly and gone to the kitchen to make coffee. But Mother and Dad were already up, phone calls already coming in since dawn. She had spotted the bird and was standing near the window: "Look at that. In the back yard." As if it were a man who'd showed up naked, lounging on a lawn chair.

I half expected Dad to interpret it and then weave around it a lovely tale that included dreams and omens and Indians. He went to the window, and, obediently, I looked past plants on the window ledge and saw the great brownish lump in the tree. I felt sorry for it. Owls are not fully alert in the daytime; it had nevertheless probably seen her long before she saw it and, if owls can be said to have hopes, was hoping she'd fail to make out the feathers blending into the general mass of trunk and twigs.

"Sends chills right through me," she said.

Dad and I glanced at each other apprehensively.

Suddenly resolved, she marched out the back door, off the porch, and approached it loudly, not stealthily, hoping to scare it off before she had to get really close, and flapped the cookie sheet she'd snatched up from the stove. The aluminum made a sound like the crack of lightning. The bird seemed to focus on her, shifting around on its perch, and then flapped away silently, as owls do, as she got nearer. I watched from the window inside.

"Why'd you run it off? It wasn't hurting anybody. They catch mice, you know."

She glared at me a moment, beyond words, aggravated that I simply did not understand. "The old folks always said it was bad luck to see one in the daylight. It was a sign somebody was going to die." So much for lovely tales.

Dad kind of snickered and told her not to borrow trouble, which was his paraphrase of the last sentence in Matthew 6. He was never afflicted with irrational fears. She always tried to hide hers by scoffing at the very idea that anybody'd ever have one.

"I am not afraid of that bird. I just don't want it there. It don't belong there."

"Nobody said you were afraid of owls," he muttered. She frowned fiercely at him, he took the hint, and the subject was closed.

A LITTLE LATER in the morning it started raining, the cool rain of early November that made you want to crawl back into your thick old quilts, a rain sure to drown the remnants of the flower garden—the fleshy, many-stalked impatiens old folks called "sultana" and the periwinkle that had already yellowed but still hung on to bloom here where you might walk around outside barefoot on Christmas Day. Mother usually left the kitchen window open a little unless it was the dead of winter or raining, or, like today, she needed to kill the aroma of something that didn't turn out well on the stove. But she pulled it shut now and glanced out into the yard—I knew it was to make sure the owl hadn't returned. Then she made what she probably hoped sounded like an offhand, casual comment: "Mama had to hire Hazel's old man to haul off a load of tin cans she found in the old privy not long ago. Porter'd heard somethin' on TV about a recyclin' center in town and'd picked 'em all up along the road and stored 'em in there."

"In the outhouse?" I laughed.

"It wasn't *that* funny. They started fallin' out the holes onto the ground and washin' on down into the creek, rolling up in Irene's back yard every time it come a good rain. Stop laughin'."

It was hard not to snicker at the picture, and even if she tried not to, I could see her mouth twitching a little. Granny Kate had had indoor plumbing for many years, but nobody'd ever gone to the bother of taking down the old privy, an object of fascination and a dare for all young cousins whenever they visited with their mamas and daddies: which one was brave enough visit the outhouse, challenging the dirt daubers and spiders.

"Falling out and washing up on Irene Posey's yard! She may have liked that better than what she must've had washing down onto her years ago. There's a story for you. Or maybe one about Porter collecting all those bottles and cans to recycle, to do his part for ecology," I mused. Mother cut me off sharply:

"Don't start talkin' about stories today. And he's got enough troubles as it is."

"So where'd Henry Rowell take the cans?" I asked to mollify her.

"To that recyclin' place, I reckon. It was right before he died last summer..." She bustled around, turned her back to us as she mumbled, and the rest of the story came out reluctantly, regretfully, as a truthful person on the witness stand will answer hard questions about a close friend's sins: June, my cousin who had legal pretentions, found out somehow and pitched a fit about the removal of all those cans. She and Dobber got together, wanted to know why nobody called one of the grandkids to do it, get the money, profit from the work. It seemed no one had given thought to Porter's having claim on it, after having scoured the countryside to collect them; and it amounted to some little money, as there were a good many cans. He'd crushed them flat, Mother said, and stacked them inside grocery bags, the plastic sort, so there was a veritable armory of them in there. In my mind I drew up another picture of what must have ensued when the emptying of this storehouse had been disclosed: the cash gone which they'd never worked for anyway, their resentment at an old Black man, sick and dying.

It came to me then that Dad was carefully gazing outside, very quiet.

"They went to Miss Hazel's and pitched a fit there. Didn't they. Am I right?"

She sighed in exasperation. "There was some words passed."

"And it was right before Henry died? Did it make him sick? Did it give him a stroke?"

"No, he had the cancer...but Hazel and him could use the money, which was why Mama hired him to do it. And he wasn't able, anyway; one of those grandboys showed up and did it. It wasn't hard, Porter'd already done the work and didn't mind them having the money. For him it was more the pleasure of havin' got them off the road."

"I wonder she came to the funeral home last night at all. Dobber must be awful broke if he needed money from a bunch of cans." When she turned away again, flinging the dishcloth around like a flyswatter, another thought came to me. "Wasn't the money, was it. Or Henry and his grandson coming and taking 'em off. It was the idea of somebody else going into the old place. They been thinking for some time it's theirs already. Am I right?"

Abruptly, "Are you goin' to get a bath or what? The two of us got to get dressed pretty soon. If she'll get out—" she motioned toward the bathroom where Amy had been doing something or other for half an hour.

"You aren't going, Dad?"

"There'll be so many folks here. She doesn't mind," he added, defensively, and she nodded agreement. "I'll just stay and put the things on the table as people bring 'em in."

Which wasn't necessary: You just left the door open when you were hosting after-funeral eats, so the church ladies and neighbors could ease in and out and not make spectacles of themselves bringing in food, not be Pharisees calling attention to their good deeds. Nobody had to be at home; none of your stuff would get stolen. Maybe in town, but not out here. We liked believing that.

"He intends to visit and gossip," she added. "Sabrina and Lilly are coming by to help him. So you need to get bathed so I can, too. Then you and me'll leave just in time for the service. No point gettin' there early."

"What about Amy?"

"She's going."

"You gonna make her? Sandra might be able to, but she's pretty stubborn."

"She's been told she has to go. And she brought something or other with her to wear; Sandra seen to that, shoved it in that old bag she hauls around."

"When should we leave?"

"We'll wait till your daddy's sisters get here. They're comin' pretty soon. Now, Maggie, I'm tellin' you, don't pick a fight with anybody today. I do not want to have to be ugly with folks."

I sighed. "Can you just tell me one thing? Does Berry know that about those cans?"

"His mama said she was scared for him to know, said he'd be really mad. He don't know, unless one of the others slipped and let it out, and they weren't that proud of themselves when Granny got through with them, let me tell you. And I called Sandra. Since you never did," she added, pointedly. "She'll be up after the funeral, too. And so will everybody else, includin' some I'd just as soon didn't show. Now go get pretty."

DAD'S TWO SISTERS were already fighting when they got

there—Lilly, the stout one who wore glasses, the older one who, despite her seniority and appearance, was cheerful and irrepressible and given to daydreaming; and Sabrina, younger by some ten years, who regarded herself as the more modern one who wasn't the country hick, who had traveled and was sophisticated. Sabrina was the kind of person who saved up and remembered things people said which they wished they hadn't, so she could remind them for the rest of their lives. Mother disliked Aunt Sabrina but tried to be diplomatic about it since she *was* Dad's sister. I heard the bickering before they even got to the porch and gathered it had to do with something from their childhood, something they remembered in different ways. They came inside and spoke to Mother. Her hands were now clumsily working on an apron, twisting and turning it. After a few kind words of condolence—"The family getting your mama buried today, huh"— and Mother's answer—"Hated to see her go, but she had a long life"—Sabrina dove right in.

"And it's bound to be a mess, what I hear, and what'll become of that crazy boy she took in?"

That had only crossed my mind once, last night before we left the wake. What *would* happen to Porter? Mother looked sideways at Aunt Sabrina: "He's not really a 'boy', you know, and he's not crazy. What do you mean, 'took in'? She was his grandma. She didn't just 'take him in.' "

Sabrina shrugged delicately. "Well, he certainly does not act like the rest of them."

Mother gave her a dark glance.

"I figured Granny Kate would've had a will," I said. "She seemed like she would've taken care of it. All that land—"

"Mama worked it out, I imagine." Mother gave me the eye again, and I hushed.

"You've moved that chair. I do like it where you put it. Gets the light better." Diplomatic, ditsy Aunt Lilly chose a place to sit as she changed the subject. Sabrina appeared displeased at this gentle digression, however, and asked suddenly:

"Daniel, you have never answered what I asked you: Do you recall what year it was we had that big snow when we was little?"

And I went to the kitchen to get them cups of coffee and to leave them to the pleasure of this argument. By the time I got back, Dad, Solomon-like, had handed down his decision in Sabrina's favor. Lilly sulked in her chair and poked her lips out a little. She sloshed the cup I gave her as if it were a finger she wanted to shake at them. "I said I was wrong."

"You change the subject, now you don't want to have to admit it, but if I'da been wrong, I'da never heard the last of it—" Which was funny, coming from Aunt Sabrina, the master of I-told-you-so.

"Oh, you two. Where's *my* coffee, Maggie?"

"You'll drink it all up before anybody even gets here," Mother said sharply.

"We'll just make more if we do," Aunt Sabrina said.

"And don't let me catch you having too much while I'm gone, either," Mother added.

"You won't catch me," he said virtuously.

Mother looked at the three of them with a pissed-off expression on her face, then tugged my sleeve. "We need to be goin', Maggie." I called Amy, who'd whined a little when I reminded her she had to go with us but had gotten herself into a somewhat appropriate dress and had put on way too much eye makeup. Hoping not to meet any cars, I drove slowly along roads that were damp and muddy, red muddy. Amy squirmed in the back seat, unzipped her purse and reclosed it several times. "Honey, you don't really smoke, do you?" Mother said.

"No! You ought not to believe everything Mama says." She stared out the window, I could see in the rearview mirror, and in a moment she added, "I don't like doing this."

"So, Mother, what's up? What's everybody been talking about, all this stuff about Porter, and the whole family here and all that?" I might be the only person who had no idea what was going on, and I told her that wasn't fair; Amy snickered a little. At last she relented, explained that things were tied up in a way that would be hard to unravel, and some of the family were already looking for a fight, saying the only way to get a fair and right deal would be to take it to court and swear she was senile, get her will thrown out, hire a tough lawyer who could do that. In the silence after those words filled the car—there seemed no room for any others as they hung in the air—I thought I could hear each pebble gritting under the tires on the road. An old saying in the country was that you didn't really know your relatives until somebody died and there was money involved. I went through the cousins, bringing up a picture of each of them in my mind—Richard, James, Dobber,

June, Jean Ann, Rhonda, all of them, even Berry—and pondered which ones I'd be willing to never speak to again. "What's in that will?" I finally asked.

We'd got very near the church by then, and time was running out for me to wrench anything else out of her; and she knew it. She'd talked in circles just slowly enough. I could already see cars pulling into the lot ahead.

"No time to go into it right now," she said vehemently. "And it's got to be settled neat before anybody talks about it too much. So just hush and quit botherin' me." She looked stolidly out her window. So that was that. In the silence we heard music bleeding out of Amy's headset, heard it all the way in the front seat.

8

IT WAS COOL and muggy, still drizzly, too. We huddled shoulder to shoulder in that unheated little church where Granny Kate had waited once to bury her husband and a couple of her kids. It stood off the ground several feet on the original great boulders where it perched, and cold air swirled underneath and around and sometimes inside. Going there, you had to rattle along washboard roads with loose gravel that threw a car around and jarred your spine; or, in the wet days, slither and slip about in fear of landing in a ditch. It wasn't just a journey of miles but of time, the old church building a destination in another century.

Berry had written about this place, saying how picturesque the frame walls were, and historic, and how drafty and terrible in winter. "Hell *could* burn with ice," he'd mused. He said people regarded it in a Calvinistic way—if you were really serious about going to church, cold shouldn't be a hindrance to you; you should flaunt your chilblains and purple fingers as holy objects.

Before the service had started, when people were still filing in solemnly, I had overheard a few whispered remarks here and there: "Were you plannin' to go to Janie's after?"

"That's where everybody was told to take the food."

"Well, I've heard they're not having anybody but just family. Never heard of such a thing. Nobody that ain't related is supposed to come. People gettin' awful big today...."

"Guess they figger they'll soon have reason to be....How much you think it's worth?"

It irritated me not to be in on the big secrets. When Sandra slipped into the pew, I leaned over to whisper something, but she shook her head once and said, "Tell you later. Amy, take that headset *off.*" Somebody snickered quietly somewhere behind us, and I heard Porter's name brought up. Where was he, anyway? Who was he coming with?

I knew why he'd ended up with Granny Kate—but I knew only when I was old enough to do the math and wonder how my grandmother could have had a baby at such an advanced age. Since Larry and Anne and Marcus always tried to keep a distance from him, I had some doubts they were really his siblings, even though people said they were. I'd always just figured he was her own last child. So one day I asked Dad: "Did women use to have babies when they were that old?" He turned red in the face and stuttered and referred me to Mother, who looked at me for a while, measuring my height and my soul to decide whether I was of an age to be let in on this particular secret. She eventually made the decision and started: "I guess I'll tell you. When Everett, that was Porter's dad—my oldest brother, you know, nine years older than me—when he was young, a fine man," she said regretfully, "in his thirties, he was found with cirrhosis of the liver and he died."

"He always was the family drunk," Dad added, sotto voce.

"*The* family drunk?" I had interrupted with the witty cynicism of a sixteen-year-old. "*The* family drunk?"

She stopped for a cool moment or two to let the two of us shrivel up again, for over on the other side of the room Dad was snickering, then continued with her quilting and the story. "Porter was born after his mother went crazy."

"A short trip for her," Dad mumbled, for my benefit.

They had to institutionalize her, Mother went on, by now deciding that ignoring us, as if she were merely soliloquizing all by herself, was the better way of getting the tale out. She was always high-strung and she just couldn't deal with Everett's drinking, which he started up while he was in World War II. And those three older kids, them so close together as they were, and Everett just drinking up money instead of feeding them all. They had to take her down to Hattiesburg, place her there for a while—"place" being a word I could translate; it meant "institutionalize." By then, Everett had really gone down bad, and Mama took him and the three older ones in to help them out. He tried bringing Pauline home once and it didn't work; she spent her days lying in bed, wailin', carryin' on...

Mother didn't like that part of the story: All the women in the family had been strong and wouldn't have done that. They'd have kicked his ass out until he crawled back and tried to do better, but Pauline wasn't one of us and didn't understand that process.

She was just one more person Mama was havin' to take care of, and at her age!, so she finally paid for them to get a place down there to live near the hospital, and sometime or other she got pregnant with Porter.

She stopped with her needle high in the air, the quilt quivering a little where she had just jerked it, that one gesture a harsh statement of her opinion of the whole affair.

They'd all thought it might do Pauline good to get out some in Hattiesburg with Everett. Her doctors would see to it she got her medication and the two of 'em came and went, he'd take her out to restaurants or a movie, like they were courtin'.

"They let her come and go from that asylum with him, not supervised," she said, shaking her head.

"It's a mental hospital. Nobody calls it an 'asylum' anymore."

She glared at me. "They were 'asylums' back then."

And meanwhile Mama still had the older three, herself, and nobody from home checked on Pauline and Everett, everybody thought it was all workin' out just fine, nobody considered they was still livin' together as man and wife, with Everett in his condition—and who was takin' care of who? Neither, it turned out.

She made several tiny mincing stitches as old spinsters sew, little prissy, prim stitches, sewing her opinion of *that* into the quilt, looking down, not meeting my eyes, as if hiding a terrible truth from me. I wanted to tell her I knew the translation of "living together as man and wife", but I didn't, because she was already mad at me.

In fact, he even died down there. It was a good thing the hospital aide was around that day and found him. The others, they were little, they had chicken pox.... So Mama had him shipped up here, did the funeral, buried him. She took the blame to herself for not going down there in person. It turned out nobody'd written down any emergency contact other than Everett, well, he was the husband, after all; and then he was gone.

So out of the blue, something less than a year later, they finally notified her Pauline had had another baby, who was in fact not even a newborn anymore—some time ago, in fact, had had it. They dug around in records, trying to find out who to get in touch with, and eventually found Granny Kate's name and just casually called her on the phone, Mother said, just called, like giving a regular update, and, oh, by the way, your daughter-in-law's been tryin' to raise this baby of hers and your son's. And when she rushed down there to see about it, the asylum administrator told her they'd hoped having the baby would help Pauline a little. After Everett died, she'd really missed him, so they'd let her keep the baby a while, under their supervision, of course, a couple of months— Yes, of *course*, they'd supervised, but it wasn't working out, and something else had to be done now. Granny Kate found Pauline didn't change him, so he had a terrible rash, tried to feed him potatoes and other things she herself ate, held him by his stomach sometimes like slinging a sack of flour over her arm. Pauline was filthy and skinny, and so was Porter—puny, not gaining weight right—and Granny Kate took him home with her and kept him with his brothers and sister. Pauline crumbled and went back to her wailing bed in the hospital. Hazel helped, more so with Porter than the others, because her own kids were grown by then and she'd have time for a baby that Granny Kate wouldn't.

Pauline eventually had some moments of clarity and said she knew she couldn't tend to him, so maybe it was better for somebody else to raise him. Granny Kate threatened the hospital: no more of them close-by apartments where nobody fed Pauline on a regular schedule but expected her to figure it out herself, "In her condition!" Mother expostulated; the quilt trembled. It was pretty strange stuff, but finally Hazel got her reconciled about it, got her to quit feeling it was all her fault. It only proved sometimes them doctors in that place was crazier than the patients. But that was the way things just operated years ago in asylums, and there wasn't much she could've done about it. You did what you could for family, what you had to.

From that point, I knew the rest. Porter had the two older brothers and a sister, all about a year apart in age, but none of them had much to do with him as they all grew up, being vaguely ashamed of him because he was weird; their shame for him shamed themselves. He was allowed to roam the roads, indulging in his interesting obsessions, surprising cousins on illegal hunts and teenagers necking in parked cars on the neglected side roads. Granny Kate saw to it that he climbed onto the school bus with Anne and Marcus and Larry, though they sat well away from him, and he slowly wended his way through an educational system which, in those days, sorted children into two categories: regular; or special ed, where sweet patient ladies loved the kids and kept them busy until they were finally old enough to age out of school.

Nobody suggested he should apply to colleges. As his sister and brothers went, and other cousins, and Berry and I, the thought that he might also take some courses may never even have crossed Granny Kate's mind. Maybe it never crossed his, either. He seemed content to pass his days growing small crops every summer to sell in town at the farmer's market, or at a stand Henry Rowell fixed for him at the end of that dirt road, near Liza's house, where civilization began; and he took care of the chickens and sold eggs. Liza took him to the county library. I'd never believed Berry when we were kids, but he was right, that at some time Porter became a voracious reader and supplemented his rustic knowledge of growing things with an obsession for ecology and organic farming.

Only, you'd never know that on just a brief chat with him. He always seemed to like alarming the people who spoke to him, made chitchat, moved on, as if he were purposefully keeping them wary of him. He reserved any deeper acquaintance for people who stuck around to actually talk after he asked them what parts of the chicken they generally ate.

A point came when some in the family—Richard, for one, and even Jean Ann—began to suggest "placing" *him* somewhere. His siblings had escaped to civilization by then and offered no opinion, but somehow Pauline found out about it—maybe he got word to her, himself, was Berry's opinion—and scrawled a strangely-coherent note she got somebody to mail to Granny Kate. The gist of it was, ***Don't put Porter in a mental hospital; it will finish him off—I know.*** So Berry took it on himself to instruct Porter about appearing more "normal", not doing things other people would find so weird, and he'd lived with Granny Kate ever since. I always thought it appropriate for Berry to do that, since he'd written his Master's thesis on him and, after its lofty, jargon-riddled main heading, subtitled it, "A Study in Neglect."

EVERYTHING WAS HUSHED quickly as the preacher came in.

"Our Sister Katherine lived a long and godly life. She was meek; blessed are the meek, for they shall inherit the earth."

I'd never known that was her real name—and I was the library.

"Everybody inherits the earth eventually," I wrote on the funeral program. "Looks like he's gonna cover all the Beatitudes." The obituary indeed stated her name as "Katherine." Underneath what I wrote for Amy, about the Beatitudes, I scribbled a note to remind myself to change her name on some sheets I kept.

Amy looked puzzled. I wrote: "Matthew 5." Sandra stared straight ahead, exhaled deeply to show her disapproval.

There'd never been a question that James would do the funeral. He'd answered the call when he was a teenager, never had much luck reforming Richard and Dobber, his first cousins and first customers, but persuaded the backwoods church Granny Kate belonged to to ordain him. There he stayed, hammering down loose boards and shingles, every nail another anchor attaching him there too. And after all, they did need a preacher who wouldn't press for raises and could earn his living without depending on tithes from this poor and dying community. At first he said he'd go to seminary later, but he never did; and finally it was his opinion that he knew everything seminary could tell him anyway, and he relied on emotional appeal. He droned along sadly now: "She had mourned; she was comforted by her children and grandchildren. She was merciful; she will be shown mercy..."

"Five to go," I wrote. We all knew our Beatitudes, having had them drilled into us for years, sometimes in this very same cold, shabby building; for even if you were only visiting some Sunday, you were expected not to shame your parents with your ignorance. Sandra turned slowly and gave me her version of Mother's warning look. She also nudged me with a sharp elbow, and jabbing her right back, I realized Amy was weeping quietly. I helped her gather her tissues and her purse and eased her out the side of the pew, mouthing, "No, no," to Sandra, who made a move to get up, too, and grasped almost desperately at Amy's short skirt only to have it yanked away from her fingers. Some cousins' faces registered mild curiosity as we slipped past them, others patted Amy's back a little; some, mine. I went outside and leaned against somebody's car and laughed, mashing my hands upon my mouth to muffle the noise, hoping they'd think I was crying.

Preacher's sermon had meandered into Ecclesiastes, that other Preacher, since he'd done the Beatitudes to death—you could hear him through the thin, uninsulated walls: "One generation passeth away, and another generation cometh: but the earth abideth forever."

"Downer," I told Amy.

"I made me great works, I builded me houses, I planted me vineyards"—he said it, "vine-yerds"—"and then I hated life, and I hated all my labor which I had taken under the sun, because I should leave it unto the man that shall be after me."

"He *knows* about the will," I whispered. She giggled a little, then stopped in horror, wiping her eyes.

"Everybody'd think the two of us are crazy. Put us down there with Pauline."

"For all go unto one place, and all are of the dust, and all turn to dust again," Preacher intoned as his closing words, and then somebody at the piano played "Shall We Gather at the River" mournfully and out of tune, and James came in with the words and made the pianist do fancy things with the timing as she tried to follow him. He always did think he could sing. There was a pause while somebody else took the pulpit to talk more.

Glancing around the church parking lot would give you a fair notion of the kind of crowd you had: mostly pickups or four-wheel-drive vehicles with rebel flag stickers on the back windows; the occasional battering-ram monsters of the old ladies; and, glaringly out of place, a few sedate imported sedans that stuck out like sore thumbs, looking self-conscious, just a little above all that riffraff parked nearby. Some of them belonged to the cousins who'd done well and came back once in a while, tugging at their ties as if they were about to choke; others, to people I didn't recognize inside, the few who sat together in business-type suits and who only nodded absently at people in greeting. I wondered about these, who they were, when they had known Granny Kate, what connections they had that we might never find out about.

The small car parked near the road was Berry's. It had sat in front of our house often enough for me to recognize it now. Suddenly sobered, I wondered where he was. I hadn't seen him inside, but, then, there were a lot of people there, more than I'd expected to turn out. And he knew how to almost disappear sometimes in a group. It was why relatives were often chagrined to find themselves and their words in things he wrote: They'd forgotten he was around.

Amy sniffed occasionally, turned away from me. I wandered around the parking lot. The cemetery was enclosed by a shiny chain-link fence and a gate that hung open now as if inviting all inside. Green canopy covered two rows of chairs near the gaping mouth of the gravesite. They would be laying Granny Kate here, next to her husband whom I couldn't remember, next to the babies she'd had that didn't live long; and over there on the right side of the cemetery were other family markers. Berry's father. One of Granny Kate's sisters. The one that read *Alexander Guy White*, had his birthdate but nothing else, but it was weathered and old.

Amy had followed me around and stood right at my back. I pointed. "That marker. There's nobody buried there."

"He didn't die yet?"

"It's complicated."

But the service was over, the coffin being carried from the building as the mourners followed respectfully to the gravesite. There we'd have more preaching; things were not respectfully concluded until the preacher spoke a little longer and people hung over the casket, wanting not to look at it. Mother sat next to Liza, the two of them steered to those folding metal chairs draped with a kind of velvet-looking fabric.

"She was meek and she was righteous and she inherited righteousness...."

I started to tell Amy that James was beating the Beatitudes again, but caught myself in time. And calling her meek: Anybody who'd seen her heading out towards the rowdy boys with her walking stick—and James had—shouldn't call her meek. Anybody that had to raise more kids after hers were all grown couldn't have been meek.

He'd described her excellent virtues already for thirty minutes inside the church. I wanted to tell them to be done so we could leave and I could find out what was going on.

The mourners shifted from foot to foot. You could just about figure out who had come in which vehicle. I watched and tried to match them up, but I didn't want to rubberneck too much, for it wasn't proper when the person was in a box right in front of you, close enough almost to touch, close enough to bring intimations to you of your own inevitable end. You were supposed to be thinking about that.

Mostly it was grandchildren here today, Granny Kate's own siblings having died years earlier, and most of her friends were dead, too. She'd outlived them, except Pauline and Mother and

Liza, who stolidly looked at the coffin the whole time. Liza'd been a good, dutiful daughter, the sort James approved: a very Old Testament daughter. I'd always felt that Mother hadn't wanted Granny Kate to take those kids when Pauline was committed to the *asylum mental hospital* after Everett died; Granny Kate had done her part in her own earlier life, and it wasn't fair for her to have to raise four more. Mother'd seldom said it that way. So Liza was the one who'd checked up on Granny Kate every day to make sure she hadn't died in the night or something, and, finally, of course, she'd done just that.

Hazel was not there.

Edna Luckey *was*, standing stolidly at the edge of the crowd. She came to all the funerals.

"She outlived others of her time, almost to a hunderd. I was born too late to know her except's an older lady, but I know that even in these last, feebled years of hers, she received joy at the thought of so many descendants, and this's what she leaves us: the picture of a long life lived with family and friends nearby."

Mother shot an irritated glare at James, but he droned right along—he wasn't her child and didn't feel it burning into him, like I would've. Granny Kate had gotten slower and slower toward the last, and she couldn't see or hear very well anymore, I knew that myself after last summer, but "feeble"? That translated to "weak-minded." Everybody here knew it did.

It seemed he was finished, couldn't think up anything else to say, and a few of the grandchildren helped Liza and Mother to the casket, and they laid roses on top of it. All of a sudden I realized Berry was standing slightly behind me. I raised my eyebrows at him and mouthed, "Where've you been?" But he was staring in the direction of the casket, where Porter's sister and two brothers stood sniffling and laying their roses. They huddled around Porter as he cried, and then the three of them led him away.

"The Duke and the King're putting on their performance," I mumbled softly to Berry, who ignored Sandra's cold, uncomprehending glare, because I knew she couldn't recall who the Duke and the King were, and she figured we were just making fun of her again, which we were, I guess.

9

MOTHER ESCAPED WHEN Sandra ordered her to ride back to the house with her. Sandra called Amy, who stood defiantly apart from her mother and said, *No*, she was going with me, and after another of those weird, disturbed gazes at her, Sandra turned away. Berry nudged me with an elbow to my back as he headed to his own vehicle. "Edna Luckey's here. Greek chorus," he mumbled. Amy heard and drew her brows downward in puzzlement.

She sat in the front beside me and zipped and unzipped her purse in mechanical, silent nervousness as I maneuvered home over red clay that had almost liquefied by then as the drizzle persisted and the cars worked the road like children stirring ice cream until it turned to soup. The cousins in their four-wheel-drives were having a hell of a good time; I could see a couple of them behind me pretending to be in trouble navigating the slippery roads, but really they were yanking those steering wheels hard to the left and then to the right just to make their vehicles fishtail around. The only thing that could've made them happier would have been if they'd had to hook one of the little sedans—maybe mine, or Berry's—up to their winches and pull it out of the ditch.

But then we were off the dirt roads again, back at Mother's on the highway, back into civilization; and her front yard was already filling up. Cousins, aunts, children, two or three relatives smoking on the porch—Mother didn't let them do it inside. The racket bursting from the house through the door almost drowned out the "How're you's" from those on the porch, spoken to me in voices deeply laced with Southern-gentleman politeness; if they'd had hats, they would've tipped them. "Fine," I told them, "How're you?" and they nodded at me and coolly, gruffly, spoke to Berry as he followed me in.

In the corner of the living room Porter's brothers and Anne sat with Jimmy, one of Uncle Thomas' sons. Various descendants milled around here and there, hovering over their children. Mother's new furniture arrangement praised by Aunt Lilly was gone. One of the cousins had dragged the seat away from the light and closer to the heater which, with all those people contributing body heat, was roasting the room; how could anybody need that heat? Dad and the two sisters had staked out one end of the dining-room table, barricaded from the rest of the crowd by stacks of Styrofoam plates and plastic forks and spoons. The swinging door was propped open. There looked like thirty or forty people in there trying to find somewhere to sit.

I walked near the table to be out of the way. Bits of conversation swirled around me, only to be drowned out by other bits caught in an eddy of noise:

Jimmy's two boys had opened up a TV repair shop in town, but it wasn't doin' as much business as they'd hoped, so far, but it was sure— Marcus' girl had applied to Harvard—well, why'd she want to go up there with all them Yankees? And the cold; well, she'd sure miss— June's youngest daughter had entered the junior miss pageant, and she might win except for that one year's English grades that pulled down her average, but— What kinda computer system you got now in the office?— You still at the power company, Richard? When you gonna retire? Or you just gonna let 'em fry you one day, cheap cremation— Ain't no good fishin' now they're pullin' down the lake; crazy, ruinin' the fishin' they say to improve it, but that's the gov'ment— What if he just showed up, just walked in here today—

The talk went up and down, came near, receded like waves as I passed through it. I leaned against the table and glanced around, feeling out of place in this house where I'd grown up, where I usually fit in pretty well, where I'd felt fine last night. Dad and his sisters, apart from the group but occasionally making comments to this or that person, were enjoying the hell out of it all.

Berry gave me a look and squeezed past to retreat to the kitchen, from which Mother and Sandra emerged shortly, glaring around.

"Maggie, come help us a minute."

In the kitchen all the food had been positioned across the countertops and the small table, buffet-style, so that people could train down with their disposable plates.

"I'm goin' to tell you and Berry quick, so you'll know." She jabbed a sausage finger first at Berry. "There's some in this house that expects you'll be takin' notes or something. It'll be better if you two stay in here as much as you can."

He turned the same quizzical glance to her.

"Why should we have to stay away from anybody?" I asked.

"You know why. For goodness sake, don't start a fight. There's bound to be one comin' as it is, and I don't want to have to run people off because of you."

"*I* don't start fights—"

"You'd run people off just for me?" Berry interjected. "Thank you."

But then she did a strange thing. She patted my hand—such a protective gesture, what you do to a scared or disappointed child. "I'm goin' to get 'em all headed for the table. There's enough food here for the whole state today. Sandra, you go out there and tell 'em it's in here and they're to wait on their plates theirselves."

"You do it," Sandra said. "They won't listen to me, you know it."

We heard Mother yell: "Everybody get quiet for a minute!" and nobody paid her any attention at first, either, so Aunt Sabrina laughed and took something metal and banged it on something else, screeching, "Y'all shut up so Janie can tell you about the food!" In the dining room there was, before Mother spoke again, just enough of a silence to show what she thought of the mistreatment of her kitchen utensils. In another minute there was a cacophony of scratching and scraping as everybody stood up for grace to be said. This wasn't a regular meal, but only casseroles, cold cuts, and desserts provided by church ladies and neighbors, but we'd have to wait out another sermon before earning the right to eat them. When James was in the house, you said grace if you didn't do anything but drink water with a pill.

When he was done, the crowd surged into the kitchen. Sandra and Amy and I stood at the side, making conversation with first one and then another cousin who ambled along pushing their plates loaded down with coconut cake and potato salad and rolls and ham and chocolate pie—not your café âu lait-colored restaurant variety but some family recipe the hue of Coca-Cola and topped with meringue dotted with tiny beads of amber where the egg whites didn't beat up just right because it was such a humid day. Sandra muttered to me that she'd better get over there to the trough and help Amy fix a plate before the hogs ate it all; so I elbowed my way into the line, too, and started spooning up what I thought I could stand. Berry waited by the sink, sipping iced tea, leaning against the cabinet, watching the throng at the trough.

It was how we'd always described our meals together, a shibboleth admitting true family.

"You know, I didn't figure you'd be here," Richard said.

"Lord, where'd you come from? Why wouldn't I be here? I grew up here," I said.

He just laughed in a lazy way and slopped a great big spoonful of potato salad onto his plate. "Thought you'd be avoidin' Preacher. Everybody saw you laughin' during the funeral. Sandra had to make you leave for bein' rude."

Sandra disavowed it quickly: "I did not make her leave. She did it on her own."

I took a quick glance at James, who stood close enough to have heard all this, and saw his sad, pitiful eyes. "And I was not laughing at you, Preacher, just in case that's what it looked like. You know how your emotions get the best of you sometime. I just wasn't handling my emotions about her passing, and then—" but I stopped, realizing Amy was staring, telepathically telling me to leave her out of it.

Richard continued: "I seen you almost run into the ditch ahead of me a while ago. Thought I might have to winch you up and pull you out."

"You wish," I said. "I wouldn't let you yank my little car out with that monster of yours. Tear it to pieces."

It was the usual stuff he and I did, insults masquerading as jokes because otherwise we'd have to get into a fistfight, and so far we were about even. Sandra and a few other people laughed, and my brother Jerry had managed to squeeze into the kitchen next to her.

"You afraid of big old things?" Richard said.

"You ain't got one," I countered, feeling pretty sharp now, and a few more people laughed, but not James.

Richard gently slid Mother's pie server under a wedge of the chocolate pie, eased around to the end of the table, glanced up, grinned at Berry: "Glad to see you, too. You make it to the funeral? Didn't see you there."

A year or two ago, Berry wrote a little piece he called "A Gay Time Was Had by All," which had everybody wondering whether he was referring to himself. "Well, Liza did use to say he had big, soulful eyes," Mother recalled, as if that explained everything about him. He looked up at Richard now, those big eyes wide, but never shifted his body as he leaned against the countertop.

"She was my grandmother, just like she was yours. You're

here. Why wouldn't I be? And nothing gonna keep us from a spread like this, right? Specially if it's free."

Richard cocked his head to one side as if considering this. "Food's always good. I'll go if there's food. But then..." he hesitated, "I don't live in fear of bein' tarred and feathered myself."

"Really? Never knew that. Oh, you talking about *me*. Should I go look in your truck? You have 'em with you last night? All that planning, I guess, and then I wasn't there."

Richard carefully ran his finger down the side of his plate where a dollop of potato salad had slopped over the edge, and licked it off. "It'd be good if you'd stop writin' stuff that embarrasses people to death. It's just exactly what people like to hear and think about us down in the South. Everybody already thinks we're trashy and inbred, goin' around in sheets all the time, that kind of crap. It don't help with you always stirrin' the pot."

"Sheets?" I said before Berry got a chance to respond. "Did you bring them, too, last night? Or just the tar and feathers?"

A momentary appalled hush fell over everybody near us.

"Maggie, stay out of this. One time you used to write nice things, about interestin' people and places. And then you quit, and he took over, and now all *he* does is be a troublemaker."

Jean Ann attacked the potato salad with vengeance, shoveling a huge glop onto her plate, then snatched up a chicken drumstick as if it would walk off if she didn't. Her breathing quickened so much everybody close to her could hear it—it was almost a low rumble, like a big cat growling. Berry turned and gave her a long, hard look.

"Richard, did he write something bad about you?" I asked him in my sweet voice that would've shut him up one time, though he didn't know now I was tense, my pulse racing, because he was like a large, unpredictable dog that could suddenly turn on you. For years and years we'd had these exchanges at the family gatherings, Granny Kate looking interested and watchful as we'd sparred; but today it was all grim and weighted with things I didn't like thinking about, and I didn't know if Richard would back down with one of his sneering laughs the way he usually did.

He'd finished loading his plate and looked down, pretending to study out which cup of tea was best. "I guess it's about all of us, ain't it," he said. "Maybe that's why I figgered he wouldn't come today, out of respect—" with the nod of his head again at Berry, disdaining even a glance at him. "I don't know why people read that stuff. Guess that's what you learned when you went off to college and got your *education*. How to ridicule folks. Maybe you should move back to Tennessee. Nobody made you move here. Why would you *want* to, if everything's so shitty? Nobody'd miss you. And, sorry, Preacher," he added in apology.

"Truth hurts," I said. The kitchen and dining room had got awfully quiet.

"Well, there's truth, and then there's tattlin'," Richard said with a grin just before he went through the door. "Which is you, I b'lieve."

"What d'you mean, that's me?"

"Well, how else would he've found out about some of the things, not livin' around here, unless somebody's tellin' him. And that would be you. *I* sure didn't. But then maybe he'll even get you one day." He glanced at Berry, who all but sneered at him. "I'd of figgered you'd take up for yourself, 'stead of hiding behind a woman. But, again, maybe not." He did a weird, obnoxious thing then: he cackled like one of Granny Kate's chickens. So he thought Berry was a coward?

"He's not hiding behind—"

"You hush, Maggie, just hush." Berry's nostrils quivered, and I realized his eyes looked even bigger, his face red, as Dobber softly crowed. Everybody within earshot who hadn't already stopped mumbling about the food did then and looked at the three of us— Berry in his white dress shirt and black trousers, tie loosened sloppily from the crisp knot he'd had it in; Richard with his plaid shirt and cowboy boots; and me with my mouth, Sandra kindly told me later, hanging open slightly.

"Well, he finally grows balls," Richard chuckled.

"Nobody oughta be doing this today, not today." Berry moved away from the cabinet. "So you shut up, too."

"You man enough to make me? Or maybe you'll hide behind her again."

"It's common decency when you bury folks. But you don't know about that. Trash don't know nothin'."

The crowd collectively inhaled and held its breath. Richard moved first.

"Maybe you just writin' about your own fam'ly, and not mine. So if they don't care, why should I." He slid out of the room amidst the quiet, banging the swinging door just a little and making it snap shut, quivering a second on its spring as it met Dobber's wood foot with a solid, dull clunk.

"Ow!" Dobber cried.

"You ain't got no toe for that to've hurt, so be quiet," June told him, and he had the grace to turn back and laugh.

"That thing's going to be a problem today," Preacher remarked, and I wasn't sure which thing he meant.

I glanced at Sandra and Jerry, expecting them to say something or take up for me or Berry, but they just stood there looking embarrassed and scared. The crowd slowly started milling around again, but more quietly now.

"WHERE YOU GOIN' with that plate, Maggie?" Mother asked resentfully.

"I'm eating in my room."

Amy was sniffling once more; Sandra heard it about the same time I did, and patted her shoulder. "Leave me alone," Amy said, shaking off her hand. She followed me down the hall. "I'm coming along. Not so much battle noise in here." She flopped down on the bed where we'd slept last night. "This family's weird. And spooky. And mean."

Coats and umbrellas had been stowed in the room; purses lay next to sweaters on the floor. I opened the closet to get hangers for a few things, get them out of the way. There was the ancient shoebox with the letters and family sheets I'd looked at last summer: So Mother'd stored that here instead of sending it on to Liza, knowing I'd find it again sometime and in the shock of the unlooked-for discovery would receive her punishment for my ingratitude concerning a gift from Granny Kate. I grimaced, took it out, laid it on the nightstand. I shoved aside several of Mother's quilts lying folded neatly on the shelf over the hanging clothes. Then stopped, and I couldn't help it: I gasped. More punishment.

Amy sat silently for a moment as I stared. "They recycle newspapers?" she ventured at last, eyeing the shelf.

They lay there, scores of them, most yellowed and brittle, stored in the back so that I'd never noticed them before. I picked one up to look at the date.

"Your mamaw kept my articles, I guess," I told her.

"Those things you did?"

"Guess so..."

"Wow. I wouldn't've thought she'd be the type to save things like that."

Me, neither. And I would fix it now so she didn't. I threw one at her—"Is This Your Ancestor?", and then "Dates in the Old Watson Cemetery".

"Was it all stuff like this?" The question chilled me.

Newspapers harbored silverfish; they ought to be thrown away. I set about lifting them down and stacking them.

"Not all. These were later. Before, I used to ride around. Got old folks to tell me their stories. That old man that ran his rebel flag up every morning, blasting 'Dixie' out in the backyard on his tape player. You ever hear about him? Probably not...I put him in, one time. Took pictures of chimneys falling over in pastures— places where people'd lived..."

"There's something sad about chimneys in fields," she said. "I always see the people who got warm beside 'em, cooked over 'em..."

I lifted down a few more.

"Charles Kuralt," she said quietly.

"Yeah—" I laughed, pleased that she understood, and she turned red. "Yeah. I thought of it as a Charles Kuralt thing. How'd you know about Charles Kuralt? I was a lot younger then, Amy. There was this little old lady that looked like she never did anything but sweep her porch. We'd drive by and it always seemed like she was sweeping. I thought maybe she'd have something interesting to say."

"Did she?" She waited, her eyes steady, almost demanding.

"Well, I passed her house a few times—I called her the 'sweeping lady'..." And there were weeds growing up under the steps, I remembered...

"But you never actually stopped?"

"Nope."

"Downer," she mumbled.

"Wish I had. Couple of weeks after the last time I drove by, a bulldozer was there, clearing the land, knocking down her old house." And that was during the early part of that first pregnancy. "Then one time the editor said it would be good to talk with this other old woman, feature her on the front page, and I'd get the byline. She changed flowers in her garden depending on the holiday—red and white pansies for Valentine's Day, orange marigolds at Halloween."

"So what'd she do on Guy Fawkes Day?"

I had to laugh. "Guy Fawkes? I have no idea. What would somebody plant on Guy Fawkes Day? How'd you know Guy Fawkes?"

"Hey, I'm not illiterate. So—did you? Did you do that article?"

"Yeah. Turned out to be his own old aunt! And she owned a plant nursery."

"Whoa! What'd you do about that? Did anybody say anything?"

"Oh, no, I put it out there, told all about that in the piece—everybody I guess thought it was okay."

"Like, nepotism's all right, because it's an activity the whole family can enjoy," she said.

"Yeah. A family tradition."

I ate a few bites and kept my eyes on my plate, making up my mind not to say anything else about those days. I *had* been younger, much younger, and then that first pregnancy ended midway through. I bought a new, better camera and drove here and there, never far away, and wrote about strange names, odd people, and for a while—Richard was right—it *was* a popular thing in the paper; people liked it. It was "nice." I did nothing but look for sentimental stuff to write about, searched for something I didn't have to commit anything to, because it required nothing except telling what I saw—no judging, no analyzing, no skepticism: That was the way that conservative old editor wanted it, and it was fine with me. It was like sitting on the porch with Dad and Jerry and Sandra, having dreamy images put into my head on those summer evenings. I took pictures of the hundred-year-old church some young couple was converting into a small house. I hung scribbled sticky notes on the car mirror reminding myself to stop here, or there, wherever.

Richard was right: hard to say that. I wrote about all the sweet interesting things I could find for a couple of years. We waited, George and I, for the new thing that would give us something else to talk about, that did not come. Then I woke up one night from a terrible dream about kudzu growing like a beast in a horror movie, which wasn't a stretch, since it could grow a foot a day in the summer, anyway—and the dusty, alarming acrid scent of sycamore trees lining creek banks thick with lush growth…. I was doing a piece on Southern geography that week, had gone to sleep trying to rewrite a part that bothered me…everything overly fertile, so green, so overwhelming it choked you, made you want to give up and just lie down in it when you were out walking on sultry humid afternoons, lie down in the kudzu tendrils that almost grew fast enough for you to see, become just a bump in the landscape the way houses disappeared under the vines. That night was oppressive, George not very pleased with me as I woke him up, entwining myself in the top sheet, wrapping my body as in shrouds. Graveclothes. The doctor said it was anxiety attacks— either that, or maybe allergies, if I wanted him to stick me a dozen times to find out.

And then later the second pregnancy was gone in one afternoon of agony which doctors deadened with chemicals but told me was healthier for my body than surgery. But had they ever tried it themselves? And when I was in a mood to sit at the computer again, George was happy; he stood in the doorway smiling, and one by one I put in the diskettes I had material stored on—it *was* floppy disks then—and formatted them all, erased everything, gone with a few keystrokes. It was amazing how fast you could do that now. You used to have to gather up the paper and shred it a few sheets at a time or throw it in small stacks into a little fire—at least there was some ceremony about it, some awareness of its passing. After I had tossed three diskettes aside, George realized what I was doing, and his smile changed into a slack-jawed look of dismay. He edged back to watch, horrified, at a safe distance—as if I were Jehoiakim shredding Jeremiah's prophesies and tossing them into the brazier, as if I would next pick up the machine and throw it through the window.

"What're you doin'?" But he shut up when I turned on him:

"What's it to you? It's gone."

But, then, it wasn't really gone, was it: Here they all were, stacked in my closet, back again, reminding me….

And he never mentioned it again. Not ever. Just tramped off on his long hikes and left messages on the kitchen counter. Because it was death, death of so many things, and what's left when nothing's there in the first place, and what you create even dies?

So I became the library, the record-keeper who wrote down the dates and names. But no more stories.

"I'm going to clean all this out," I said. She shrugged. I wanted to tell her, Don't look at me for your role model, girl, for I'd be a poor one to follow.

"Can I come in?" Sandra asked hesitantly but then did anyway. Amy made a sullen moué and turned her back on her mother.

"Why're you shut up in here by yourself?"

"Out of sight, out of mind," I told her.

"Yeah, well, now they're all gonna think you're pouting."

"Whatever. They don't like me, no matter what. Better that than having to call Edwin because I was beating the crap out of somebody. If I can't depend on you to take up for me, I'm not going to force myself on anyone."

She poked her finger into Amy's chocolate pie and licked it off. Amy turned further away and quickly put the pie down with a display of exaggerated disgust.

I didn't want to tell her I had seen a little piece of masking tape on the side of the dish with Mrs. Posey's name written on it; she'd made that pie and brought it over, and as I looked at it I couldn't get out of my mind the thought of Porter's cans falling out of the privy, him refusing to eat that coconut pie years ago because he "knew things." Well, we all knew hers was the food you avoided at Sunday dinner-on-the-ground if you had the connections to find out things like that, or we just raised eyebrows as food was laid out on the long board-and-sawhorse tables: This'll be gone fast, it's Anne's old recipe; or, Don't touch that, Irene made it; she told me three days ago she'd made it.

But I didn't tell Sandra just yet; I'd save that as a little surprise maybe.

"This's a homemade pie," Sandra said with a kind of respectful awe in her voice, as if she meant something deeper.

"All hail the homemade pie," Amy sneered.

Sandra looked disapproval. "Homemade pies're better than store-bought ones."

But I wouldn't stand for that. "Are they? Store-bought ones have quality control. They're always gonna taste right. No bad meringue."

"Nothin' unique about 'em," she countered. "You know the homemade ones had love mixed in with 'em."

Amy sighed deeply.

"You want bad meringue, so you can stick to your principle?

That makes the love taste better?"

"Why do you always want to make somethin' more out of a simple thing somebody says?"

"Okay, you're right, I'll shut up. You're right."

She plopped down in a chair next to the window. "God, what a mess you've made in here."

"Amy and I are recycling. We took Porter's example and looked around to see what we could do. We'll take care of it, don't worry."

"Mother might be keepin' 'em for some reason. Better ask her first," she advised.

"By the way, Amy promises me she does not smoke." There was a soft snort from the other side of the room.

But she ignored that. "Mother wants you to come on out there soon as you eat. They're about to start their fight."

"She wouldn't tell us what's going on."

"Maybe she didn't want you to know."

"If I'm going out there, I'm gonna know what I'm getting into. What makes you so special? What's so horrible about it that I can't be told? Since I'll know in a few minutes, anyway."

She glanced back and forth between me and Amy, who caught on sooner than I. "You aren't *her* mother," Amy said. "It's not your place to say who gets to know and who doesn't."

She glared at Sandra who seemed puzzled at her words, or maybe surprised at the challenge. Whoa...you're in for a few rough years, I thought. Sandra stuck her chin out all of a sudden and started very fast: "Granny Kate tied everything up legal before she died. But, long and short, it's all going to be divided, or it's going to Porter, depending on what they decide to do with him. And the real big question is, will they just go to court and get her will voided because she was senile."

"But she wasn't. She couldn't have been senile and kept him out of trouble all the time. And a lawyer wrote up that will. They would've known if she was senile."

Sandra raised her eyebrows. "All I know is they're gonna fight it out. They want this done before they all leave today, before everybody gets a chance...a chance to...."

"To get greedy?" I said.

"-*Er*," Amy supplied.

Sandra gave her another look, a kind of assessing look, and

spoke fast: "They're fixin' to do this. And Mother wants you to come on."

"Only if you agree to help make Richard keep his fat mouth shut, and Jean Ann too. If they pick on me or Berry again. Fat lot of good you were a while ago."

"You ever think how you got it fixed now so Berry can't even come back here to apologize to you? Everybody's watchin' him now." She cocked her head to one side. "He can take up for himself, Maggie, or else he better learn. Anyway, come on out. Amy, you, too, spend time with your relatives."

Amy stuck her tongue out and fake-gagged with her finger.

"Lovely. Your manners really have improved since you haven't been in *my* house these couple of days. 'Bout time for you to go home and straighten your attitude out. I guess you're not going to clean up after yourself, either." She picked up Amy's plate, turned to leave with it, glanced at the pie, took Amy's spoon and ate another bite next to where she'd stuck her finger in.

"You really want to know why I didn't want any of that pie? Irene Posey made that," I said.

She just barely flinched for a fleeting second. Then, bravely, "Nothin' wrong with Irene's food. She's a sweet old lady."

"People have got sick on it before, as you well know, but whatever." I shrugged. "Talkin' about Mrs. Posey—I heard something funny this morning. Mother and Dad told me Porter's been stowing cans and bottles in Granny Kate's old privy. You know how he's into recycling, well, he saved up about five thousand cans, if you believe what Mother said, and stowed them in the old outhouse, really neat. You know how they've been saying all these years they ought to tear it down sometime or other. But there were so many, they got to falling out and ended up in Irene's flower garden she likes to pick her bouquets out of. She always has some pretty ones on her kitchen table. She grows pretty zinnias."

She was not fooled: "The zinnias have died off by now," she said flatly.

I shrugged. "Oh, yeah you're right." Then I started out of the room and found Amy behind me again—my little shadow today. Maybe it wasn't true about the flowers, and anyway it really didn't have anything to do with the food except to chain together a little connection to worry Sandra all day, but that was us, and it would make another good article for Berry to do some time: How we all liked to talk about food and make jokes about private parts and shit. Except, of course, he couldn't put it that way in the story.

I WALKED RIGHT up on Jean Ann in the middle of her lighting into Berry in the semi-private hall. "I got somethin' else, too," she was saying. She turned slightly. "And you might as well hear it, yourself, Maggie."

"Sorry, Jean Ann, my dance card's full, and Mother wants me for something or other," but she wasn't going to be put off by that for long.

"She does not. Nothin's goin' on right now that can't wait. I want you both to hear this." Richard and Jerry were standing within listening range, and they weren't even pretending not to hear. "I don't appreciate you makin' fun of me, Berry, and I'd've sued you if Bob hadn't stopped me and said that was just what you wanted, more publicity."

"Your own brother!" Berry said in mock horror.

"Yeah, my own brother. You just mind your business hereafter. And just wait a minute, Maggie." Her nostrils trembled. She most certainly did not ram her car into Bob's shop, she said; she hadn't even been mad at him. What it was, was the transmission had been going out on her car, and that day no matter how many times she'd put it in reverse to back out of the driveway, it had jerked back into drive and before she could lift her foot off the accelerator, there she was bumping his building—not ramming it, just bumping, and it had not done a thousand dollars' worth of damage, she had no idea where I'd come up with such a ridiculous thing—

"I came up with?" I interrupted. "Why me? Why're you raising hell at me about it?"

"Everybody knows it's you's been tattlin' to Berry all the time. Like Richard said. Get your numbers right next time," she said with disdain. "Do your research, like he'd say."

"Told you so," Richard interjected.

"You didn't think about putting it back into park or just turning the engine off after the fifth or sixth time?" Berry asked.

She ignored that. "I was humiliated," she said, "and you'll hear from a lawyer if you write stuff like that about me again."

"Somebody told me you laughed about it," I told her.

"Whoever said such a lie?"

"Besides, why'd it embarrass you? Nobody used your name."

"But everybody knew it was me—" She closed her mouth quickly.

"Because everybody knew when it happened. You broadcast it around the whole family yourself. Mama heard it from four different relatives before I was told," Berry said.

"So *she's* the one—"

"No," he interrupted quickly, "I said, 'before I was told.' I didn't say it was her doing the telling."

"I am one-hundred percent sure it was Maggie or her, one of them."

Mother came around the corner of the hall right then. "Oh, Jean Ann, you know you was just mad because Berry made it look as silly as it was."

"I want everybody here to notice, she was the one who as usual picked a fight, not me," I said.

"Don't start up in my house," Mother told me.

I elbowed Jerry out of the way. "By the way, thanks for nothing, Brother."

"Maggie, I need you to help me sack up the trash," Mother said. Jerry told her not to worry about it, he'd get to it, but she insisted he go on out to the living room and take it easy for a while; she and I could manage, maybe, with Berry helping.

"Oh, God, we've been summonsed!" he exclaimed.

Except for Amy, who had her fingers hooked tightly under my arm, they all cleared out; everybody heard that tone in her voice she got sometimes. She gave the swinging door a nudge. It smacked closed like Jean Ann's mouth had a moment ago. Funny thing about that door. Dad never used it as punctuation. But through the long years, Sandra and Jerry and Mother and I all had, employing it as a sort of exclamation mark at the end of an ultimatum screamed out loud, but a little different from slamming a solid door, which always seemed really permanent, a final termination; the swinging door held hope that a reconciliation might be possible. Then on other days it was a way of changing the subject when the subject had become too painful to keep talking about; or a metaphorical road-not-taken, the turning of our backs on one alternative and closing it away for a while. It was certainly being abused today, too much punctuation from wannabe raconteurs. Berry wandered over to the kitchen sink again, looking out the window this time, and I told Mother to go ahead and dish it out to me so I could get over being mad at her.

"I took up for you this time," she said sternly. "I ain't doin' it again."

"I didn't start it."

"I don't care," she said. "You bite your tongue till they leave. You won't have to be around 'em after today if you don't want to. And one more thing," she added. "You better take a back seat while we talk out Mama's will, because there's some that don't want you or Berry"—she raised her voice loud enough for him to hear—"here atall, afraid what they say'll end up in some magazine next month."

"You'd run me out of your own house? Your own daughter?"

"I say you have's much a right as they have, but there's stuff that's got to be discussed today, period. If it ain't, it may not be done at all—or not the way it was intended.... Fights gettin' started won't help."

"They're just camping out here because there's some money and they want a part."

She snorted a little. "You sit out of the way. Don't say a word, and"—this again loudly to Berry—"*you* pretend you're about half asleep or something."

He turned to her with a small laugh. "Yes, ma'am."

Then she gave me another one of those strange little pats and looked regretful, as if she felt really sorry for me, and I propped the door back open and, to make it legit, picked up a bag of what looked like it could be trash and passed it over to Jerry. "Go put this in your truck with all the other garbage you keep in there," I told him; he gave me a funny look and headed outside.

In the living room Aunt Sabrina had a cigarette hanging between her fingers. The room was hazy and exotic-looking with ribbons of smoke in the air; it was surprising how such a small thing could change a room you knew, a plain, familiar room, into something almost spooky. Mother caught her eye and glared at her until she mashed the cigarette down inside her coffee cup, crushing the lit end in an exaggerated way, rubbing it out slowly, like you'd erase a long sentence you'd written on paper, laughing a little and at last brandishing the butt for Mother to see.

"Let's open a window," Mother told her sweetly, "so we can let some fresh air in," and she raised the one right next to Aunt

Sabrina so that a cold breeze blew directly on her face.

10

SOMEWHERE IN THE background a muffled clatter of spoons and dishes punctuated by occasional, louder clunks filled in a kind of hissing quiet noise that made it hard to hear every conversation in the living room and dining room. Somebody was still in the kitchen organizing the leftovers, covering the plates and trays, washing the serving spoons. When I flopped down on the couch, and Amy next to me, and Berry took up an inconspicuous chair opposite me, oxygen seemed to refill the room: People considered us disposed of for a while, a typical human cleanup going along the way it would've after any other family gathering.

Eerie little wisps of smoke—remnants of Aunt Sabrina's cigarette—lingered here and there; the afternoon darkened, the men lounged near the door. Amy whispered to me, "I hate every one of them," and then seemed to doze off—how did she do it, with all the laughing, and people getting up to smoke out on the porch, and kids tearing around everywhere? There were in fact so many kids roaming about that after a while I decided she might as well stay slumped against my arm: They were probably roaming around in my room, too, so she couldn't lie down there.

The talk swirled around me like streaks of Aunt Sabrina's smoke, one strand floating near enough to get my attention, then another. Sometimes it was jobs: Logging was booming lately, lumber going for a premium, but hard work, hard work...and it'll kill you while you're still young... Then a few words about the economy or the governor, voiced a little louder than jobs; a word or two about what kind of satellite dish was best to pick up stations out in the country, if you weren't wired for cable...nervous, aimless, edgy talk that was a sort of prelude, a time-filler ahead of what would be said later, after all the cleanup was done. It was hard sometimes to peer through the fog of words and remember that most of them were decent respectable people, some of whom held down good-paying white-collar jobs. When they came home—that is, when they returned to Granny Kate's old house or even gathered in the hospital corridors when she'd been sick—

when they in other words reconnected to her and, in her, to their last real tie to what they remembered as the way things used to be—then their accents gradually deepened as if they'd been drinking, which they hadn't always been, and somehow their hair became less tidy and groomed and their clothes looked more like the things shipped in from God knew where and hung outside the one men's clothing store in town, Clearance!, claiming they were only last season's.... It was strange how it happened. And then they went back to their jobs, then they were crisp and professional again.

I knew them all better this way, the way they were here today, but I didn't like them so much.

Amy was sticky. I wriggled from time to time to shift her, and each time, she roused and looked wide-eyed at me as if I'd pinched her; and the eyes would dart around at the relatives and she'd close them, quickly, shutting it out. So maybe she wasn't dozing at all. Her brown hair was shiny and clean and straight, her eyelashes dark upon her reddened cheeks. She looked the way she had last summer when, after one of her spells with Sandra, she'd begged to stay with me for a few days and had gone to the town swimming pool in the afternoons, diving gracefully in at the deep end, her eyes not squeezed shut tensely but merely closed against the rush of the water, her thin teenage frame one long straight form gliding under the surface like a smooth young otter. All the way from the deep end to the shallow, where I sat aimlessly at the edge, dabbling my feet to stay cool. That shiny dark head, dripping water like melting silver, popping up near me: "Come on, get wet, Aunt Maggie! Can't you swim?" And I would demur, saying I didn't want to mess up my hair because I had some other place to go later, and she'd dive back off again, leaving me swishing my feet, recalling the cool pleasure of swirling water....

Somebody over in the corner started talking about the body found back in the creek last summer. It was Rhonda's opinion, seconded by Marcus' ex-wife, who had come for God knows what reason, that maybe it was an Indian's baby; they had roamed these parts once, so it could be— And Richard turned and interrupted with laughing scorn: "No, Indians never buried their younguns, they let the crows eat 'em"— And so on. Jimmy said maybe we all had Indian blood in us, and that allowed Jean Ann to poke her head around the edge of the kitchen door and give a report on her DNA test. Berry's eyes lit up; but, she said, she didn't think those things were accurate, because hers didn't at all show what she'd always known to be true; so you couldn't believe them, anyway. Somebody else opined that the baby could've been some pore thing left after one of them fever epidemics way back yonder long time ago.... Then they considered conspiracies: "Coroner said there were questions he couldn't answer"—from Jimmy again—"but that's the gov'ment for you. Probably got a good idea who it was. Probably something they don't want out."

"Better not say anything else, or Berry here'll have it be one of Jean Ann's love babies."

And Jean Ann heard that and shrugged her shoulders: "None of mine."

Amy stirred and gave Jean Ann a glance; the movement drew Richard's attention: "Where's your old man, Maggie?"

I stared coldly at him. "Busy."

He laughed. "Busy stayin' away." —Loud enough so a good many cousins heard him. Some tried to be kind to me, asked what they were doing over at the lake. Before I had a chance to answer, Richard scoffed: "Ruinin' the fishin' for everybody. Don't know why they can't leave well enough alone."

There were some questions then about what those wildlife guys were trying to accomplish, draining the water down to nothing, and he took it on himself to answer again before I could. His opinion as always was: The gov'ment just wanted to show they were the bosses and keep honest fishermen out, guys maybe who'd had a bad week and had to bring home supper on a hook. The cousins, some of them, didn't buy that and let him finish his rant before looking politely at me for my take on it.

"They're trying to kill off some of the invasives," I started. Richard snickered again.

"Just stop 'em at the border," he suggested. This time the silence gave him to understand his brand of sarcasm wasn't going over well. His face went a little red. "I for one am pissed they're using funds to tear up somethin' just because they can. Keep the water in, I say. Nature takes care of itself just fine. Don't need no help from us."

"It's not a natural lake, though. It was built," Marcus said.

But Richard wasn't having it, and flailed out with one hand, his face grim. "There's no need in takin' that water out, ruinin' the fishin', messin' up the boat ramps. They just tryin' to throw their weight around." Nobody said anything to affirm that; Dobber might have if he'd been inside, but he'd gone to the porch for a smoke, so Richard was on his own, and it was not like the old days when he could depend on his toadies. Berry looked solemn, stared at him. Richard stood and fumbled in his pocket for a cigarette, headed for the door.

"Just my opinion, as good as anybody's," he concluded. "Get your panties out of a wad, Maggie; I ain't insultin' your old man." He joined Dobber and another relative; we could hear their voices, low, outraged.

"Why'd he care if the water's deeper in one place or another?" Larry mumbled. "He'd go find him a spot anyway, legal or not." Some chuckled; Berry frowned and looked out the window at the men smoking on the porch.

A few years ago George blundered on a group of road-hunters who'd had no luck that day and were consoling themselves with a few six-packs of beer. They were also out of season, and it was his job as a game warden to put a stop to that kind of thing. He called out a warning, but by then they were drunk enough, he said, that it just seemed to scare them, and one fired off a last shot that hit close enough to dislodge a chunk of bark from the tree he'd wisely stayed behind. The missile struck his head and sent him to the ER: Head wounds do bleed inordinately. When he yelled, they cranked up their trucks and tore off down the road.

George got Edwin Bonner to nose around and find out what he could. Tongues would loosen up after they thought they'd got away with it, he figured, and somebody did eventually tell him they'd seen two vehicles like what Dobber's cronies rode around in, but Dobber wasn't with them that day, they insisted to him when he tracked them down. George, however, never believed that and laid in wait for Dobber when he left work one afternoon. It was all words, he told me later—turning around and holding out his arms to show me he had no bruises—he and Berry thought Dobber was just all words.

MOTHER WALKED THROUGH the swinging door, and a change came into the room with her. The smokers came back in, anticipating her opening remarks. Little by little everybody got quiet and attentive, and at that point somebody happened to be directing a comment towards where Porter's family was sitting. Anne and the brothers looked the way I must have earlier when Richard jumped me in the kitchen, but they were silent, just sat looking tense and scared and resentful.

"...I mean, Godamighty, we ain't talkin' knick-knacks and pots and pans here. I don't care about the knick-knacks. Y'all want 'em, you can have 'em all."

It was Dobber. I expected James Preacher to get up and leave the room, his way of showing he didn't like somebody's language. But today he only shook his head sadly and asked them all please to not take the Lord's name in vain.

I had no idea how Dobber got that name; it was something to do with the wasp that made mud nests, little caves constructed on ceilings and inside your lawn mowers. About half the cousins had nicknames like Peck or Tater or Dobber or something. You didn't ask about it for fear of what you'd find out. Maybe Dobber'd played with mud a lot as a kid, or maybe one of the bullies had decided he looked like his namesake. "I mean, it's gotta be more than five hundred grand," he went on. His rough, thick hands combed his hair in agitation, disturbing his carefully-arranged style. Whatever sort of devilish appeal people had thought he'd had as a young man was pretty much gone now. You'd call him these days a hard-working poor relation. All four of them, Great-uncle Thomas' kids, were just hard-scrabble, never-got-a-break types. Some families are that way: You have the branch that made good, and then you have the ones that always look burned-out and used-up before their time, working at hard, minimum-wage, manual-labor jobs. Jimmy, Dobber, Linda, and Richard, who was the younger brother—Richard was about Sandra's age; Dobber six or seven years older than that, and he looked old enough to be Richard's father, his complexion red and coarse from days spent working in all kinds of weather.

A different person realizing most of the room was listening, paying attention to his ill-chosen words, might've sheepishly stopped; but not Dobber. He had the floor and made a fast calculation about keeping it and how that would advance his propositions. "I know somethin' 'bout timber. And I'm tellin' you, there's people would easy pay five hundred thousand for that land, or more. You realize what that'd give each of us? There's eleven of us—"

Richard took out a grubby piece of paper and started figgering. Dobber waited until he'd got through.

"At the least, forty thousand."

"Forty thousand," Dobber repeated reverentially, enjoying the sound the words made. "We ain't talkin' knick-knacks here. But we probably gonna have to go to court."

There was a sudden hush. It was the sort of quiet you hear when a doctor tells you you have to decide whether to continue life support on somebody. Aunt Sabrina had evidently decided she wasn't in the family and should keep her mouth shut; but she looked on, an interested, keen glint in her eyes.

"Are we ready to do that?" Richard asked thoughtfully.

"I just don't think she was all there to've done her will the way she did. That is, what I've heard about it. Which could be wrong." He looked hopefully, expectantly at Liza, but she stayed quiet. Mother also said nothing. Dobber sighed: "So we may have to go to court."

"Or one of us's goin' to have to take him in," Jean Ann said clearly. "You're not sayin' it, Mama, but everybody already suspects that's what it's all about. And we're right, aren't we?"

Liza's eyes narrowed as she stared at Jean Ann. I would've thought she'd have had the gumption at least to turn away, but, like Dobber, she didn't; she stuck out her chin a little and glared back.

Then they all glanced toward Anne, Larry and Marcus.

"I figure I'll have Mom one of these days, and I cannot take care of both of them," Anne said defensively.

Jimmy tapped his knuckles on his chair-arm. "I thought she was still in that hospital."

Anne said nothing else.

"Alicia and I've got our hands full with our kids. They're just now turning into teenagers. We can't handle another kid." That, from Larry.

"Usually your own family takes care of this kind of thing. I mean, he's *your* brother, not ours," Dobber said in a judgmental tone, and Larry looked down at the floor. Anne's face turned red, and Marcus fidgeted.

It was like a jury deciding a capital offense there in Mother's living room and dining room in the damp gloom of the rainy afternoon. Porter's mother didn't count as one of Granny Kate's offspring, she wasn't blood, and nobody wanted to claim her as blood right now. Two of the original eight babies had died early, leaving the six who grew up in various states of poverty and alternated shifts watching the dirt road in front of her house for something new to come along and change their prospects. Mostly, it hadn't. Yet somehow Granny Kate had managed to hang onto those eight hundred acres of one-time farm land that had not grown anything but trees for forty or more years.

Everybody in the family thought she was leaving everything to the grandchildren; in the last ten years or so she'd started saying it herself over and over, either right after we'd finish eating, or right before people splintered off to escape back to whatever lives they had. They'd tell her she ought to sell the land in her lifetime and make herself more comfortable with the money, and she'd laugh and say she wasn't comfortable anymore anyway. She rethought that when Everett and Pauline's children became hers. Times were different, and as with Pauline, she wanted her wards better took care of; so she sold off some timber behind her house and had a new bathroom installed in one of the old bedrooms. Which was why the privy became a storage place for Porter's cans and bottles.

She'd sold timber just one other time, to pay for Everett's funeral and buy him a marker. She never farmed again after she took his kids in to raise, not farmed for a living but only for her deep-freezer. Anybody thereafter daring to tell her to sell off and build herself a better house got a sharp answer for their efforts: She was leaving it so the grands'd have something after everything and everybody else was gone.

So they all sat glancing around suspiciously, wondering which one might get saddled with Porter.

"What *is* in her will?" June, James Preacher's sister, asked. "Liza, do you know? Aunt Janie? I heard she left it to us; but some've said, to Porter. It don't make a whole lot of sense to me."

"If all of you think this's the time to *talk* about it," Liza started grimly as if to remind everybody her mother had just been buried, "I'll tell you what she told me." She gave Mother a strange glance and paused, but Mother just glared back. "I haven't looked at her will with my own eyes, but she said she fixed it so the land would be sold, all together, when she passed on—"

"I figgered that"—that was from Dobber.

"—and I was to get a sixth," Liza continued. She stopped at the general soft gasp in the room, and looked coolly at them. "There was just the six of us that had kids of our own, and all the others's passed on now, well, not Pauline *but*...except Janie, and she'd get the same as me. And Willis' part would've gone to Alex."

I thought again about Porter's mother, locked up these many years in the asylum, and wondered if arrangements had been made for her.

Jean Ann laughed a little nervously and fiddled with her hair. "I am truly not trying to be greedy. I am not needing money. I'm just asking. Did she leave anything to us for right now?"

"You get your part when I die," Liza said coldly. "The other grandchildren don't have their mamas and daddies anymore, except Janie's three. So it goes straight to them."

Richard did a little more arithmetic surreptitiously on his scrap of paper. He scratched his head and stuffed the pencil and paper back into his pocket.

"Well, that's fair," he said. "Anybody'd see that's right. Anyway, it still leaves at least four, maybe a little more, hundred grand to be decided about. Now I *know* it ain't really ours, not yet, not any of us, so ever'body just keep your feathers smooth. But if it's in her will, we'd find out sooner or later, and we might as well think about how to handle ever'thing while we're all in one place together. Might not get a chance again, except in a goddamned lawyer's office." He ignored James's deep sigh. "So what else is in it?"

Maybe Jean Ann was trying to decide if Liza could possibly go through a hundred grand before she died; she glanced from her mother to Richard. Berry gazed steadily at the floor, his mouth a hard, thin line turned up so slightly at one side. It was just the two of them—Jean Ann and him, with three stillbirths after him, so he had about as much financial interest as she did, yet he was silent.

"The rest of it's to be divided into fifteen parts all the same," Liza said. "One part for each of you grandkids. If Dobber's got his figures right, that ought to be, it would leave..."

"Could be twenty-seven grand apiece," Richard said. He nodded. "No need to be greedy about it. That's twenty-seven thousand none of us's got now."

Liza waited. It didn't take long. I was the library: I knew that with Liza's children out of the picture, there were only eleven.

"But I said it was eleven. There ain't fifteen grandchildren alive. Where'd that come from?" Richard said in a minute.

Mumbled variations of "I told you she was getting' senile—" went around.

"She counted Alexander Guy. She always hoped he'd show back up one day. She put somethin' in there if he didn't, by the time she died. So I guess his part would be added in. Fourteen."

"So, eleven, then, if he don't show up at the lawyer's office that day. Not likely he will, now, am I right?" He chuckled a little; the others mostly didn't. "That bumps up the total. But it still leaves three parts. What about the rest of the money?"

"Well, Janie...?" But Mother just shook her head one time, held out her hand as if to say, *Go on, you started*. "That's where Porter comes in," Liza said all in a rush, a little loudly, as if it was a challenge. "One of you that agrees to take care of him'll get the interest off the other three parts. And when he dies, if it's a natural death"—she paused, looked coldly at all of them as if she really wondered if somebody might do Porter in—"the three parts goes to the one that did take care of him. And he gets his share outright, too, like the rest of you. And if nobody agrees to do it, then the money goes to him, all the rest of it except a hunderd dollars for each of you. She had the bank president and the sheriff and the county supervisor witness it and tied it up all legal with the lawyer."

So that was it—another strong-woman story to tell around. Two or three other cousins laughed softly with me because of new respect for Granny Kate and, for that matter, for Liza too, who seemed to be enjoying this.

"A very Old Testament way of dividin' it all up," James said admiringly. "Three parts for the son. He ain't the oldest son...but very Old Testament."

"Well, that does it," Dobber said. "I say that proves it. I say we take it to court."

"Oh, no, you don't. You ain't gettin' me to say *my* mama was crazy," Liza said firmly. "Because she wasn't."

"Well, then, maybe you oughta be the one to take care of him," Dobber said sarcastically. "He's your nephew."

"And so're you, I hate to say."

"If you're gonna be the one to keep the rest of us from gettin' our parts— She told us we was to get it all," he continued plaintively. "It was to be ours. I think he must've influenced her mind. Everybody knows they got to roamin' around lookin' for that cemetery that dead child washed out of, like it was one of her own. Out half the nights. She went crazy, I tell you."

"This will was done long before any of that," Liza said.

"By rights the family oughta take care of him," Richard put in. "He's their responsibility." At that, Anne, Marcus and Larry froze again. "Or put him away. He's feeble-minded."

"He's not feeble-minded," someone said.

"Or, anyway, not normal. I've always said so."

"I know about the law," June said. She was receptionist in one of the lawyers' offices downtown and always promoted herself as the go-to person on small legal things when we were together. Sitting near her, I saw a crafty, self-satisfied expression on her face; or was it just the darkening afternoon? "I know a man can't leave money to his wife and say she can't have it if she ever marries again. Well, this's like that. I don't think it's legal."

"But this's a grandma," Dobber said. "It's not the same."

"I don't know what the fuss's about," Richard interrupted firmly. "Looks to me like all somebody's got to do is take care of him for just long enough for the land to get sold and the money to get divided, and then send him off with his mama."

"That's our mother you're talking about," Larry warned, his brows lowered. "You better be careful."

"Yeah, and it's your brother we're talking about, too—you could solve all of this, do what you ought to do." There was silence again. "Guess not," Richard went on sarcastically. "Where is he, anyway? Y'all take him some food? Didn't think about that?" There was appalled silence, and with grim satisfaction he glanced around at the shocked faces. "Guess not," he repeated. "Don't be self-righteous with *me*. So what would anybody do if we just handled it the way I said? They'll never collect all that money back. Not if nobody pitches a fuss about it." He frowned slightly, almost menacingly, at Liza. "He belongs somewhere else, anyway. Somebody like him could not look out for hisself. You know it and so do I. That's why he stayed with *her* all those years."

"I told Mama I didn't think she should do it this way," Liza said. "I told her it'd cause nothin' but trouble. She just wanted to see him looked after. She shoulda left you all pieces of the land."

The telephone rang in the kitchen, and Aunt Lilly got up to answer it.

"I'd just as soon had the land," Jimmy said. "Some land to hunt on, put a cabin on, part of the old home place. I'd sooner had that."

"Land's just somethin' else you have to take care of," Richard said.

"She couldn't figger out how to divide off each piece. Some of you'da complained about the part you got," Liza told him. "If it was a lot of the creek bottom or something." She appealed to Mother again with a glance.

"Well, who's to do it?" Dobber said. "Who's to take 'im in? I'll give a thousand of my share right off the bat to anybody that'll do it. Hell, I'll give it today."

He glanced around the room again when everybody kind of sucked their breath in at this offer. Some of it was the shock of hearing it actually said; or maybe the thought of another pile of fifties. Everybody was glancing around the room now, back and forth at everybody else like kids in a game of musical chairs. Then three or four people were talking at the same time in a rush to get their say in, and I heard somebody remark it wasn't any need to hurry in such a way, it didn't look good, right after a funeral, and somebody else said it wasn't just being greedy, it was taking up for yourself, and over it all I heard Dobber insisting that now was the time, while we was all together, and there shouldn't be any going back on their word, and Richard was insisting with a cold gleam in his eye that it was simple, they were making it out to be way too complicated. They argued back and forth a few minutes like that. All of a sudden Richard met my eyes and laughed. "What's the matter, Maggie? You eat that bad pie?"

Aunt Lilly was back at the door, silently motioning to me with a kind of desperate look on her face.

"You sound like you're talking about a used car."

"If you're offended, *you* take him."

"Stay out of it, Maggie," Sandra said in an urgent, anxious voice.

"I'm in the house I grew up in, thank you, I'll say what I want," I told her. "I would've thought *you'd* remember that, too."

"Just because it sounds a little rough doesn't mean it don't need to be said. Unpleasant things do have to be discussed. It's just a legal thing."

"I don't need your opinion, either, June," I told her. I knew I was getting shrill and silly and that some of them were smiling condescendingly and some were gritting their teeth, but I plowed on: "If I could, I'd give every penny of it to him, or I'd give it away."

"I don't doubt you would," Richard interrupted. "All you do-gooder liberal types do stuff like that, even if it don't help nobody. And usually it don't."

"That's a great Christian attitude, Richard." It was the first time Berry'd said anything. He'd stood up by the kitchen door, applauding softly. "Preacher might not agree, I guess."

"I told you earlier to stay out of everything today," Jean Ann said loudly, "or you'll wish you did."

"I am terrified," he scoffed.

"Good Lord. We had to put up with the niggers and the crazy folks already yesterday; now we got to hear from the queers, too?"

There was a loud sucking sound as everybody took a deep breath and emptied all the air out of the room, and then it was extremely quiet in the vacuum, and everybody stared at Richard.

Dobber shook his head. "That's what's wrong these days. They think they got the right to run everything."

"I won't have this startin' up," Mother said—her first words.

"Shut your goddamned mouth, Richard," Berry said.

Another kind of hushed gasp.

Richard swaggered near the door, his eyes level, meeting Berry's. "What'd you say?"

"You heard me," Berry went on, an icy smile dragging at his mouth. "I say it to you and about half of everybody else in here. I ought to feel sorry for you, except you're not worth it."

"There ain't going to be a fight in my house," Mother said firmly. Dad was pushing his chair away to stand by her in support, and everybody else was sort of moving apart into a semicircle, apprehensively, and eagerly, the way kids do around a schoolyard fight. Richard took one more step toward Berry.

"Back off," Berry said extremely quietly, almost a whisper, his stare deadly cold. "This ain't no back-street honky-tonk, where you got people to lie for you. And it ain't midnight on a dirt road somewhere, either. You think *everybody* here'll help you this time?"

Richard's face turned slightly redder. He seemed as confused as I was to hear Berry's speech change, without ironic overtones, into what everybody else's was like today.

"I never had the chance to beat your ass, but I'd love doin' it,"

Berry continued. "And bein' in better shape than you are, you fat-gut clown, and knowin' more about how to do it, I'm tellin' you now, I'll shove your sorry butt out that door in half a minute."

Dobber was edging forward, but Richard's face seemed to register some shadow of uncertainty, and he hesitated. He finally motioned Dobber back: "Naw, not now or here."

"No, your way's backwoods somewhere, ain't it?"

The side of Richard's face twitched. "Besides, no tellin' what I might catch, these days."

"Maggie, darlin', George's on the phone for you," Aunt Lilly interrupted anxiously.

"Maggie to the rescue," Richard crowed as he sat back down straddled of a chair.

"I'll be there in a minute, tell him," I said. "Richard, you forget, this was my house, one time, and, for my part, you're not welcome. Act like you got some sense for a change."

"Aunt Janie, I am sorry to see her creatin' a fight in your house, at a family gatherin'—" Jean Ann started.

"Oh, shut up, Jean Ann. You upset because your mama's getting what's rightly hers and you don't get anything yet?"

Bob told me to watch what I said to his wife, and I told him she was my cousin and he wasn't even blood kin and ought to keep out of it, and couldn't she take up for herself? and it just looked like it was going to be a regular old brawl in spite of everything. James Preacher wasn't even trying to calm anybody down. Mother stood up and told them all in the next thing to a scream that this *was* her house and she wasn't having no name-calling and no fighting and no yelling and no swearin', they'd just all have to leave and go somewhere else if they was going to do it. Aunt Sabrina's eyes gleamed.

Richard leaned his chair back a little. "Well, Aunt Janie, why don't you take Porter? I say anybody tellin' the rest of us what to do oughta be ready to put their money where their mouth is."

"You know, I have never liked you, Richard," she said calmly.

I shook Amy off onto the couch where she sat staring at the angry faces. Richard watched me, not realizing until I hooked my foot under the lifted leg of his chair. It skidded nicely on Mother's polished hardwood floor and sent him down with a loud crash, his head bouncing against the wall. Everybody gasped; Dobber started for me, and I shoved him back before Jerry stepped up and stared him down.

"You get out and cool off for a while," I screamed. "You can't just say whatever you want to in here!"

Richard eased up with as much dignity as he could show the crowd and threatened to whip my butt or sue me or both. I bellied up to him, shoving him backward with my hand—"Out, get out on the porch!"

"I ain't fightin' a woman. I won't call you no lady. But I ain't fightin' no woman."

He ambled toward the front door, fumbling in his shirt pocket for a cigarette, which some thoughtful cousin lit for him just before he went out.

"You might get your ass beat," I yelled, and with a black look at me, he went outside and stood on the front porch, glancing back into the living room every few minutes, his cigarette hand trembling a little, and after a second of hesitation Dobber joined him.

"You don't talk ugly in my house," Mother said to me.

"Well, make everybody else stop it, too!"

"I will!" she said grimly.

Amy jumped up to follow me as I limped to the kitchen, where I could pick up that phone. Just as I was leaving the room, Richard stuck his head back to the door and asked me if my old man was still playing with his stuffed animals, and I told him he'd be the next one George caught, and it'd be in *all* the papers if I had anything to do with it, and I kicked the swinging door shut, which just made my foot hurt worse. I picked up the phone. Aunt Lilly had laid the receiver down on the table, so George had been able to hear a lot of what was being said in the background and wanted to know what the hell was going on in Mother's house.

"Everybody's fighting over Granny Kate's will, and nobody wants responsibility for Porter, and I can't explain now, there's too many ears close by. Where are you?"

He had got home just a few minutes ago, he said, and was about to get cleaned up, if I wanted him to put in an appearance there or if I needed any help beating Richard up.

I told him not to bother. They wouldn't think any better of him if he did show.

Amy was trembling. Something to eat might help her a little; she hadn't had much all day. I saw that Aunt Sabrina had brought her coffee cup ashtray in here, hidden it behind the extra styrofoam plates on the countertop by the sink. Maybe she'd finally been a little ashamed of irritating Mother. Or, again, maybe she just planned to let mother find it later. It was as bad as seeing crumpled toilet paper dropped on the floor, and I picked it up to sling it all, coffee, grounds, butt, out the door; but there on the back stoop, I swear, was Porter himself, leaning up against one of the porch posts and gazing out at the rain that was turning the masses of fallen sweetgum leaves into matted brown islands that looked like discarded paper sacks in the back yard.

11

I PUT MY head back into the dining room. "Mother, could you help me a minute?" In her voice. So there I was, wearing her old socks after all.

She glared generally around at everybody in the room before leaving it. "What?"

I motioned out the window.

"Oh, my Lord," she said. "I thought they'd sent him to stay with Hazel," she said, shaking her head. "You sure he didn't just wander up—"

"From where? He's not even wet. He wasn't at Hazel's house. And why send him to her, anyway? His family is *here*. And somebody in that room there brought him."

"This's the last straw," she said. "Don't just stand there. Tell him to come in out of the damp. Ask him if he wants some salad or pie. We still have plenty of them. My Lord. I guess they didn't even feed him."

I heard her light into the cousins, and from their silence I knew it wouldn't be long before they'd all swear they thought he was somewhere in the house, or somewhere else entirely, and then they'd all be asking each other, "Weren't you supposed to've taken him to Hazel's?" and there'd be a rush to the kitchen so that the first one in there could demonstrate the right thing to do— And there I was, vacillating the same way I was giving them down-the-country for doing. It sort of put you in your place.

I opened up the door. "Porter, nobody knew you were there. I think you ought to come in out of the weather."

He smiled a secretive smile. "Prob'ly safer here."

"Come get something to eat. There's still plenty."

"The shoutin' over?" he said. "They finished?"

"Come in and get something," I told him again and inched back inside. By now the parade had begun, led by Marcus and Anne. "He's going to catch pneumonia," she said.

"Didn't he ride back with y'all?" I said.

"We brought him, but we just—"

"We thought he was in the bathroom—"

"You been here an hour. You didn't any more think he was in the bathroom than I did."

There was a disconcerted silence, and I, being able to feel superior—I *had* tried to get him to come back inside, after all, whereas they hadn't—I waved my hand and ordered them to go to their comfortable seats, go on back where they'd been. The embarrassed quiet in the other room had been broken by voices expressing excuses and defensiveness and rationalizations, and a few of the more conscience-stricken cousins saying they were leaving, it was just too bad this was going on; and others telling them they couldn't leave yet; and above it all, I heard Dobber stubbornly saying over and over, "It don't matter anyway, he might's well know—money don't mean much to him, and maybe he'd say who he'd live with, if that person'd have him. Why don't we just ask him? He ought to have a say…"

"Ya'll come back in here," Mother ordered in that voice. "Let Maggie look after 'im— You just come right back in here and we'll get somethin' settled—" and she frowned meaningfully at them.

I had kind of bullied them through the swinging door by then, and let it shut in their faces. But now what. There he still was, watching the rain, and Amy shivering in the corner by the door, and I didn't want to have to fool with him, either. But he was, as Mother impressed on me, family, and that had to mean something or other. A thrill of pity, perhaps, or shame, went through me as I peeped through the window at him. You just didn't feel that way about somebody who didn't matter at all to you, did you?

"Come in," I said again, "and let's get some food. Or cake or pie or something. It's too cold and wet to stay out here on the porch."

He shambled inside, looking weird in the unfamiliar suit somebody had got him to wear. I took Amy's arm, gently steering her to one end of the table away from where the food lay.

"Maybe a sandwich? Some salad?"

"It's not chicken salad, is it?" he said. "I don't eat chicken salad." He laughed at me, or, rather, sort of chuckled, and winked the way Granny Kate did that time in the hospital.

"It's potato salad," I said stolidly. Then—wanting to giggle as I had at the funeral a while ago—I could not keep myself from adding, "We had chicken salad last night."

He glanced up at me quickly, then back down at the food. "Was it good?"

"As chicken salad goes," I said.

"Well, I don't eat chicken salad. Familiarity breeds contempt."

And suddenly I saw him and Berry on that fence.

Behind me Amy laughed in a strangled, horrified way.

He wandered around the table from one end to the other, lifting up the plastic wrap on the ham, running his finger along the edge of the cake plate and licking off the icing. "Looks like the throng's done been through most of this food."

I got busy filling a cup with ice for his tea. Amy just stared at him.

"There's plates over there," I said. "Why don't you get whatever you'd like."

"Think I'll pass on the chocolate pie," he said, smiling his secret smile downward.

Dad eased through the swinging door. "Believe I'll sit in here with y'all."

"Safer in here," Porter said. "Get yourself some salad. I have already eaten."

Well, that was news. "When?" I blurted out.

"I stayed out here for a while, and when everybody was pretty much in that livin' room, I come inside and got what I wanted. But I could eat a little more. What about you, Daniel?"

Dad told him he'd already eaten, too. Porter slid a slice of pecan pie onto a plate, a piece of ham, got a fork. They both took chairs that Mother had pulled away from the table and lined against the wall to keep people from spilling food on the seats.

"Be careful with your chair," Porter said. "They fall sometimes."

Evidently nothing escaped him.

"Well, Porter," Dad said, watching—as I was—while he shoveled pie into his mouth with a fork. "You takin' it all right?"

"Ain't bothered me yet. Didn't spoil sittin' out, did it?"

"What? —Oh. No, nothin's been out more than an hour. No, I mean Granny Kate. You holdin' up okay about her?"

Porter looked down while he chewed, his brows lowered just a little in a frown. "She was so old," he told us at last. "Ninety-nine is *old*. She'd started havin' more bad days than good ones here-lately. Got to where she couldn't see's well as she used to. No trouble with her hearin', though, no matter what ever'body thought. She could hear plenty. Even through walls. Never let on, though." He chuckled. "Not many knew she had a hearing aid."

I glanced toward the quieter living room in spite of myself. Mother had evidently calmed them all down some.

"People are kinder to dogs than they are to humans: They gently put them to sleep. She often told me she had no earthly idea why she was still here. I had no answer for that. Do you?" He waited a few seconds, but, like him, we had no answer. "I had no answer. I believe I will feel the same way, sometime. She wanted to get out and walk towards the last," he went on. "Took it in her head to ramble a little. I didn't let her go far."

"What was she lookin' for, do you think?"

"I don't know that she was lookin' *for* anything. She wanted to look *at* things—the fences, the old bridge, even, like she wanted to be sure all the things were safe. She'd say, 'We need to go look around,' and if I asked for what, she'd just tell me not to worry. Maybe she did think she'd lost somethin'. Not a real thing, you know. Somethin' she *thought* she had. I just went when she said to. I had to look out for her. Lots of things you can see if you walk and look," he added, turning towards me with eyes hooded, the corners of his mouth lifted. "I done what I could for her, but I never fig-gered why she wanted to go walkin' when she was so old. And then sometimes she wanted me just to drive her around the roads out here.... Ask Berry." His uncertainty changed quickly into decisiveness, and he nodded.

Dad raised his brows at me and rolled his eyes. "Why him? Ask him what?"

"Maybe he understood it better than I did."

A strange remark, and I reminded myself to remember it for

later. "What're you going to do now, Porter?" I asked. "You going to keep on living at the old house?"

"That depends. I am sure goin' to miss her. I seem to have no say-so in this. To me that is strange. I do realize I've never done for myself. But why do I have no more say-so than those teenagers in that room?"

"You need to think about what you want to do. Where you'd *like* to live. You know the relatives are gonna want to sell the house or something, and they can, I guess, legally, and, anyway, you ought not to live out here by yourself. Where would you want to be?"

He put down the fork and stared at it with the little smile on his face again. "I'm not sure I'll be making that decision on my own. She already saw to it that some things were decided."

Nobody said anything for a few minutes, during which he picked his fork up again and finished the pie.

"And I have to get my driving license," he said. "Somebody needed to drive, after she got to where she couldn't see. But nobody wanted me to do it. She let me, because somebody had to. None of the others could understand that."

Dad cleared his throat. "Shame the old place'll be sold off. Everything goes. There used to be just about anything you could think of on that land. Wild turkey, deer, bobcats. I wouldn't'a been too surprised to run up on a bear some day."

I was annoyed suddenly, knowing what he was about to do. "Used to be panthers around these parts," he went on, with that intent, faraway look in his eyes—was he trying to scare Porter out of thinking of staying in Granny Kate's house; or was he in his story-telling frame of mind; or was he just being mean?

Porter frowned a little, glanced sideways at him. "I never saw one," he muttered. "Been out in those woods a lot."

"Oh, you wouldn't. They're extinct now—it's a shame," Dad went on. "But, one time, they were around."

"Thought I saw an owl off in the woods a while ago, earlier," Porter said. "You or Janie ever see it around? Sometimes they start hangin' out in the same place after a while. Some people think they are bad signs."

Dad cleared his throat again. "I wouldn't be scared of an owl. But I used to go huntin' when I was younger, and one time—"

"Excuse me, but I've heard this one," I interrupted. "Porter, if I were you, I'd let 'em all know right now, today, what I wanted to do; you got rights in this, you're a grandson too, and you've lived there a long time. You probably wouldn't *want* to be there by yourself, like I said, way out in the country, but you go on and have your say, too."

"You know they think I don't have good sense," he said coolly. "Whereas, I could tell 'em a thing or two. But then they'd probably make me go back to that doctor." I sucked in my breath at this remark. Even Dad was staring at him. "So, no, I'm just gonna let 'em figure it out, what they want to do with the property and all, and I'll discuss it with 'em later. Plus anyway, she told me the lawyers would help me if I needed it. She planned things out. I might live next to Larry. Or Anne. But, nope, I think I'll go set out on the back porch again. It ain't so chilly I'll get sick."

After a moment of silence, I couldn't think of anything to say; and then, with another kind of sideways look at me, he did ease back outside, taking a glass of tea in one hand and dragging a chair with the other.

12

WHEN I LEFT the kitchen, Dad was serving himself and Amy another slice of cake, and though she made a move to follow me, Berry beat her to it and was chasing out a couple of Marcus' kids and closing the door behind us when I entered the room.

"Couldn't stay in there, your mama'd have to run me off, I'd have killed Richard by now. Somebody'd've had to call Elvis Bonner," he said. "Or I'd've had to run off to Texas the way they said those old ones did. I figured you'd sneaked out to drive back to town yourself."

"I was in the kitchen with Porter. What's going on now?"

"Mama was crying and making no sense at all, and your mother was still saying things in that voice of hers—I always *was* afraid of it, and I still am."

"Did you hear yourself there before I left? What happened to you?"

He winced. "It always comes out sooner or later, huh. You know, the scary part is, legally, Dobber's right. They can't enforce all those stipulations, if somebody pushed hard enough. Granny Kate had to know it, too. She probably made the lawyers put it in to try and keep 'em honest, make 'em think about it. Appeal to their 'better angels.' "

"They don't have any 'better angels'," I scoffed.

"I hope somebody does. I think about it a lot now. She must've, too, because she did write her will a good while back, before they had any reason to call her senile."

"You accused Richard of some bad things a while ago. I mean, 'sheets,' really? You think he has that in him?"

"I don't know. Do you? I mean, I really just told him, 'Thou art the man!' He can interpret it however he wants."

" 'Thou art the man.' Second Samuel. Old Testament."

"Very good. All those Bible drills paid off."

I crawled up onto the bed and stuffed several pillows behind me, leaned back against the headboard. "We're gonna have to leave that door open a little, or they'll have something else to talk about."

He grimaced. "No, they won't. Remember, I'm gay." He parked himself astride the little round wicker stool Sandra and I had used as girls in front of the mirror.

"That will not hold you up," I told him. "Don't break it."

"I'm just powdering my nose."

"Shut up." Somehow all of a sudden I was about to cry. I didn't want to wipe my eyes and expose myself; maybe blinking would solve the problem. A great blob of tear slopped out and started tracking down my face. "Dammit."

"You haven't grieved at all that I've seen. It's just delayed sorrow."

"Oh, yeah, like at the funeral. You should've seen me. Laughing like a hyena. I had to use Amy as a human shield to get out of the church. Yet it seems they all saw me anyway."

"Most people thought you two were overcome with grief. I knew better." He stopped, fumbled in a pocket and produced a handkerchief for me.

The mild answer somehow made me sadder.

"I saw you wandering around in the cemetery with her. You show her Alex's grave?"

I wiped my eyes. "Yeah."

He laughed softly. "What'd you tell her?"

" 'Ain't nobody there.' No...body." I passed the handkerchief to him.

"I still wonder where he is, what became of him."

"Look 'im up on the Internet."

"I've tried. Nothing there. Guess he *did* what those old ones did, left for Texas, changed his name." He snorted. "He was pretty thick with Richard. I bet *he* knows where he is."

I turned away. "I'm sorry about what Richard said."

"You didn't say it," he pointed out. "Anyway, you got sweet revenge for me. I wonder if his head hurts."

"God, I hope it's banging like an anvil about now."

He laughed softly. "I loved it. You've never been able to properly take up for me. You couldn't tell 'em what would shut 'em up. It would've turned on *you*."

He did: He'd said it, what we'd not talked about for our whole adult lives.

OUR TURN HAD arrived to sit on the gate and watch when we were almost out of high school, not really, not actually, because we'd already done that as children and were too old for it, now; but figuratively. The last summer before we turned eighteen, the last year we could officially claim to be still children, Granny Kate lifted up a bushel of black-eyed peas one day and found herself in the shape of a lower-case "r." Her doctor prescribed three weeks of rest and muscle relaxants, which might make her act a little strange, he said, so people were going to have to help her out with meals and the like. He doubted Porter could do it all, especially as her vegetables were coming in and needed preserving. The pills did relax her, to the point where she lay in bed day after day and gazed up at the ceiling with vague, bleary eyes. Anne and Marcus and Larry had escaped by then, gone off to town and got jobs or got married or got whatever bought their freedom. Mother bullied everybody and organized a schedule of relatives to bring at least one hot meal a day for the rest of the time Granny Kate had to be drugged up on the pills. Somehow, Sandra and I hadn't considered we'd be included in the schedule. I slouched in behind Mother when her turn came to ferry the food over—slouched in, bitching softly, until I saw Liza was already there when we arrived, which meant Berry would be, too, and there'd be commiseration, at least. It turned out that Liza decided the house needed cleaning, and

Granny Kate, a good bath. She'd made arrangements with Mother to come and help her.

Berry and I wiped down the table and countertop together. "This place's so old, the dirt's dirty," he said softly; we snickered, threw the sponges at each other.

Liza and Mother cast exasperated glances at us.

Berry nudged me, tugged at my arm, called to Liza: "We're gonna get out of the way, get some fresh air."

"You can stay right here and put this linen in the washer."

Obediently he picked up the pieces, threw them into the machine. I pretended to be helping; we quietly debated the quantity of detergent to add and twisted the knob to start the washer. Then he jerked his head at me. I scampered to the back door: "Berry isn't supposed to see any bathing done, he's not a woman."

"Come here and pick up—"

But we were gone, laughing like crazy, before we heard the rest of that command. Sandra, being a couple years older and more responsible, opened the back door and yelled at us to come here; but we, being eighteen or so, didn't answer to her. We ran across the back yard, heard Porter's complaint—"Y'all are goin' overboard with this cleanin'!"—and raced to Conjure Creek where we took off our sandals and splashed downstream a long way, scrambled under the bridge where the riprap was thrown, kept going until we were well out of sight and hearing of anybody. We threw ourselves down on the shallow side of the bank and sloshed our feet through the water that ran quietly onward. It was ninety-three and unbearably humid. In a while I rolled my shorts legs up even higher and fanned my button-down cotton shirt to let air under it and sat down, dabbling my toes in the only cool spot around.

"I feel bad we didn't get Porter out of there, too."

I considered that. "I don't. He gets on my nerves. And he's old, anyway. He's older than we are. He won't be mad at us. He'll think it's his job to stay."

"He's not so much older."

I closed my eyes against the bright haze overhead, heard him move away and splash quietly. I had nearly fallen asleep when a double-handful of the cold creek water hit my face. I grabbed the front of his shirt, and he stumbled and fell against me.

We stared at each other maybe a half-minute. The creek that

had drowned a child years ago and swept him along in the flood when it was running high made that sensuous *shisshing* at our feet. When Berry clamped his mouth onto mine, I knew why Liza and Mother wanted us in the house, where we could be seen. They knew; somehow, where we hadn't. In a long while something like a shiver brought him up away from me; in one convulsive move he sat back in the water. "We better be getting back before they come looking for us, or send Porter to."

"No reason to hurry," I told him thickly. "I don't want to sweep floors or fold towels. You rather fold towels than stay out here with me?"

He looked at me, faced the water again, slowly walked upstream under the thicker trees, places we usually avoided because the snakes liked them as well as we did. He didn't see me ease up from behind. "Let's go back. Just let me cool off a little first," he went on, and I bent my knees into his suddenly and he tumbled into the creek, his hands sinking into the silty bottom, his face dripping with the sandy water.

"Did that help?" I took out at a run. I had a good start but let him catch me a time or two. It was a while before we stumbled into Granny Kate's back yard again, and as we did, he was pulling at my shirt again and stopped abruptly. Mother stood akimbo, glaring at the sight of my rolled-up shorts, my nice little checkered shirt pulled tight in his grip across my chest and up on my midriff where a big damp spot darkened the fabric. He shrugged and let go.

"You two tryin' to get drowned down there? What've you been *doin'*?"

"Give it some thought: She's mostly dry and I'm not."

But I spent the rest of the afternoon washing sheets and bedding while he played chess with Porter. On other days, Porter sometimes let Berry win, I knew; it was another one of those things Porter was good at, and, then, he *was* older and had been playing longer. He took the game very seriously, never lifting his gaze from the board until he'd checkmated whomever he was playing. This time, though, Berry lost, fair and square, over and over, to Porter's disgust. And we were both being watched by Sandra and Mother and Liza, all of whom had *known* before he and I even knew, ourselves. They had *known*.

We worked a lot that summer, preserving Granny Kate's garden for her. They stationed us in the back yard by the kitchen, easily seen as we shelled peas that stained our hands purple; or shucked corn, mechanically stripping the ears naked, pulling down the outer green leaves with strong, sudden motions, running our fingers over the firm kernels covered with cornsilks like soft hair. Looking at each other's hands the whole time. I stared as he gently rubbed off the silks, his long fingers working between the kernels up and around, delicately brushing away the strands.

But there were always times they couldn't watch us, times we weren't at Granny Kate's house; and we savoured all of them.

"NOBODY'D BETTER COME in here and catch you sitting in front of my makeup mirror," I said.

He laughed and, rummaging through one of the little dresser drawers, fished out an old makeup brush and dusted his face with a gaudy flourish, put the brush down. Neither of us said anything else for a long several minutes, and the memory was gone, and there was only melancholy now. I wanted to ask him questions that I couldn't really ask, that were not my business—the sorts of things everybody in the family had wanted to ask him all his life. I wanted to ask if he would've liked to bring somebody with him to the funeral, for emotional support. I wanted to ask him if he had somebody *to* bring, or was alone, sitting in his comfortable house in silence as I did in mine. But then, if he did say he was alone, what would I do—be glad? Would I wish that upon him?

"You used to have a feather boa from some prom or something. I remember it. I could put it over my shoulder before I go back in there. That would clear out the house."

"Shut up," I said again.

"Did you ever wonder why we kept going up to Granny Kate's all those years? To keep her company? Hell, no. If we wanted to do that, we'd have done it the right way, on a regular basis. And Mama or your mother wouldn't've had to goad us into it. And we'd've seen to it she was taken care of better. We'd've persuaded her to get out of there, get some decent little retiree apartment in town or something, we'd've got Porter something meaningful to do, some kind of job, some more education. But we kept her there—"

"Nobody made her stay; she wanted to."

"Well, then, enabled her, because as long as everything was kind of frozen in the moment, our lives were, too. Like there was still something we *could* all get back to if we wanted it. Like we had all the time in the world. Hell, it's why I came back, you know. Why this meal at your mother's today, why not at the old house?"

"Well, I told Mother it was to keep everybody from picking out what they'd like to have, then helping themselves to it, while they were there and it was handy."

"Damn! Missed our chance. No, really, seriously?"

"Well, seriously, *my* mother says it was to spare *your* mother. *My* mother says *yours* wasn't in any emotional state to do it."

"Maybe. But also because it would've been too scary there."

"Scary?"

"Too many ghosts."

"I don't believe in ghosts."

"You know what I mean: not that kind of ghosts. Ghosts in our minds. We'd have to admit she's gone. And that whole kind of life's gone. Like we'll be, too, some time or other."

The knob twisted; the door opened gently, an inch at a time, and Amy put her ravaged little pale face inside. "Can I please stay with y'all?"

He gestured for her to come in. She slid downward against the wall near that stack of old newspapers, drew her knees up under her chin, pressed a hand against the door; but he shook his head: "Let's leave it open a little to hear what they're saying."

She didn't buy that, I could tell; she turned quick, assessing glances on him, but she did leave the door open.

"Mamaw's scary," she said. "She whipped 'em into shape a few minutes ago. You're not gonna hear 'em yelling anymore."

"Strong woman," he told her.

"You won't have memories like I do," I said. "And that's sad. Used to, we'd go to a river or a pond and catch fish and cook them right there, over a fire we built. People'd huddle up and eat and go over all the family legends. The women always did the cleanup, so nothing much's changed; they'd dump the oil they'd fried the fish in, and we'd get back around the fire. By then it'd be getting dark, and everybody'd listen to the stories."

"And all the stories were about strong women, Amy," he added. "Oh, they talked about men that did funny, stupid things and mutilated parts of their bodies, they walked into hornet nests in the woods, or they had to leave the area to stay out of trouble." She laughed a little.

But the ladies were always shortchanged in those stories—so it seemed to me when I was a girl; the women were above reproach, steady, sustaining, mildly sacred, in the Southern way: the nurturing women, backbones of their families, salt of the earth, at least the old ones; the younger ones who drove big trucks and got in your face when you challenged them commanded a different kind of respect.

It was a given that the women *had* to be strong, a long-suffering wife attached to the rapscallion: the toeless one, the one that had bashed a friend's head in during a drunken fight and yet somehow got off scot-free, the brooding one ever'body knows to steer clear of, he's crazy when he's had somethin' to drink, and he's *always* had somethin' to drink—all married to ladies, whose lives through long years became examples of forbearance and forgiveness.

"The women were the strong people," he added. Then he put a finger to his lips: "They're pulling straws; let's listen."

As Amy said, there was no more loud talk in Mother's living room. Relatives took it in turns, earnestly explaining why they couldn't accept the responsibility of tending to Porter; the one who gave the flimsiest excuse would have the short straw. I wondered if Mother was pointing to each in an orderly way, commanding a recitation. Anne pleaded her mother, even though Pauline had been locked up many years and wasn't likely to get loose now unless she climbed out the window. Marcus told them he traveled too much and, being divorced, didn't have anybody to help, and it wouldn't work for his kids to have that responsibility. Larry insisted his own teenagers took up all his time. So that was Porter's immediate family; and it came back to Liza and the cousins.

"It's gettin' late," Dobber suddenly announced loudly. Beside me, Berry flinched.

"Yes, it is, and we have to get home," Jean Ann said. "Whatever y'all decide's fine with us." She stood at the hallway and we could just make her out, there, fidgeting with her purse.

"What if it's you we decide ought to do it, after you leave?"

She stopped and considered Dobber's threat.

"Nobody leaves till we all agree. I said that already. It's got to be agreed on before the lawyers gets it done. We done asked *him*, and y'all heard what he told us."

The three of us in my room stared: we'd started eavesdropping too late. Amy raised her hands—clueless, that meant. I had no idea where she must've hidden after Berry and I had left the main room.

"You willin' to accept what he said? You think he can sort somethin' like this out?" —That was Rhonda.

"You all heard him—he sounded pretty reasonable to me. He very clearly said it don't much matter, he knows he can't live out there by hisself. To me that means he has enough sense to make a decision, and his decision was to let us decide. Now since there ain't nobody here got any guts, I'm goin' to say what I feel, and those that don't like it can just shut up. I say she left it for us, she told us that, over and over. It was meant to be ours, and I intend to get my part. If it means I put up with Porter a while, I'll do it. I'm sayin' it now. I'll take him for a while. And I want ever one of you to know right up front that after it's all settled I'll situate him somewhere to get some regular treatment. I ain't squeamish about it."

"Wouldn't be right for you to keep the interest money if you did that," James Preacher put in.

"If it makes it easier for all of you to swallow, I'll put that part in with his to help take care of him wherever he goes later. I ain't greedy. I just want my fair part."

There was a little quiet discussion about how to arrange legally for him to sign over the interest from the other three parts without arousing the suspicions of the lawyers. Eventually everyone decided that if Porter was moved in with Dobber and it was handled with discretion and the money turned back right at the first, it would just look like a generous gesture, which it was, anyway, Dobber insisted angrily.

"These things must be done *delicately*," Berry whispered in a Witch-of-the-West voice.

It evidently hurt Dobber's feelings that the other cousins hadn't immediately endorsed his plan: He could lie as well as the rest of 'em, he went on, just as well's they all had through the years when they claimed to feel sorry for Porter, when they didn't want no part of him. At least he was honest enough to admit it.

"I'll do it myself," Liza interrupted. "He's my brother's boy and I'll just do it myself. Mama done it for years, and nobody ever heard her complain. Did we?" A heavy silence followed this question. "At least I'll know he ain't rottin' locked up in a room somewhere. The money don't mean anything to me." Jean Ann said urgently, "But, Mama, it'd be yours fair and square, and it'd have to go to somebody—he'd never be able to handle it—" but Liza ignored her and went on, "The money ain't important. He's my nephew. He can just live with me, and we'll put a stop to all this. I told Mama I didn't think she oughta done it this way. Now it's settled, and I hope everybody's satisfied. Let's all go home. You need some more help, Janie?"

Mother, sternly: "Thank you but we will manage."

"Who's gonna clear the flowers off the grave tomorrow?"

James Preacher sorrowfully volunteered, and Jean Ann told Liza of course she'd be by to help, and the scraping and creaking symphony of the chairs began again as they all started to get up and leave. "No, it's not all settled," Larry said unexpectedly. "We, that is, us three"—he motioned to Anne and Marcus—"we don't like how it's been done, and he may be your nephew, but he's my brother, and by rights it's my job to see after him, I'm the oldest. I'll fix him up on my property. I'm not sure how I'll manage, but I'm ashamed of myself for not already sayin' I would. She had it hard for years, with the four of us, and it's my turn. I'll use that interest to pay for extra things we need to do for him, maybe send him to community college. Well, *now* it's settled."

Everybody apparently decided to get up right then and leave, before Larry changed his mind. We heard him calling his teenagers, who, along with some of the other older kids, had homesteaded Mother and Dad's bedroom with a music player. Unfamiliar with the sleeping arrangements in the house, he shoved open the door to my room, apologized for doing it and surveyed the three of us, then left the door open and hunted down the faint strains of canned music like a dog scenting a deer. Anne wandered into the hall, kind of wringing her hands together. She asked Larry if he was sure about it, said she'd help when she could, and he told his kids he was leaving and they needed to find their coats.

I pushed the door almost shut once more. The stack of old yellow newspapers on the floor shifted and spilled neatly into a diagonal swirl like a deck of cards. Amy, sitting there next to the mess, tried to straighten them.

"Do me a favor, Berry, haul these things off when you leave, okay? They probably got silverfish."

"They your mother's? I'm not messin' with anything of hers. Besides, she must want 'em or she'd've thrown 'em out herself."

He scanned the mundane headlines of one, held it away at arm's length to read the date. Then another. With a skeptical look at me he riffled the pages. "These're your old pieces. She saved 'em for you." He studied me for a moment, then shrugged and laid the paper down on top of the messy pile. "Whatever. They're on microfilm or something somewhere. We better get out of here."

"Oh, and this is yours." I handed him the box on the nightstand. "You remember, we left it last summer. Then your mother gave it to my mother, and she made sure to shove as much guilt as she could on me for not taking it from Granny Kate that day. It's all stuff about your dad's family," I added uncomfortably; he and I didn't talk much about Cal.

He picked up one of the letters, then another. "I don't recognize any of these names."

Knowing he might call me the library again, I anyway explained how they'd been sent to one of Granny Kate's nephews, a man who'd also been the data repository before he died—I put it that way, lightly, ironically, to forestall him. He opened one of the crispy old envelopes and scanned a page, put it back, glanced at the family sheets. "I'll go through it some time."

"No, you won't, but it's out of my hands now, so you do what you want to."

He reached out to Amy and hauled her off the floor, and she blurted out a strange thing, the thing I'd wanted to ask and couldn't: "Berry, didn't you have anybody you'd've liked having along today for all this crap?"

"That would've have made it easier?"

She didn't answer.

"I have you and Maggie. By the way, Amy, you're thinking it might be a man I'd bring. Don't necessarily believe everything you hear from your relatives. You coming back out tomorrow?" he asked me.

I shrugged.

"Well, if you do, before I leave, I'll visit for a while, nice and quiet. So I'll see you then. Or if you don't come out, I'll try to catch you in town."

We edged around each other in the doorway of the bedroom, watching and listening as the cousins left, one after another. Finally, out of nothing, Amy asked, "Who's Edna?"

"Edna?"

"Over at the church. You told Aunt Maggie you saw Edna Luckey. Who's she?"

He snorted derisively. "Your mama has seriously ignored your education. Greek chorus."

"Yeah, what does that mean?"

"What on earth are they teaching you in school? Here's the way it is: Edna's the commentary in a Greek tragedy."

Amy's mouth pulled sideways. "I know *what* a Greek chorus is. I don't know what you mean about *her*."

He smiled a little at tone in her voice. "How old do you think Edna is, Maggie? She lives a ways down the road from here. She always comes to funerals if they're not too far from her house. Any funeral. All funerals. Funerals of people she knows, funerals of people she doesn't know. Equal-opportunity funeral participant."

Amy grimaced. "Bad enough when you knew them. Why would anybody do that?"

"Well, she'd probably *say* she does it because she knew their nephews, or she was a friend of their grandmother's or something. She'd have some reason for it, if you asked."

"*Have* you asked?" she said slyly.

"In fact I did." Amy laughed as he continued: "I did it tactfully, you know. I just eased up to her one time and asked if she was related to the deceased. She gave me some answer. And the next time I saw her at a funeral, I asked again."

Amy laughed again; then, "How is it *you're* at enough funerals so you see her that often?"

"Not by choice. But folks out this way have a habit of dying off."

She asked another question: "Has anybody ever told her to leave?"

"Why should they? She always slips away without making a scene. She's harmless."

"So I see why you say she's a Greek chorus."

"But a silent one," he agreed. "She makes the comment by just being there."

"What's her comment?"

"What comment do you think would be appropriate for funerals?"

"Hmmm. 'We're all gonna die.' Did you ever write about *her*?"

"Yeah…one time…."

One of his very first pieces was about her, calling her that, wondering if she came because she was trying to fend "IT" off with familiarity. I told him that was just about the weirdest thing he'd ever written, and he told me she was the weirdest thing he'd had to write about, and it took some doing to be that weird; but *I* had given him the idea about "IT", so what did that say about *me*?

"She avoids Berry now," I told Amy. "If they happen to show up together, she stays away from him, or she just leaves."

"But we aren't at funerals much anymore," he said gloomily, "because everybody's died."

"Oh, no, there are still plenty, just a new crop," she said. He started picking up the old newspapers to haul them out.

13

THEY ALL BEGAN to clear out, and the house was quiet again as before but changed, filled with the scents of different people, the trace of Aunt Sabrina's cigarette lingering, and the furniture disarranged. Relatives roamed in and out of the bedrooms, looking for the jackets and umbrellas they had stored away on my bed and on Mother and Dad's.

Amy followed me to the kitchen where a final mild, exhausted cleaning was going on. Aunt Lilly and Aunt Sabrina were gathering the plastic cups and Styrofoam plates. Anne had offered for Porter to stay overnight with her, but he said he'd be fine in the old house, and nobody argued. Larry told him he'd drop him off there before he went back to his own home, would make sure there was something for breakfast tomorrow in the refrigerator, packed up some of the leftover food for him to eat at lunch; and so he was disposed of, too, as Mother stood over Jerry making him sack up the garbage. She collected assorted pieces of rolls, a chicken bone, used napkins, and crammed them into an overflowing plastic trash bag, continued her busy seeking out of the leftovers, and, "I declare I'm glad that's over with," was all she said.

Aunt Lilly kept her mouth shut. Aunt Sabrina could not: "I have to say I've never seen the like of it. I've seen family squabbles but nothin' like that. And all over money. Ain't it disgusting. People'll sell anything these days for a few dollars."

Dad glanced nervously toward the sink where a clatter and bustle defined Mother's agitation. "Well, I guess it shouldn't'a been tied up like it was," he said. "It was a mistake. Brought out the worst in 'em. They ain't usually like that."

Aunt Sabrina shook her head. "Oh, I've heard of some of their shenanigans. *Our* family never has ended up in the newspaper."

Bang. Two serving spoons hit the floor, splattering potato salad against the cabinet. Mother took a paper towel and savagely cleaned it. Aunt Sabrina kept on wiping the table. "I think it's the young generation comin' on. None of the old ones would've done that, but the young ones don't care no more."

The water gushed a torrential flood at the sink. Lilly jumped back a little to keep her clothes dry.

"You seem awful stressed," Sabrina continued. "You had a lot on you today. Why don't you take one of my Valiums and go to bed? Me and Daniel and Lilly'll finish cleanin' up."

"I don't take nerve pills," Mother told her. "I don't need 'em."

"Anybody could use one now and then."

Mother scrubbed the serving spoons with a vengeance and slung them into the drain board.

"You need a big dishwasher for times like this," Aunt Sabrina rattled on, and I wondered how long it would take. "I have really got the use out of mine. Maybe you could catch one on sale. Or at least you oughta wear rubber gloves or something. Start savin' your hands."

"You forget I'm going to be rich," Mother said all of a sudden. "I'll have enough money to put a dishwasher in every room of the house, if I want to. That way, I wouldn't need any help cleanin' up."

She threw the dishcloth at the drainboard with both hands, slam-dunking it like a basketball, and left the kitchen, saying she was going to change out of her good dress. I followed her. Behind me I could hear Aunt Sabrina telling Dad he really ought to get her to take something for her nerves.

I EASED INTO her room behind her. "You ought not to let her bother you. Geez. I sound like you every time I turn around today."

"I feel sorry for 'em," she said. "Every one of 'em. You needn't look at me like that. I can't imagine why Mama did this. If she'd actually tried to, she couldn't've stirred up any more trouble. Made 'em choose between what they need and what's the right thing to do."

I told her they'd all done okay so far without thirty grand, and probably most of them would end up blowing it, anyway. "Thirty grand's not enough to really change much of anything for them. It's like getting a piece of cake when you really need a hamburger and french fries. You're gonna eat that cake because it's better than having an empty stomach, but it's just sugar. Go right through you."

"You just don't know," she insisted. "There's Dobber. Never had a pot to pee in. So he's got a chance to do a little better, but it might slip out of his hands. Porter's the one that'll blow his money—or give it away to anybody that walks up. Nobody ever taught him nothing about money; he don't know how to use it." She pushed hangers around, sort of shoving at them in a way that brought back to my mind me pushing Richard out of the living room. "You and Berry don't get along with none of 'em much, but yet here you still are—and there he is, back again. Everything he is came from here. He wouldn't have nothin' to write about if things had've been different long ago."

I would have to ask Berry about this one; there was a truth in it that made me uncomfortable.

"You are what you are," she rattled on. "You don't get away from it by makin' fun of it. You end up just makin' fun of yourself." She started undressing and put on a heavy robe over her slip, her hands moving in a quick, clumsy rhythm. "The ones that don't really need that money, they'll go home and it won't be nothin' much to 'em, just buy 'em a new car or something. But the others, the ones that do need it...they know they ain't nothin' much, and likely won't ever be. But it hurts when somebody points it out to 'em." She slid the dress onto a clothes hanger and stabbed it into the closet where it quivered a time or two. She whirled around at me, her eyes big and sparkling with impatience. "Don't any of you understand we're all scared of gettin' old and just bein' that—old—and nothin' else? It don't matter what age you are, and you don't just get used to it when you do get old. We ain't any different, and that's why I feel sorry for 'em. None of 'em likes theirselves too well right now. It's true. They don't. And they ain't all bad. It was hard to admit they could use that money so much they'd even think about goin' to court and fightin' their last two remainin' aunts."

"It was forty minutes' work, that's how hard it was, and then finally somebody says *maybe* he'll figure out some way to look after his own brother after all. They didn't fret much over it."

"Mama's generation's done. You saw that today once and for all." She tied the belt around her waist with a snapping chokehold and turned her back on me. "Your time's comin' one day, too."

She whirled out, her robe flapping around and reminding me of the time when we'd been outside with Dad while he told his tales, and we came in to smell a strange odor, a hint of burning cotton, and discovered she'd caught her housecoat afire in an old gas space heater and then, calm as you please, reached down with her hands and patted the flames out and went about her business, and hadn't even yelled or told us...and I shivered now, rabbit-running-up-my-back, as I thought about that damned dream, and her wrapping her quilted self around me, rescuing me.... She went back to the kitchen, but I sat there a while. Eventually, Amy's sad face peeked around that door, too. I jerked my head. "Come on." She edged in and stood there, her headset hanging around her shoulders, leaking music out.

Sandra threw the door open. "Amy, get your purse and come on. It's late and we'll have to leave early tomorrow."

"Can't I stay here tonight?"

"It'll take too much time to come back out tomorrow. Besides"—she was trying to be calm and reasonable—"all your clean stuff's at the motel."

"I could get my stuff from there and go spend the night with Aunt Maggie," she said.

I started to tell Amy she'd just about got the bluff on her mother; but at fifteen maybe she was still a little young to know it.

"Aunt Maggie's too busy to fool with you tonight," Sandra told her.

"Plan on visiting with me and George the weekend after Thanksgiving. That's not too far off."

Amy turned to me, hopeful. "What could we do?"

"I don't know. What do you want to do? See a movie? Go skating?"

"Make fun of the relatives?" Amy suggested with a sly glance at her mother.

Sandra stolidly looked from one to the other of us. "Go on and find your purse; I think it was in the kitchen." Her eyes settled on me as Amy slouched away. "I'm not going to let her hang out here much anymore," Sandra said bluntly. "She'll be okay soon as she gets back into her routine. She'll get to running around with her friends. I don't want her to spend any thought on this. She needs to forget it."

"You're the one who made her come, you know. But, yeah, she'll put it away inside herself, like the rest of us. You don't just walk away from it."

"Wanna bet? I'm not gonna let her turn into this. She's my child. You remember that—she's *my* child. She's not yours."

"You think I'm a bad influence on her?"

"Today was a bad influence. She'll be okay."

"You're right. She *will* forget it. You keep her away, then." I was suddenly tired of all of it. Forgetfulness looked good to me, too.

She stood, obviously holding back words, snatching them like angry children before they slipped out of her mouth to inflict some unhealable injury, stared at me for a moment, started to say something else, turned and left.

I sat on Mother's bed thinking nothing. It was a relief, thinking nothing much at all, your mind almost blank. Mother's latest quilt was bumpy underneath me, new and stiff, not used enough yet to be comfortable. She made them, slept under them for a while to soften them and then packed them up or gave them away. I searched for the name on this one.

Amy.

In a little bit I heard Sabrina and Lilly exchange goodbyes with Mother and Dad. I went out one last time that day into the once-again straightened living room that was different now and hugged them myself, and they left.

MOTHER HAD SKILLS. She could see through things, find the outright lie or the slightly-off dissimulation. Maybe it was because she was left-handed and had more of the intuition those types had. I'd taken one last nibble of caramel cake and was headed out of the kitchen when, out of nothing, she ordered me to promise not to tell the thing she was about to divulge.

"Sure," I agreed.

Her lips tightened. She assessed me, unerringly detecting the failure to give the formal vow. We held each other's gaze, knowing neither would give in. Dad, however, absent-mindedly restacking magazines somebody's kid had strewn around, took her silence as mere disgust and said, "Somebody dumped a big sackful of garbage right in Hazel's driveway last night, late, Maggie. Strewed it out all over the place. Lots of beer cans in it," he added. "Like a message, sort of."

"Daniel, I told you not to tell." She turned on him, aggrieved.

He was suddenly defensive. "Well, *you* were just about to.... Weren't you?" he said.

"Not till she said she wouldn't spread it around. So now she knows anyway."

"It may've just been an accident," he said tentatively, an effort to ameliorate the damage with an implausible alternative.

She glared at him, turned back to me. "You really need to keep this to yourself," with a final probing, soul-freezing scowl, knowing she had nothing to hold over me. Her voice was flat as she told it: Hazel didn't come to the funeral because she thought she'd be aggravating a bad situation by showing up. No matter how she'd loved Granny Kate, no matter how close they'd been through the years: She stayed away to keep a family pacified...*our* family. She did that for ours.

Her original move to get the ironclad promise from me having been thwarted, Mother resorted to negotiation: "There is some things you just can't tell, no matter how bad you want to. Because it won't help. Will tellin' keep it from happening again? Right now, you and your daddy and me're the only ones that know. She didn't even tell Liza. Some of 'em would get mad to know it happened, but others wouldn't care."

"Then you ought to tell the ones that *would* get mad."

"It wouldn't stop there. You seen that today. —Daniel, I wonder where your mind is sometimes."

He edged apprehensively toward the kitchen.

She turned back to me with purposeful energy: "You'd best forget about it. For whatever it's worth, Edwin's looking out for her."

"You said it was just us that knew."

"Well, of the family."

"How'd *you* find out, then?"

"Sally called me this morning; real early."

So that explained why I'd got up at dawn only to find they'd already arisen themselves. "Who told Edwin?"

She pounded the couch cushions fiercely. "Don't matter. He's watching. Look, you are stayin' again tonight, ain't you?"

"I planned to drive back to town. George's home now."

"It's awful late. George will not mind. He probably wouldn't even want you on the road. And you look tired and sleepy."

And I realized I *was*—sharing a bed with Amy, dreaming of fires and my mother suffocating, and saving, me, and then the betrayal of the cousins had extinguished the last leftover energy I had.

"I could wash what you wore yesterday, or find you something. Let me look and see what's in my closet." She turned away, pretending that was the main task on her mind.

I always sought whatever privacy I could find when I talked to George and found her nearby...it was something I just had to do, so I didn't look up and find her watching, listening to my words and adjudging them sufficiently affectionate, or not. So, later, I went to the kitchen alone and gently nudged the swinging door shut. "Everybody's gone now. If you want to, you can come and visit in peace and quiet and then follow me home."

He hesitated. "There's a lot of laundry to do. I'll get somebody to bring me over tomorrow. So we don't have two cars out there, and I'll ride back with you then. It's late, and raining. Stay and keep 'em company."

"I could help with the laundry."

"I know how to do laundry."

"Not worried about me with Richard? Kissin' cousins, all that?"

"Well, you said everybody's gone. Anyway, I can't see you getting cozy with Richard."

"You never know. By the way, I told him you'd catch him one day."

"Yeah, I heard you over the phone. And I will catch him sometime. I nearly did two days ago," he added grimly. "Although, from the direction he was shooting, he wanted to catch me. But he's got smarter: He did have a license."

Mother gently pushed the door open and brought me a purple sweatsuit, handed it to me wordlessly, her lifted arm a question mark. I shrugged and took it with me to my bedroom.

GEORGE AND I had run off to Alabama and got married after college; no long-thought-out plan for me. I might not have done it at all if I'd had to consider flowers and dresses and combined finances and mortgages and losses. Doing it fast kept me from thinking too much. We bought a little house, and for a good while I seldom saw many of the relatives.

Mother figured I was pregnant. She arranged a family gathering at Granny Kate's so I could show everybody I wasn't. And they did look.

So now I lived in town, where you had your social life run by the Baptist church and the high-school football games. Out in the country, it sorted out into degrees of ruralism—the farther away from town you got, the farther back in time. Town in those days was still the same as all the other small urban areas in the South, not changed just yet into bland asphalt mall smoothness.

There was one television station.

With federal grant money the police department bought modern equipment. The sheriff's office regularly bought ads in the county directory to publicize their anonymous tip line. If they'd also advertised rewards, they'd have had more calls, though perhaps not many results: There weren't many crimes for those tips to be given.

Berry got his degrees, went into education, moved to Tennessee. Before you could Google somebody, I had to depend on the random bit of information through his mother, and then through mine, and that was undependable. Liza said he got married, had a child, even, a girl—"But it turned out not to be his," Mother told me, and her quilt shuddered at the thought of it. "So he's divorced now," and she gave me a look, but I turned away from that. George and I were trying to create our own by then, without any success; and he, good superstitious Primitive Baptist that he was, believed it a judgment on us for sleeping together long before we ran off to that j.p. in Alabama. And I secretly wondered if it was a judgment for having slept with Berry my cousin that summer long ago. When Jean Ann's unmarried daughter Susie had one baby and another on the way—"Million wonders she didn't pop it out at that altar," the quilt shivered—it didn't feel fair to me. God must use a bad set of judgment scales.

Other cousins moved and we lost track of them, too, but I took it personal in Berry's case. Jean Ann didn't talk much about him, as if she didn't claim him as a brother at all. Time passed. People left the outlying parts of the county in droves and got jobs in town, or in places like Jackson or Birmingham or Atlanta, where they changed into the personalities necessary for life, learned to wear dark business clothes buttoned up tightly. But when they returned here, then in an hour, or half an hour, or ten minutes, they changed back, loosening a tie, undoing top buttons, shedding heels—as if like chameleons, their skin camouflaged dull brown for so long, they couldn't revert too fast to the bright, gaudy, raw green it really was. Conjure Hill stayed as treacherous in rainy weather as it had always been. Fewer cars passed now. It was hard to justify paving the old road Porter wandered along—finally they quit trying to justify it at all, certainly not just for three or four old ladies who persisted in living there out of sheer stubbornness, defying their own fates; so it stayed dirt, and the county scraped it once in a while, poured a little gravel in the winter and spring, and otherwise ignored it.

Middle age stalked the way Richard hunted deer—not in a friendly way, not according to rules, but sneakily, setting traps to catch us glancing at a cold reflection in our mirrors as we groomed ourselves for the workdays that became weeks and months and years. We made our dutiful, regular pilgrimages to Granny Kate's beat-up old house to observe—from safe distance of the decades between her and us—the gradual passing of her generation. We sat on the cypress porch in our small groups, the dirt road undisturbed except by an occasional car, her chickens clucking in the background. All Granny Kate's mirrors had turned foggy, mildewed and indistinct, reflecting an older sort of world unchanged. She sat enthroned with grandchildren around her, sometimes asking somebody if you wanted a Coke, looking over the whole brood with what struck me as annoyance and amazement. Rip Van Winkle would've had that sort of look—the kind I saw more and more on Mother's face just lately and sometimes even caught on mine when I passed by my reflection somewhere.

Porter followed her around on those days—had she told him to be her helper when they had company, or something?—and to him she slipped things to be put into the sink or up high where a child could not reach. Later, in other years, he just glided around without her telling him to, and took care of the knickknacks and figurines by himself.

There was a peaceful, humming quiet out there at her house, one the older cousins wistfully referred to as the way it used to be. You'd think nothing ever happened, or ever had.

"It's so still and pleasant. I do just love it," Rhonda said one time, fanning her hair around. "It's a haven from all the stuff that goes on these days. So peaceful. Don't you wish we all could just live back in the country again like we used to."

Granny Kate sat behind her in the porch swing, the ball of her right foot touching gently down at the nadir of each arc like a soft-sole tap dance.

"It will all be left to you grandkids one day."

And they'd look around, glance at the hardwood and pine trees, the edges of the cypress swamp down the road; and I pictured them in their jobs, sitting in front of their computers, going home to the sealed, climate-controlled houses we all had. And I knew they'd never give that up in exchange for this. *She'd* lived in it, knew it intimately, as you know the old man's body lying in bed next to yours for forty years of nights. But no matter how they might deceive themselves, it would only ever be an occasional retreat now from the life they preferred.

"Peaceful and quiet," Rhonda reiterated, her eyes half-shut in somnolent rapture.

"So quiet you might could hear your fingernails grow, and you sure wouldn't have nothin' better to do than watch 'em growin', while you was at it." This was Porter's mumbled response, a comment that shut everybody up. Granny Kate smirked. No one had too much to say after that, at least not that day, though several people gave the two of them a look.

GEORGE HAD WORKED at the refuge for several years before they started sending him places, a couple of days at a time, a week at a time, maybe close to a month at a time. He'd go here and there to fight fires, to run a seminar on water safety, to get some more safe-practice training—it was always something. Days would stretch into weeks, and I lay by myself wondering if he secretly enjoyed all that time away as much as I did.

I started missing Berry about the time I had to admit I could not pass for nineteen anymore, about the time George and I had given up on kids, about the time I found it just as comfortable, whenever he was away, to sleep by myself on the little daybed in the room I called my office, about the time we started meeting in the halls of our vanilla house with gracious smiles, as if we were sure we knew each other from somewhere, but couldn't think just exactly where.

Berry didn't come to the reunions, to Granny Kate's birthday parties, to the funerals of her last two remaining sisters. Many of us did our duty, brought flowers to her for happy or sad reasons, hugged her and left her with Porter in the old cypress house at the bottom of Conjure Hill. Maybe Berry couldn't face that anymore with everybody staring at him. Maybe he had got high and mighty and didn't think he should associate with us—that opinion was passed around a few times; it was easier to say that than the other thing, that he didn't want the pain.

But when she was ninety-four, Liza reminded us again she wouldn't be there forever; so we gathered for another celebration of sorts, and she extracted from him a promise that he'd attend that one. Mother told me all this when she passed along Liza's fiat. "Sorry, can't go with you that day," George said, leaving me to ponder whether I was unhappy or relieved about that. For how did you greet a person you'd sat on a fence with and shucked corn with and loved, who'd left you for all those years and was coming back at last, different and old?

He brought a little bouquet of tea roses to her, which she looked at and set down on the porch beside her rocker. Then he sank to the floor next to her; and, pretending not to be all that interested, really, we listened as he told a few stories from when he'd been a principal, then a superintendent, at a last-chance school for kids who had nowhere else to try. "Oh, you rehabbed the hoodlums?" Dobber chuckled; Berry gave him a grave look: "Sort of." We knew already he wrote scholarly essays about educational things—Liza'd always been proud of that, and bragged on it. Now, he said, he'd retired.

"Retired? You ain't old enough to retire!" Dobber scoffed; but that was jealousy, and got him another solemn glance. Retired, yes; and he was doing more writing, but it was for magazines, now, and they might see some of his things here and there in the regional publications they knew of, hunting magazines, outdoor ones, if they wanted to look. It wouldn't be education stuff, he added with a laugh.

"Like what Maggie used to do?" Dobber inquired; I deliberately tried to freeze him with a cold look.

Berry frowned at me, however. *Used to?*, I could see him asking. "Yeah, that," was what he said, though. Oh, and he'd bought a house in Jackson.

We knew he'd come home regularly through the years to look in on Liza, and occasionally on Granny Kate, too, but he'd never showed up at the large gatherings. And he didn't stay long that day, either, but eased down the steps, patting a shoulder, giving a quick hug.

Granny Kate's ninety-fourth birthday was the first thing we knew of that he wrote about. Liza made sure to tell most of us where to find it. "Conjuring Up the Past"—he was proud of that title, but also a little touchy, I found out when I called him.

"Was it just too clever of me?"

I told him I didn't think it was clever at all. We were swinging our legs on top of that fence again, poking at each other.

"You ought to start back yourself, uphold our family tradition," he told me gently.

"Compete with you? Nope. Through with all that." I said it with superiority. Just like Dobber asking about that early retirement.

How do you conjure up the past? he'd asked. Can you feel it in a yellow veil of dust drifting down over a house that has always sat there within your memory, settling into and softening the wrinkles of a person who started the process of making you what you are? Or is it the more concrete things, the old roads we take past nearly-forgotten homeplaces in our travels to the one we remember growing up in, the one we always search for, some time or other in our lives?

He told about Granny Kate, talked about the hill and its name. Nobody'd ever questioned why it was Conjure Hill—it just was. It was there, would be there in some form or another, would endure, its identity in a name magical and incongruous.

Everybody in the family was pleased, even the ones who weren't entirely sure they liked him. Berry, that weirdo, could be tolerated, even bragged on now as Berry, that relative who had made good and was back home. Some of them said they, too, had things to write, and would he sponsor them; and he told them that wasn't really how it worked.

He showed up now at places they frequented—the Wagonwheel, a greasy spoon and bar out on the highway; a rodeo sponsored by a rich guy with a ranch on the south side of the county. "Gathering material," he told me, as the two periodicals he favored ran a couple of generic pieces on places he'd visited.

The months passed, fall blending into mild weather that was Mississippi winter. Thanksgiving that year was quiet, all in all. Granny Kate was always getting deafer, we observed, but she didn't look any different, and the house was pretty much the same. We didn't really believe she was able to keep it this clean herself anymore and knew it had to be Liza. We had brought in the turkeys, the ham, the pecan pies dripping dark Karo syrup, and we made on affectionately about her rolls, the only thing we allowed her to provide, which we knew she had Liza buy at the Winn-Dixie these days. The afternoon was warm and rainy, and after huddling together for a group picture to be copied later for anyone who wanted it, the crowd thinned. Relatives with toddlers and babies left early for home. Chatter died down. It was hard to find something to talk about these days; it was always a fake intimacy created at her house. In a bit someone mentioned Berry's "Conjure" story: "You gonna do some more things like that first one you did? What you writin' about next time?"

He'd been leafing through an old photo album and glanced up. "Workin' on 'em."

"How do you do that—decide on what to write, and when? Is it like they tell you to do one on some subject? Like Maggie did?" That was Richard, and you'd have thought a normal person wouldn't keep on, after seeing my frigid glance; but, no.

Berry looked sideways at me. "I get to decide myself for my 'Down Home' pieces."

"So what you doin' for the next one?"

"Don't want to give it away; then you wouldn't read it."

The silence grew. Richard made a scornful, windy noise.

"Don't wanna tell the ignorant kin, do you," and Dobber cocked his little finger in the air and sipped from an imaginary cup.

Their eyes met, and Richard snickered a little in the background. Berry could've laughed it off, could've said something like, he couldn't think up anything just yet, it took time…but he only glared and then abruptly got up and left.

"A Gay Time Was Had by All," was his very next column. It was just a kind of funny, double-entendre piece about family reunions and hunting and how some men had big long guns and others, just short little pistols, and how they were all pretty much the same, guns for all that, no matter what they shot, the brand didn't really count much, but some people couldn't see it that way and wanted the biggest gun to belong to the biggest man.... Dad laughed as he read it, insisted on reading it aloud to me and Mother with a raconteur's style, emphasizing some words. I was visiting at their house that day, and Mother said, "Hmmph," when he was finished and never mentioned it again; but her mouth tried to smile.

Berry started writing something once a month about the family or local people. It was funny stuff—how "Cousin Dinger" got caught spotlighting deer and ran through the woods, leading the local game warden through bogs and poison ivy until he finally lost him, but then "Cousin Dinger" couldn't very well brag about it because he also lost his gun and his spotlight, and anyway if he did brag he'd be prosecuted by the very annoyed warden who was recuperating with calamine lotion and steroid shots.

And how "Cousin Janette" got mad at her husband and left him for the seventeenth time, but chose to crash her car into his little metal Sears workshop over and over, just for vengeance, right before she pulled out of the driveway.

And how "Cousin John" wanted to find an ancestor who was an officer in the Civil War—but he called it the "War of the Rebellion"—because that would earn him points in the local Civil War club and let him sit at the top table at their meetings.

And how the local constable had an Elvis thing and dyed his hair and appeared in impersonation contests.

And so on. When Berry showed up at family gatherings, it got to where nobody talked to him, so he quit coming; maybe Liza told him to. Maybe he figured it out on his own.

But he did get invitations to speak at business club dinners in other parts of the state to speak at after-dinner meetings. One of the magazine editors suggested he ought to publish a collection of his pieces, a proposition he discussed with me. I was ambivalent. Mother had offered her opinion: "He's just makin' fun of people now. He's just gettin' back at them."

"They deserve it."

"They might. But there's something mean about a person that

enjoys makin' people unhappy. That's what they done to him all them years."

While I repeated her comments, Berry pulled at the skin under his chin. "You think I'm mean?"

I changed the subject, because he and I both knew Mother was right in a way. Fingers in the sugar bowl again.

James Preacher lost sleep over the "Gay Time" story and did sermons on him for a while, without mentioning his name, actually, the sort of sermons he always did: rambling denunciations that Liza told Mother about, which Mother told me, and which I passed on to Berry, which made him laugh but not really laugh. James pulled out themes on reaping what you sow, living sinfully and paying for it, the tongue being a fire and a world of evil. He was, after all, named for the Book of James. After a while Berry got tired of it, and we hatched our plan with the CD. I was apprehensive.

"It's not illegal or threatening. Just music. He'll like it." So Berry said. He'd burned one track of "Revolution", followed by several seriously X-rated rap pieces—"just in case he tries to skip over the first one. But I think 'Revolution' is a good choice for his club."

Mother told me to apologize to James; and I finally did, just to smooth things over. "Gave you the wrong CD; sorry," but he looked mournfully shocked: "You *listen* to that kinda music?" And offered to make and give me a tape of songs his gospel group was plannin' to record, whenever they got some money.

Edwin Bonner took his county constable job seriously; I had to give him credit about that. After the "Dinger" story, he paid a visit to Dobber to warn him that just in case it might of been him that time in the woods, it would be better if he didn't never do no more spotlightin'. Dobber called Liza and wanted to know Berry's phone number, which she gave him, and which, Berry told me, Dobber never used. I reminded him Dobber never went anywhere without a shotgun in his truck.

"Talks big, but his gun has no ammo," he said.

For a few months whenever Mother or Liza called—mostly because of the ever more frequent hospitalizations Granny Kate endured and which we sat out like the near-wakes they were—I realized everybody had developed the habit of glancing sideways at each other, watchful of a slip of the tongue, carefully censoring words. Liza checked in on Porter during those hospital times, cooking food and taking it to the old house to prevent his eating only corn flakes. People whispered around about how long she might last, and what was going to become of her place when she was finally gone, speculation which she perhaps heard, for the relatives in their years of desperation got careless. What's gonna happen to all that land?—worth a lot of money, somebody would ponder, and the silence would shame him for a while, for having asked that instead of, "Is she better today?"

AFTER THE BABY had been decently interred and before Granny Kate died, things had quietened down. I haunted the library, staring at page after page of microfilmed records in search of names of long-dead families, trying to define their lives neatly by where they'd lived and what they'd done. George couldn't stand it, glanced loathingly with even a little fear at the notebooks I left open on the kitchen table after the library closed and I had to go home. It was as if he thought I'd summarized his own life into one of those pages, and the summary had the wrong details. One night he looked, grimacing, over my shoulder at my account of an ancestor who'd moved a lot, had lots of children, outlived several wives. George picked up one sheet, tossed it back to the table. He clumped over to the sink. The water burst on; he fumbled with a glass.

"Did you ever hear about Berry and Porter?" he asked me all of a sudden, his back still turned.

"What about 'em?"

"I'm surprised," he continued. "I figured you'd know. I figured somebody'd told you, your mama maybe, or Liza. *He* told me a while ago, after he moved back. We were talking about that time I caught Dobber in the woods spotlighting, that story he wrote about it. And he told me he wished I'd shot him, left him for somebody else to find. I thought that was strong. I told him so."

I started laughing. "But you blame him for saying it?"

"I reminded him he *was* his cousin, and he said, Well, he wouldn't've necessarily wanted it to be fatal, just painful.

"And then he said, 'Like he did me and Porter,' and I'd never heard about this, either, but he said when he was young, seven or so, Richard and Dobber, maybe even James, got him and Porter to go off with them when y'all were all up at your granny's some time or other. They took the two of 'em and stripped off their pants, pinched around on their little dicks a while till that got old, made 'em do it to each other, then tied 'em up outside the old chicken coop, looped the cord around one of the fence posts so they couldn't reach it, tied bandanas around their mouths, strewed corn all over the ground next to them, into their shoes and shirt pockets, tied their hands up, left 'em that way."

"My God."

He drank from the glass, drank deeply, kept his eyes on the table and my papers; I sat, taking in this new revelation. The room was very quiet already, and he spoke in a soft baritone. "Porter never said nothin', never complained the whole time. Told Berry they'd done it before, to just *him*, and somebody'd eventually come around, they always did. I guess they figgered Berry'd do the same—just not tell. Silence and shame are how that kind of shit gets swept under the rug."

I touched the papers. "Yes."

"But Berry got his hands loose and ran out screamin' murder, and after that time, your granny always made sure she could spot the younger ones easy when they were at her house, so nothing like that would happen again."

And so we had sat on the fence. "Did he ever say anything to Richard or Dobber later, when they grew up, or James? James is a preacher! Surely James told him he was sorry, sometime or other."

George shrugged.

"Berry's always said people walk around and carry awful secrets inside. I guess that includes him. Mother says he uses his stories to get even with them."

"It's not good to hang onto that stuff."

"How can you say not to hang onto it when somebody's done something like that? Even if it was a long time ago?"

"You have to or you're just stuck in the mud, like that road up to your granny's house: When it's rained a lot, if you don't keep moving, you get stuck."

There was a picture now in my mind of Berry, a seven-year-old, tied up next to his cousin while the older boys went off laughing at them, and I wasn't sorry I'd slipped James a vile CD, and I wasn't sorry Dobber'd been written about, or June, or any of the others. "Awful to think kids can grow up to be sonsabitches."

He set the empty glass in the sink. "He'll never write *that* story, you know. But maybe you should, instead of doing that. That tells more about how somebody lived." He gestured dismissively at the documents. "What'll we have for supper? Want to eat out?"

He'd grown a beard for the fall season; it was easier than shaving every morning, and warmer when you were tramping through woods most of the day; and it made him look like somebody you wouldn't want to meet in a swamp, some wild backcountry fellow from a century ago. I used to like it when he didn't shave for a few months. He was exotic and different to me, someone I had to reacquaint myself with.

"Maggie, I don't mind, you know; I've never minded about the babies." He looked anxious, as if he had not said it hundreds of times to me, as if he thought I might believe him this time. There was nothing to say back, and I didn't try. I always just shuffled my papers around every day he was away; and then finally at last I left him that note saying my grandmother had died.

14

LIZA CAME BY with Jean Ann in the morning, on their way to clear the dead chrysanthemums and carnations and ferns that had been plastered by the rain onto that fresh grave yesterday. Oh, and Granny Kate had told her to give me something, she said, although she, Liza, hadn't wanted to say anything about it in front of the others in case they might feel bad they hadn't been specially, individually mentioned. It crossed my mind just for a second that maybe I'd come into a little money myself; but then she said it was the family Bible, the one Granny Kate had put up on the top shelf of her closet some time back.

"She couldn't see them little words much anymore, it didn't bring her much comfort anymore," Liza said, frowning a little at the heresy, "so she put it up. I guess it was five years ago, she told me I was to give it to you, since you was the historian."

Ironic: All the others, so determined to hang onto their traditions, had bartered their souls and consciences for money, and yet she'd decided to pass to me the most traditional thing of all.

"I didn't want the whole bunch around when I told you, which is why I'm mentioning it now. You go on up there and get it."

I shook my head. "Last summer she said she'd give it to Berry."

"When did she say that? She never said any such of a thing," Jean Ann declared.

"Oh, yes, she did. You ask him yourself."

Liza sighed. "He stayed with me last night; I'd've mentioned it then if I'd known. He's gone now to look up somethin' at the courthouse."

"Well, that's convenient, him gone, not able to be asked."

Liza turned a cold look on Jean Ann: "He'll come out in a while when he's through in town."

"See, just wait for him," I said.

Liza rose from her chair in an agonizingly slow manner and took Mother to the kitchen with her; through the swinging door I heard the low murmur as they talked. Jean Ann sat glowering at me. "Why do you deserve the family heirlooms?"

"Because I keep *all* the records. The deaths and births, divorces, marriages, remarriages...remarriages..."

She looked as if she might smack me. "And that's another thing: Why do you keep it all to yourself?"

"I don't; can't you read what I email?"

She narrowed her eyes and warned me it was everything she could do right then not to snatch out my hair, so I leaned over and offered it if she wanted to try. But Mother and Liza stepped in and told us to behave like the grown women we both were.

"Larry's up at the old house today helpin' Porter get his things packed up," Liza said. "He wanted you to know, Maggie."

Mother looked relieved. It *had* worried her a little, she confessed, that maybe Larry'd just renege on his word after everybody went home.

Well, it was his job anyway, Jean Ann sniffed, his and the other two's.

No, the rest of us aren't our brother's keeper, I put in; and she said she didn't hear me volunteer my house yesterday.

"I think I'll go out on the porch," I said.

"Too cold out there," Mother scolded.

"Not as cold as here."

Jean Ann stared me down, and I heard Mother's exasperated sigh just as I shut the door.

The drizzle had given way to a cloudy, cool chill; before long the few struggling plants in Mother's flower bed would be completely gone. I shoved my knees up under my chin, pulled Mother's huge old purple sweatshirt down over my legs, put my hands inside my sleeves. And waited. I waited the way I'd waited with Sandra and Jerry for Dad to come out on those warm evenings at dusk, the way we had all waited, on a fence, in the yard, in the old house. This time I was cold and felt a fool to be sitting outside. Nothing stirring. Nobody on the roads, no stray dogs roaming up from the woods. An eerie, abandoned feeling, being there all huddled up in myself, nobody in sight. I heard behind me Jean Ann's treble voice once in a while, sometimes a few short, gruff syllables from Mother.

Berry showed up finally, parking near Jean Ann's car, turning back to glance at it as he approached the steps. "Why's my sister here?"

"She brought your mama."

"Ah. I remember. The cemetery. A family outing. My, what a lovely ensemble you're wearing. Just a little purple lump, aren't you."

"If you didn't notice, it's cold."

"So go inside."

"You've heard of hell freezing over. Hell's in there. Go see for yourself."

He laughed, an edgy sort of uncomfortable laugh, a laugh bracketed by that slight frown that made me do a quick review of my words.

"Sorry, shouldn't have said that. That's your sister."

"It's all right." But he looked out at her car and the frown stayed; I apologized again, and he waved his hand as if to swat at a gnat.

"Sit down."

He did, on one of the other chairs, and we had peace for a few moments before Jean Ann peeked out the door. "Didn't I hear a car?"

"Why, yes, you did." Berry looked gravely at her. "I wanted to come by today and thank Maggie's mother for putting up with all of us yesterday. I *know* you're here for the same reason. Tell me how you worded it to her so I can do it right."

She was disconcerted. She allowed a puff of exasperation to escape.

"She did a good job. She told Mother she appreciated her...wait, no, first she called me a liar. Have you got around to appreciating Mother yet?"

"I don't appreciate any of *this*," she said.

"And then she wanted to pull my hair out, so I offered it, and she turned me down. You could loan me your car, and she could get into hers, and we could ram each other a few times."

"Mine? Why mine? There's yours, right there."

"I'm not messing up my car. I got to have something to get home in. Just give me your keys."

"We could do paper rock scissors," and he held out his hand.

Jean Ann might've gone along with it and even contributed in other days, but today she decided not to, and tears began rolling down her cheeks. "I'd of thought you of all people, you of all people," she cried to Berry, "would've not deliberately tried to hurt somebody's feelin's."

"You're right," he said soberly, "so I apologize, which is more than you've ever done."

Because Jean Ann had not returned into the house, in a rush and followed by Liza, Mother stepped onto the porch, ignoring Jean Ann's snuffles.

Liza spoke diplomatically: "Berry, there's a little controversy."

He rolled his eyes. "Always."

"Maggie was to get Mama's old Bible—she told me five or six years ago, before you came back. But Maggie says Mama wanted you to have it."

"I already got it. So no controversy, about that, at least," he said calmly, looking around at our faces, judging our various degrees of surprise, or outrage in Jean Ann's case. "Well, you remember, Maggie, that day last summer, she went to get it, and then Edwin drove up asking about that coffin he'd found. So nobody remembered right then. But I went back later that afternoon"—he turned to Jean Ann—"I was afraid she might forget, or, well, at her age, something might happen before I could get back up there," he finished mildly. "You remember, Maggie. We got to Mama's, and then it hit me I'd left that Bible. So I drove back."

"He did that," Liza said. "He didn't say why he was going back."

"Did you ask her for it? Did you go up there just to beg her for it?" Jean Ann demanded.

"Why would I do such a thing? I went with Maggie that day because Granny had some stuff for her to pick up. Papers, documents... Oh..." he turned to me for a moment. "You sure nothing'd been taken out of that box?"

An odd thing to ask. And I didn't like talking about it in front of Liza and Jean Ann, after what Jean Ann said earlier. Mother's sharp eyes were on me, observing my hesitation, and of all people she came to the rescue. "She took the pictures out to put 'em in her computer, was all. Now, about this Bible..."

"You're just gonna let him keep it?" Jean Ann turned to Liza.

"And I still won't get an apology," he told me.

"It oughta go to somebody that'll keep passin' it on down. Which don't look like it's gonna happen with him, is it? A year from now he won't even know where it is. It needs savin' so some-body down the line'll have somethin' of hers, so part of her'll be like continued. Who'll see to that with *him*? There it is with a person who'll just probably put it up and forget about it. Or whoever cleans out his stuff when he's gone will do it."

Berry and I were both watching her somberly. "Who do you want me to leave it to, Jean Ann?" he asked softly. "Whether I have kids or not myself, I can make sure it goes to somebody else. Who you want it to go to?"

"Well, somebody...maybe even Susie's little boy."

"Granny Kate told Berry he had to read it. Can Susie's little boy even read yet?"

She didn't like that, glared at me. "He'll eventually read it. Anyway, he'll do it as much as Berry ever would."

"About that you are possibly right," he agreed. "I already put in my time Bible-readin'."

Liza shrugged. "It was Mama's business. Maybe you'd like somethin' else, Maggie. Why'nt you run up to the old house and look around for some little thing?"

"Mama!"

"I know what's there, Jean Ann, would you just calm down? Larry's up there with Porter, anyway. You wanna go along with her, since you don't trust her?"

"I did not say that! Aunt Janie, I did not say that about Maggie," this to Mother, who had turned a cold gaze upon her.

"I'll take her," Berry offered.

He waved broadly, Richard-Nixon style, as we left. Jean Ann was arguing and Liza was shaking her head and looking off into the distance; Mother stood akimbo and glared at them.

He drove past his mother's house, turned onto the gritty lane and headed back to the last century.

"Why didn't you tell me before now you'd been back? Why didn't you say something about it?"

"I'm supposed to tell you everything I do?"

"Well, dammit, it would've made *that* not happen. Nobody knew you already had it. Not even your mama. I don't like fighting, I really don't," I told him. "Jean Ann, she has a grudge against you. But she was taking it out on me."

"Maybe I actually did embarrass her with that piece about her car. But, Maggie: *Was* that everything Granny gave you?"

"Why do you keep asking that today?"

"It just looks like there's a gap. A gap in the letters, something that got taken out. Maybe it was never there, in the first place," he mused.

"Well! So you did read them!"

"I did." He'd hesitated before saying the words, as if the two of them had to be considered carefully.

"Why'd you have to go to the courthouse?" I asked.

From the passenger seat I could see him consciously make his face blank, no frown, no emotion. "Something to look up."

"About her will?"

"Not really."

We'd arrived by then at the bridge over Conjure Creek, where the bank had been cleared of debris from the storm three months back. He stopped and killed the engine.

"What're you doing?"

"I'm going to throw you over the bridge. I owe you from years ago." He reached into the back seat and shuffled papers around, manila folders, a briefcase. "No, I always wondered. Didn't you? Where that box came from? I'm just like all the others. I want to know. You can get a geological survey of the county at the courthouse. It breaks down into little sections, terrain rises, the creeks, all that. You see?" he said, spreading across my lap a large white sheet, frayed a little at the edges. "Here we are." He put a finger on a point. "Her land's cut in two with this ridge, at least road frontage. You following me?"

"Yeah. But..."

"Just get out here a minute." He stood beside the car with the map and pulled me to the other side of the bridge, the upstream side. "You see, see on the map where the creek rises, I mean? Off to the right—" he motioned in the direction of where the back of her house would be. "And you see the topography lines? These circle things—"

"I know what they are."

"Ah, yes. I forget from time to time, you're the library. So, there's no doubt that little box had to come off her land. Somewhere. The creek rises here. It comes down here. There's no usable burying places over here, because of the swamp. You see?"

I stared up the stream which was now placid, amber-clear and wading depth. It had taken a monstrous cloudburst to dislodge something and move it to this spot. The tree branches, cut back now so that, at least at the bridge here, they no longer hung over the creek as far as they had last summer, waved bare in the cool November wind. "Somebody'd been on her land without her knowing?"

"Doubtful. If she didn't know, Porter would've."

"Or there's a little grave or two, maybe settlers that moved on before she got here.... What's wrong with you? Why'd you go to the trouble of getting this map today?"

He gave me a solemn look: "Oh, I didn't get it *today*; I had other business down there, this morning. Something I needed to find out, for myself. This, I've had this a while."

"Why?"

He looked upstream, and after a moment shrugged. "It just didn't seem right, not knowing something about it. It passing through this world, and nobody ever knowing anything.... Like my *sister* just said: gone, and nothing to remember." He stopped, and we listened to the gentle swish of the water across the gravel.

"But this paper hasn't given me any answers. We better get up there before Larry leaves, to have a witness we didn't steal stuff."

He turned around at the bridge, instead of going on toward the old house, and took a left onto another dirt road, one even less traveled. We came to other intersections where he'd pause and smile to himself before choosing one of the lanes and continuing. There were so few of them left now, and you didn't know whether to be sorry about that or glad, as you listened to the crackling noise of small gravel and almost-dry mud smacking upon the sides of the car as if thrown in handfuls by children hiding in the woods. He glanced now and then at me as he turned down assorted roads I'd forgotten about, some I hadn't traveled since George and I drove them. Some were ancient—you knew this because they were sunken, the banks heavy with leaning persimmon trees and honeysuckle vines and poison ivy hanging a good two or three feet above the road bed. And then others were newly scraped and ditched just before you rounded a curve to find a raw, freshly-built house positioned between trees in an excavated yard, because somebody wanted a true home out in the country.

Last summer when we'd gone to Granny Kate's, the big storm had washed the dust off everything the night before. There was no dust now either, and yet I shivered again, as if the very leaves hanging overhead were grasping at us as we passed. But this time, in November, they were dying—the first frost hadn't yet come to kill them, but they were dying and just didn't know that they were.

"You cold?" he asked.

"Let's just get there," I said. "No more sightseeing, okay?" And without another word, he found a trail that took us back out.

15

WE SOFT-SHOED INTO the house, avoiding each other's eyes, feeling foolish about tiptoeing, about being so quiet. But it felt right to tiptoe, to touch nothing we didn't have to. It had become that museum, a display of random pieces from a life, and you were careful in museums. I noticed the details, fresh to my eyes now, as you do in museums: The walls inside had been built with just boards laid horizontally over diagonal ones tacked onto a frame— three layers of boards, one on top of the other. You could see that in places where they hadn't been finished off. But, in other areas, sometime or other, someone installed a little cheap fiberboard paneling with a pastel rosebud print.

A discount-store picture of a woodland scene hung over the fireplace in what she had always called the parlor. I had sat in that room many times as a girl looking at that picture. Jerry told me there were two deer hidden in it, if you wanted to find them. I had tried but never did.

We heard Larry's almost-patient voice asking, "What about this? You want this?" over and over, and in the background, Porter's monosyllabic replies and occasional silences.

"We're here," Berry called, then turned to me and raised his shoulders. "What else could I say?"

Larry appeared from a back room, combing his hair with his hand in a frazzled way.

"Mama sent Maggie," Berry hurriedly told him. "Told her to pick out some little thing she'd like."

"But I don't know if I will," I added. There was a look on Larry's face that spoke annoyance and frustration and resentment, and I really didn't want to cross him right then.

"Well, hell, I don't know why not. Porter said Jean Ann come up here late last night. I don't know what she might've got. You may's well join the crowd. —Not to speak ill of your sister. But I don't want responsibility for keeping folks from taking things. It's not my job."

Berry shrugged. "I'll ask her about it in a while. She's at Maggie's mother's, she must've forgot to mention she'd been here. Go on—" He nudged me, and Larry, distracted by a sound in the back, turned away.

"This's like picking somebody's bones," I said.

"Yeah, apparently you're not the first."

The house was unfriendly now; it seemed unwilling to allow anybody to be warm and comfortable and familiar there anymore. The few chairs, with threadbare spots on arms or seats, sat stolidly, as if disapproving our being in the house. I could not bring myself to go through other rooms, certainly not her bedroom. A light scent of dust and old chrysanthemums hung around me. It felt like the funeral parlor the other night, even smelled like it. Or like my house—I stood still, realizing it smelled and felt like my house now, not like hers particularly anymore or really anybody's. "Let's just go," I said.

Berry thoughtfully surveyed the room. "Whatever's left here'll mostly be gone, for sure, in a week or two. If Mama doesn't get somebody to put it all in storage, it'll probably just mysteriously disappear by increments. And anything here after that won't be worth taking. Granny said all along she didn't have anything of value to sell with the place, and she wouldn't try to dole it out, this or that little thing, to so many descendants. So you have about as much claim on it as anybody else."

"What would you have?"

"I've already got it, remember? Hurry up. It's creepy in here."

I turned slowly around in a circle in the middle of the room. All these things belonged nowhere but here, these few things she had accumulated to make her life meaningful or comfortable...they seemed to huddle in the room, trying to avoid being noticed, worth nothing, as she herself had said, but in some way valuable to her, and when they were gone, then she would be gone too. What to pick? There was the picture— I looked at it, swept my eyes over it closely. If there were deer, I still couldn't see them.

"You want that?" Berry asked.

"No. Just remembering something. You see any deer in it?"

"Ah, that old story." He edged up to it, ran his fingers over it, squinted. "Afraid not. You're not going to get anything?"

I turned to him. "We've all got part of her already. I can't take any of this."

"A very poetic thought. I think I'll use it some time."

"Feel free."

He shouted over a sudden din in the bedroom, "We're leaving, Larry—" and "Yeah—" he hollered back at us.

"Can we please not go back to your mother's just yet?" He squinted at the choice before us: to the right, back to town; left, into the old, the milieu we'd descended from.

"What's wrong with you?" I asked.

"I just can't. Not yet. Maybe Jean Ann and Mama'll be gone if we don't rush. I just can't talk to them again right now. Is it okay if we ride around a little—not much," he added, and turned to me, a sort of desperation in his eyes. "Just far enough. And I got something to work out; I need a good brain, an extra one, for it."

I held my hands palm-up: Proceed, if you must. He turned left and eased carefully up Conjure Hill, pulling the steering wheel hard to the left to make the muddy curve. As the road straightened out halfway up, we could feel the transmission switch to passing gear to pull the grade.

"One day they'll come in here and shave the hill down and put up some railings or something, and make it safe for us."

—A simple, casual statement, but the edge in his voice belied the words.

HAZEL ROWELL'S WAS the next house on the left, neat and painted, newer and updated, not like the weathered gray one we had just left. Hazel had always been better off than Granny Kate; her house was well insulated, sheetrocked and wallpapered and should have made Liza and Marcus and Richard and perhaps even Mother ashamed to have left Granny Kate living the way she had for so many years. All up and down the highway sat government-loan houses, built from similar blueprints and bricked and centrally-heated and air-conditioned, houses available because people were poor and could apply for low-interest payments. Granny Kate might have qualified, raising all those grandchildren. Berry and I had passed the double-wides somebody or other had bought recently and moved in; even one of them would have made a tighter house for her and Porter, a warmer one, more comfortable. But nobody'd pushed the idea hard enough; after a few stout *No*'s from her, the proposition was always dropped. It was if they really didn't want to replace the old house, even for her sake, and so sometimes they papered and painted and bought new curtains, and area rugs to cover the bare floors, things like that, which were really just like lining a cave with fabric. It was still a cave.

And yet Richard, Dobber, June, the others resented Hazel, who had been her friend, who had more. Maybe it *was* the house. Maybe they never wanted somebody they thought ought to be less to end up with more. Maybe that was why Richard and Dobber had been so mad at her kids when they walked past Granny Kate's, down the road and out to the highway: fear that some day they'd be more, and themselves, less.

He stopped beside her mailbox, where a large bag of garbage slumped in the mud. Grimly he lifted it into the trunk, slammed the lid. Her car wasn't in the drive; I hoped she wasn't home to wonder if another group of delinquents had stopped to harass her. He eased on past her house a ways, then executed a nice three-point turnaround and stopped at the edge of Conjure Hill.

"Mama told me about it," he said. I didn't go to the bother of asking how *she* knew.

WE STOOD HALF-LEANING against the hood of the car, breathing in the humid melancholy cool air of Mississippi fall. Whenever as an adult I had stood at this point and closed my eyes, I used to fancy I could hear in my mind shrill laughs and screams of children playing in those woods. But it was an illusion; they were gone, and there was no noise, not even of leaves blowing about, for it was a fairly calm day and the limbs were mostly empty except for the occasional oaks. We saw the roof of Granny Kate's house below, the chicken coop way out back, and much further to the rear, the privy where Porter'd stored his cans. From here we could even see the creek, where it turned back towards the homeplace before hills hid it off to the right. But there were no children.

"Why do you have that map, really?" I blurted out.

Hazel Rowell drove by, waving at us as she continued to her house. There had not been enough drizzle the past two days to make the ruts bad, because up here there was no traffic, no four-wheel-drive trucks slipping around in a funeral procession to churn up the mud. He let her pass before saying anything. Then, abruptly, "Granny Kate had to have known the baby was buried on her land. She had to. Just, she was as surprised as we were when it washed up. She didn't expect *that*. Who would've?"

"Well, then, she knew who it was."

He didn't argue but went on: "It wasn't from some early settler long ago; I asked the coroner. He told me, maybe within this century. That was what went in the paper. How'd there be anything left of a baby buried in a wood coffin a hundred years ago? It would've never washed down. It would've been in pieces strewn everywhere. The box and everything else."

I wandered to the beginning of the slope downward and broke off a shaft of broom sage at the edge of the road. "She had two babies that died."

"Both in the cemetery with her. She made out like she didn't know anything about it that day; remember what she said? Something like, 'People should see to it their folks is taken care of.' I didn't think about those words at the time. Later I did. I got the map. And there's no way she couldn't have known about that baby. Not where the creek runs, not it going back any more years than it did."

"What if somebody sneaked back in there and buried it without telling or asking or anything? The woods might be full of things like this."

"Occam's razor."

"I don't remember," I said.

"Simplest explanation's usually the answer. But I can't find the answer now."

The broomsage crumbled in my fingers as I worried at it like a string of rosary beads. No: The answer didn't come to me either. I tossed aside the bare stalk. Some part of me was annoyed, and felt betrayed even, that he would invest so much thought into the question, something dead that would never bring changes to our lives and didn't matter. I told him that, headed back to his car.

"That's ironic, coming out of you," he said, and he wasn't smiling.

"And it's ironic you're so obsessed with this thing from the past. It's not your problem. If you care so much, get it dug up, do a DNA on it if they can." I flung myself into his car. He stared at me; I glared right back, until he got in, himself, turned sideways and contemplated me coldly.

"DNA's your thing," I said. "Back last summer, you told me it'd always trump my genealogy work. So go do it. You can probably compare it to whoever else in the family's done it and find out if it's at least related."

"I could." He seemed about to say something else, changed his mind and turned another hard glance at me. "Wanna see how fast we can take this hill?"

"No, I do not."

"Oh, the ditches aren't deep, and I've always wondered." He cranked the engine, revved the motor, and for a moment it kept time with my pulse.

"What's the matter with you today? You trying to get even with me about something?"

He scoffed, pushed down on the accelerator.

"Or is it all that yesterday?" I hesitated but only a moment or two: "I know about what they did to you and Porter when you were kids. Is it that? Did it all come back to you? Because I don't blame you, but I'm not responsible. I didn't do it."

"Who told you? George, I guess. Doesn't matter. Did you ever wonder why I never told you myself? Because all us boys were raised to be tough. Telling somebody, it would make us not tough. I don't like thinking about it."

"I said I don't blame you, but it's pointless letting it rent space in your mind now. Just write them all off. I mean, you've done that, literally, with most of 'em; now do it in your mind."

"DNA, huh..." The motor screamed. I clutched reflexively at the door handle, and he laughed at me, laughed with a terrible, unhumorous bark. "You afraid of me? Am I a bully too? All in the family."

"If you're gonna be an idiot, I'm getting out."

"Oh, we'll get down the hill just fine. Nobody around to run over, either." He grinned a scary smile, mashed his foot down hard. The car strained against itself, wanted to careen recklessly ahead. Again he pounded the accelerator. "I always wanted to, and Dobber's not around to watch out for. I might not watch out for him anyway. It'd be fun to get the rest of his foot."

I opened my door and waited, challenging; he gently eased back on the accelerator, and I heard the silence—you can hear silence. It's the noise of wind whispering through dead, dry grass beside you, then drifting down the hill.

"I won't crash us," he said. "Buckle up and let's go."

We hit thirty, but that was about it. At the bottom he stopped and laughed and pointed to Larry, at the expression on Larry's face as he stood on Granny Kate's porch, apparently astounded at the roaring, mud-spewing racket we had made coming down. Berry lowered the window.

"I always wanted to do that, Larry."

Larry nodded as if he understood completely.

16

I KNEW WHY Berry had always planned to escape, and it wasn't just about chicken coops.

He didn't know I knew. It was one of those secrets, but one I could not tell him I knew, and which at times like today I wanted to tell him I knew.

He was fifteen. Liza came to Mother's house, a big knot on the side of her head.

Cal had found out what the boys had done to Berry and Porter long ago, she said, had taken Berry to the barn to show him how to fight. That was what he said he was doing. Later I understood Cal was ashamed that his son had never fought back, hadn't dealt bloody noses or broken teeth to his cousins, no matter that he was younger and smaller; Cal took it as a reflection on himself, and maybe he even wanted some revenge for his own loss of pride and took it by shoving his son around. Who knew; to men of that generation out in the country every day was a struggle against age and time and even their own better natures.

Cal had also heard the other insinuations and was afraid where smoke was, there could be fire. That he loved Berry in his own way wasn't disputed, and nor could you say his vexation wasn't mixed with disgust. So he would teach Berry self-defense, he said.

Berry didn't want to hit his father. That infuriated Cal: "Be a man, for God's sake," he'd yelled; and, "I am one!" Berry had yelled back. "Then show me you're the same as they are," Cal taunted. "I don't wanna be the same as they are," Berry shouted, and that was when Liza thought she should intervene: Berry's face bloody from an upper cut and Cal standing nearby with clenched fists, panting like an overworked horse, a triumphant, tense look on his face. Liza rushed over, Cal shoved her—"Godamighty, Eliza, stay outa this, get outa the way"—and she stumbled back against the corncrib, stunned, and Cal turned and looked at her, irritated with this distraction, and Berry swung a decent haymaker that laid Cal out cold.

Two days later Cal went to the sink for a glass of water and fell down dead. Liza called Mother, and Edwin's office; possibly he might be patrolling, she thought. The two of them arrived about the same time. He took in the healing bruise on Cal's face and the broken-open spot beside Berry's right brow before he bent over and put his ear to Cal's chest. "I'm sorry, Liza. There ain't nothin' to be done now."

Mother took Liza by the hand and sat her down in a chair and made Berry sit next to her while Edwin made phone calls to the proper people. Then he took her aside and nodded towards Berry and pointed at Cal, whose body he'd placed on the couch with Liza's help.

"Anything I ought to know?" he asked.

"Not a thing." Mother bristled even reliving the scene for me. "Ask her, she'd be the one to tell you, anyway, wouldn't she?" Liza turned her white face to him and shook her head just a little; he nodded once and continued with his calls to the coroner and the funeral home.

Berry hid his bruised knuckles at the funeral by keeping his hands turned over, palms up, as you would, taking Communion, and to explain the cut beside his eye he told me some sort of lie about an accident, and I just let it go. Fathers surely did put their sons through a lot sometimes, I thought.

LIZA AND JEAN Ann *had* left.

George had arrived somehow, and was passing the time of day with Mother and Dad. They asked if I'd picked out a thing; I told them I didn't feel right doing it, after finding out Jean Ann had gone up last evening. Then I remembered again and said flippantly, "Sorry, won't disrespect your sister," and he shook his head.

"DNA always trumps," he said. "Thank you again, Aunt Janie." He hugged her and half-heartedly shook Dad's hand. "G'bye, Maggie." He didn't look me in the eye, hurrying past.

We walked him to his car and sent him off, and George turned to me. "What the hell was that about?"

"Just being a jerk."

"You or him?"

At the porch Mother stood waiting for me, judgment on her face. I poked my chin out at her: "Well, go on, say your say."

"I asked you not to pick another fight."

"I'm tired of being accused of starting everything," I said. "How was I supposed to've started it this time? Jean Ann made it her business to follow me outside. Then she made the first smart crack; I didn't."

"You're s'posed to overlook some people. You ought not to let 'em bother you."

"Yeah, like you didn't let Aunt Sabrina bother you yesterday."

"Y'all come on in and get lunch," she said. "That's different."

We followed her to the kitchen where I continued: "It is not different. It's the exact same thing."

"I never did try to get back at her till yesterday. She just pushed me too hard yesterday."

"Jean Ann just pushed me too hard, too."

"You know what I'm goin' to do? I'm goin' to buy a real expensive dishwasher. One of those big ones that'll do anything. And then whenever your Aunt Sabrina visits and offers to help clean up the kitchen, I'm going to make her wash everything by hand. I'll just tell her there ain't enough things to run that big dishwasher a whole cycle, use all that power to do it." She raised her brows and smiled coolly at me. Dad cast a wary glance.

Mother might open a window on Aunt Sabrina, or glare at a cousin's little boy, or tell the relatives she wasn't going to have no cussin' in her house, but she didn't often show her temper in a crowd. It wasn't good manners. I tried now to digest her giving advice on revenge as she slopped a wet dishrag across the kitchen counter.

"But I tell you one thing. I'd never be dumb enough to lean over and offer Jean Ann my hair. It'd be like askin' Porter if he wanted to go through the garbage." Her shoulders shook a little.

"Or getting him talking about chickens," I said carefully, since it was hard to believe she was joking in the first place, and, of all people, about Porter.

"Oh, Lord," she said. We all started giggling. "I declare, I ought to be ashamed, laughin' about him. Poor old thing." She shook her head sternly. "No tellin' what'll become of him."

I told her I guessed Larry'd be doing the worrying from now on. She said maybe and maybe not, then glanced out that kitchen window again and shook her head once more. "For a while. Not for long, though. But I don't expect there was any other way."

IT WENT HOW they had said it would. Porter moved in with Larry. Larry's kids yelled about not being able to have any of their friends over because their crazy uncle might be saying stupid things and acting weird. It was also rumored that his wife Alicia threatened to leave. But the lawyers were as anxious to settle the will as everybody else had been, Granny Kate having added a neat little provision about their fees and timely disposition of property. So there was no opportunity for Larry or Alicia really to back out of the deal before it was a done thing.

No more than a week after the funeral, Robert Beck, who owned about half the town and some of the county, approached the lawyers and said Granny Kate and he had discussed his buying everything, and he had the financing lined up and wanted a meeting with the heirs named in the will, wanted to make his interest known officially and put an option on the property. Mother took me with her; and, around a long oval table, there sat all of us apparently congenial cousins, dressed in whatever professional-looking clothing we'd scratched up out of our closets, passing around the sheets of paper like trays of food at a feast. Berry was there, also, next to Liza, glancing at me from time to time across the table. When it was all done, Robert Beck stood up and shook everybody's hands all around, and Berry said, "I know about you helping her out before, and I appreciate it." The man gave him an annoyed look and turned away suddenly. Mother brought it up as we went home: "What on earth d'you think Berry meant by what he said to that man?" But, like Porter, I had no answer.

After waiting ninety days for debts to be settled, and then however long it would take the lawyers to do their filings after that, the grandchildren and Liza would get a bit more than Richard and Dobber had figgered. They had several months to pleasantly anticipate it. In the meantime Thanksgiving and Christmas and the new year would give them other things to think about; and so everybody was happy, except Larry's kids and Alicia. In a couple of weeks Larry went with Porter to buy a little one-bedroom house trailer and set it up in his own back yard. Alicia told him he was crazy, it must run in the family, because the trailer had a gas furnace and stove; and sure enough, in another week or two Porter had turned away from the stove one noonday, not being familiar with gas cooking; and the resulting fire burned up most of the kitchen and almost himself with it before the volunteer fire department arrived.

By then all the paperwork had been settled on the other things, and while Porter was being treated for burns, a psychologist dropped by his room in the hospital. This time the family doctor and the psychologist diagnosed several high-function personality disorders and prescribed a few calming medications. Porter didn't seem at all his old self, Mother said, the day he was settled into the adult group home associated with the mental facility in town: Times were different now, as Granny Kate herself had learned, and people were no longer locked up on a family member's word. Mother told me Larry cried when he left Porter there. And Porter had just turned away and started hanging up his clothing.

THANKSGIVING CAME AND was gone before new red dirt had to be shoveled to fill in where her grave had settled after a few weeks, but nobody suggested a family gathering this year—it was just too soon after the funeral, too hard to even think about getting together until we'd forgotten some things. Amy did not come over to make fun of the relatives, either. "Some other time," was all Sandra said, smooth as silk, to me.

Porter had been moved to his temporary place by then. Clouds slumped across the horizon every day. About a week before Christmas, James Preacher mailed off his yearly diatribe about the misuse of the season in general and the substitution of "Xmas" for "Christmas" in particular. It was the same letter to the editor every year, which he fetched from some file cabinet at his house, retyped, and submitted with misspellings and incomplete thoughts.

Things felt unfinished, as if maybe even Granny Kate's death and the funeral had been a strange dream and she was really just in a nursing home, ignored; or forgotten, like Martha, some cousin or other of mine, whose parents had gone home from a church service one Sunday night unaware that Martha was not in the back seat with her other siblings. Maybe somebody ought to check and see if Granny Kate'd been left asleep on a bench, and we would all feel guilty.

Winter arrived, what passed as winter in the South, half-hearted, sullen, humid, but not cold, turning the remainders of the plants that hadn't yet died into mushy decay like overcooked greens. I sat in the vanilla kitchen and drank too much coffee and, taking the cup with me, meandered aimlessly into the vanilla living room to hold the edge of a curtain between my thumb and finger and watch the street, not with any hope of seeing something different but because there was nothing else really to do. George was gone a lot. He left at six most mornings, came back at nine, or later. When a job kept him out late, I stayed busy making pilgrimages to the library. At the lake the final stages of the draw-down were commencing, cleanup from that, boat-launch repairs and public-beach re-sanding; and then, George said, the spillway would be partly closed once more and the water level brought back up. Meanwhile, he was on overtime patrol, dealing with the eager fishermen who, greedy for an easy haul, were pulling stunts like sweeping up the desperate fish in huge illegal seines or—if they figured they could get by with it—dropping a little electric current in the water.

Sometimes he left very quietly, tiptoeing around and even easing the door shut to lock it from the outside. He thought I was asleep; but I knew. Sometimes I gazed blearily from under mostly-closed eyelids and saw that he stood for a moment or two, watching me with a puzzled expression on his face. But then he did always leave, and I was back in the house alone.

17

"WE ARE ALL going to meet one more time up in the country," Mother said sternly to me. "You may as well plan on bein' there." As at Thanksgiving, nobody in the family suggested a Christmas reunion at the old house. No longer "Granny Kate's", it was now simply "the old house" to us.

"How'd they pull that off?"

"Jean Ann asked Robert Beck if the family could use it a time or two."

"Didn't they turn off the power and water?"

"Not yet. Liza started to, but he said he might need it if he was workin' up there late, it getting dark so early these days. He told her he'd pay the bill." The silence that followed these words seemed to be one of those carefully-placed blank spots Mother would insert into a conversation to provoke me to ask more questions.

"Why would he be up there working at night? Doing what?" I said.

She sat at my table, fidgeting with two spoons I'd left from breakfast. "These are dirty," she announced. "It looks like your dishwasher didn't get 'em clean. Or did you use 'em and forget to wash 'em? He said yes, they could go there, at least, they could until he started taking it down."

"Taking it down." She said those particular words flatly, grimly, as she had delivered other grim news to me through the years: *"Cal died this morning. Your cousin Anne's house got hit by that windstorm yesterday and she has a broke arm and leg."* Dad glanced covertly at her, cleared his throat, and it came to me that she'd spent a lot of time in that old cypress-board house herself, and, flat and grim as she might try to be, she couldn't tell me this. And he knew and was trying to help. I gave him points for that.

"Several of them decided they'd ask what he meant. Him wanting the power on, they figured he'd probably be there, so they drove up. It was about the first of the month, I b'lieve. He was repairing the fences. They look nice now," Dad mused. "I went up there not long ago myself just to see, and he put up some of those new metal posts and barb wire."

"He took down the old wooden boards we sat on?"

"Well, Maggie, they were rotten, you know," he went on reasonably as Mother stared at the spoons.

"Go on."

"Well, those grandchildren told him he didn't have a legal deed to it yet—"

"Liza said he told 'em he didn't think the folks'd mind him doing a little repair, as they'd already agreed to him buying it," Mother interrupted, her voice strong and tense again. "He intends to have the house all pulled down one day soon after that will's probated." She stopped there again, yanked the spoons up and went to the sink. "These are dirty." She turned on the water and began scrubbing them fiercely, so Dad finished the story, embellished it, added details, and I could visualize how it happened as he spoke:

"But we didn't know you were just goin' to tear down Granny's home," Jean Ann wailed.

Liza took it with silence.

He was calm, as if he was surprised at them somehow. "Well, you know, she and I talked all this out, the last few years, and it really wasn't her desire for youall to hang on to it after she was gone. She told me many a time it would be fit to give it up, when the time came. It had outlived its use. 'Let it pass,' she said." He looked at them, Jean Ann wiping her eyes, James Preacher shaking his head sadly. "She never said that to any of you?"

"Yep. I've heard her say it," I affirmed. Mother turned from the sink, her eyes slightly watery, and gave me a dubious glance, as if she thought it was an all-too-convenient memory.

"Well, you remember," I insisted. "It was something she'd always say about things. When somebody needed to move on, she'd say it: 'Let it pass.' "

"Well, others has said it too," she sniffed. Dad continued:

Robert Beck turned back to his fence-mending. "I don't mind if you get together here a time or two more, but I'll be taking it down when I get the deed; you need to tell that around. I can't have vagrants using it as winter quarters; that's the way fires start, and it might get a good hold out here and burn up some fine timber before they could put it out." He turned once more with a speculative look on his face. "Any of you want to have it moved, I guess that would be fine with me, though I'm not going to finance that, myself; you'll have to do that part. And you really ought to remember that wasn't what she wanted done."

When Dad finished telling the story, and I finished envisioning it, Mother turned again and stared hard at me as if she were waiting for me to cry a little, too, like her or Jean Ann, or put on a sad face, like James, or something. But time had already started building that callus in me as I had known it would in Amy. Sometimes I did think about Granny Kate, the afternoons up at the old house long ago, thought how very weird and maybe even boring it would be to last to that age, but I didn't think of her that often anymore. She was already a part of the past, so the fate of the old place didn't bother me much. Mother exhaled loudly.

"So, we are getting together up there one more time. And you need to come, too. We are going to get along, so do somethin' nice for everybody. Like, maybe, bring your family notebooks or those old pictures or something."

"When?"

She told me the date they had set and made me write it on the calendar to prevent my having the excuse of forgetting, or of not knowing in the first place. She and Dad had dropped by the house that morning on the way back from another appointment with the doctor, this time an appointment she'd made for herself. I wanted to know if she was sick; she sniffed haughtily and told me her eyes weren't so good right now, because of cataracts, but they weren't ready to come off yet, so she guessed she'd just have to keep working that quilt and hope that at the end the stitches didn't look like mine did. I let it pass.

SO THERE WE were, driving up again into that yard. The ghosts were all around. But not sitting on the fence, looking at us, for they wouldn't have been able to balance on the new metal posts and barb wire.

It was cold. Nobody wanted to light the heater. Somebody—probably Richard—suggested right off that if we accidentally burned the place down, Robert Beck would just deduct it from everybody's settlement, regardless of whether he himself intended to tear it down. All the grandchildren kept on their coats as the soft winter rain misted down outside. After a while, Marcus said, "Screw this," and lit a match to hold to the old clay grate. The gas caught up quickly as he eased the valve open a little.

"Them things ought to be outlawed," James suggested.

"Mama tried to get her to put in a unit," Jean Ann said.

When we'd arrived, Liza and Mother were already there, sweeping out dead bugs and mouse droppings, a handful of crushed leaves by the door—as if that would matter in a few weeks. Sweeping seemed to be a way of rearranging your life, trying to clean up the ragged leftovers and mistakes, even if, at the end like this, it was a pointless exercise.

Everybody had nervously smiled and greeted one another, catching up on news, remarking about how nice it was to get together again like this; and then a great mournful silence had fallen like that misting rain outside, cold and depressing.

"We won't stay too long. We're goin' to take a look around one more time and decide about a few little things still here at the house, and then we can leave if we want to, if we get too cold. We may as well start with these few chairs." Liza gestured vaguely at them.

They were three old cane-bottom ones, not worth anything, really, except for sentimental reasons. The huge ancient table she'd served food on was long gone; I didn't ask who'd got it but hoped that person was Liza. Picking up one of the chairs now, Dobber reckoned he'd take them home because he could use them in his shop. Nobody said anything. Liza went to the kitchen cabinets and opened them—a few jars of canned tomatoes, a couple of cheap bowls, a stack of plastic cups from the dollar store for times when everybody had come over with kids and she didn't have enough stemware. Liza took all the items and laid them down on the countertop. Dobber strolled over to look.

I realized the others were kind of hanging back now. "I guess I could use them bowls and cups, too. Wonder how old the tomatoes are?" Dobber mused.

Mother lowered her eyebrows and shot him a look. "They are just from last summer, and canned tomatoes don't go bad that fast," she said. "How are you goin' to use all those bowls and cups?"

"Well…" He hesitated, turned and realized that everybody else was kind of staring at him, but not quite, the way Porter looked through or around you. "I ain't bein' greedy. If anybody else wants anything, you have as much of a right to it as I do. Step up! Say so!"

But nobody did. Mother glared at me. "Maggie brought her

notebooks for anybody to take a look at, if you rather do that today."

I froze for a moment, then nodded and headed back through the light mist to my car. There was Rhonda, right on my heels. "I'll help you," she said, but there was an edge in those words, and she kind of stared at the house as we took my armful of boxes and books back inside.

"You don't want to be here any more than I do," I whispered.

"I didn't want to come at all. James called and told me I needed to, and he got in touch with some others, because he said otherwise it might be just one or two people getting everything that was left."

"Not much of any real value," I muttered, holding the screen door for her at the porch.

"Yeah, but would it be right for one person to walk in and get all of whatever it is? That one person who's doin' it, by the way?" she hinted, raising her eyebrows, waiting just at the door, the screen resting against her back. "Because, just so you know, he's already said he's gonna put it in a yard sale. I doubt any of it'll end up at his shop."

I winced. She met my eyes for a second or two. "I guess, really it *isn't* worth anything much, and who cares, right? I mean, you, or I, or maybe even Liza, might put it in a yard sale someday ourselves. But just—"

"Just not tomorrow or next Friday," I finished. We went inside.

Dobber had got a couple of paper sacks and was packing things into them with Richard's help, the two of them oblivious to Mother's sullen glare. "Well, what else's left?" Richard asked.

"Do you know, I think we'll donate whatever else to the shelter," Liza announced. "That okay with you, Janie? Everybody all right with it?" People nodded.

I spread the books out on top of Dobber's old chairs, and various relatives eased over and started flipping pages. Nobody had ever really seen my records—I'd never let them, not because they were secret, but because I suspected they'd want to change things, or tell me to leave them out entirely. It was easy for me to write down all of Richard's marriages, but maybe he wanted to forget some of them, wanted them expunged from pages as well as memory. Maybe Susie'd want me to adjust the date of her wedding to make her baby a little less premature; or Jean Ann'd say there wasn't no reason to put down all three times she'd married because it was to the same man each time. When I was younger, I might have given them some consideration—what harm in those little things being changed? Only the few exemplary ones had lived exemplary lives; why should they be able to hold it over the rest of us, who'd just made a few mistakes here and there? Give 'em enough years, they'd make some too: So I'd thought, one time. But then I got old; and today it had to be real, it had to be true. If the little part wasn't true, what was?

But nobody said anything to me for a while. There were a couple of small groups huddled around two of the chairs, people kneeling and squatting and sitting on the floor. James and Rhonda took the photo album and started going through it, quietly remarking on the old pictures as they recognized people. Someone moved one of the notebooks to the floor, so all in that group could examine it better. I leaned against the wall, watching and waiting for it to happen, and at last it did:

"Maggie, not sure this date here's right..."

It wasn't Richard, and it wasn't Susie, and it wasn't any of the several others who might be embarrassed by an inconvenient number. It was Anne, her brother Marcus near her, who met my eyes. "Mama's birthday's not right."

"E-mail it to her. Or write it down on something."

I hadn't heard Berry ease into the room. His car hadn't been outside while Rhonda and I were hauling in my genealogy crap. Or had it? I hadn't looked, because she'd been right at my elbow, whispering.

"Instead of making your own corrections on her book," he continued. "That's the right way to get facts straightened out."

I gave him a look, because what would *he* know about that kind of thing? Anne took the paper I offered and began scribbling.

"When did you get here?" I asked.

"And why?" Richard said, a little just-kidding smile on his face.

"Why're you always asking me why *I'm* here? Maybe I ought to ask you, for once." He leaned over the big photo album James and Rhonda were examining. "Maggie, did you bring those other ones? The ones from last summer?"

"You want those? I don't have them with me. I did scan them into my laptop. You want me to email them to you?"

"What other ones?" It was Richard again, and the tone in his voice made me and several people nearby glance at him; he'd evidently not appreciated Berry's last remark. He went on: "Why'd he get to see 'em and we can't?"

Berry rose from the squat he'd been in. "They're my dad's family. You wouldn't have any interest in 'em."

"Speaking of pictures, shouldn't we take some?" Marcus interrupted nervously. "The house'll be torn down one day, and this'll probably be the last time any of us'll see it. Ought to be some pictures."

People glanced around. Berry pulled his phone out of his pocket. "C'mon, let's group up."

Mother announced firmly, "I will take the picture—I do not want to be in it," so Berry handed her the phone and told her to press the button, it was all ready for when we got into the frame. The silence was broken by a few "Sure's", some grumbles as people rose from the floor, and then he said, "C'mon, Richard, Dobber, get in here, too!" For Dobber'd stood up from his packing and was watching us, and Richard's mouth was a straight line of cold antagonism.

It was a ghastly moment. They stood at the side of the uneasy group as Mother backed up. Berry directed people: "No, you're too short, you get in front. Anne, over beside James. Mama, you get near the middle. Aunt Janie, you *should* be with her...the only two children left..."

"No. Not today. Maggie, behind Liza. Richard, you and Dobber get close to Liza, too," Mother ordered. "You're too tall to be on the side."

Richard and Dobber had distinctive ways of getting around. Richard always kind of sauntered, as if there was nothing on his schedule to hurry him; Dobber moved about with jerkier, clumsy little motions. They repositioned themselves closer to Liza, and I moved in behind her.

"And now, me," Berry said.

He went behind the apprehensive, silent group and jostled into the pose, throwing one of his arms over Richard's shoulder and the other over Dobber's. Richard turned around and glared at him.

"I just realized there aren't any kids here. Didn't anybody bring your kids?" someone said.

This was true. The relatives in the room were mostly my age or older, a few slightly younger. Mother hesitated, held the phone aside, an odd expression on her face. "So it's just gonna be this generation in the picture." She and Liza shared a glance across the room.

"Okay, get ready," Berry said in Mother's direction—"one, two—"

Just before the flash went off, with all of us still maintaining the sickly smiles we had stretched our lips into, Richard stepped away from Liza: "Nope, I ain't gonna be in no family portrait with that little bastard. He ain't *my* family;" and all hell broke loose.

IT WAS WORSE than after the funeral, because there weren't so many men here today. I learned that afternoon Richard really was scary.

Berry swore when Richard made his comment; then swung out at him.

Richard stiff-armed him backwards, pushing him towards the kitchen sink.

James yelled, "Whoa! Whoa!" and threw Dobber aside to try to step between the other two.

Marcus pushed Anne behind him and Larry.

Mother flung Berry's phone to the kitchen counter and put her fists on her hips. "I told you before, don't you start nothing in this house!"

"It ain't your house this time!" Richard yelled, flailing at Berry and James.

"I grew up here!" Mother shrieked.

Berry yanked Richard's arm and somehow, in a quick move I could hardly follow, twisted him so his back was against Berry's chest. He leaned into Richard's ear.

"Everybody here sees it today. No sneaking around. You won't get by with it like you did with Alex."

And then it got weird. Richard's expression changed from fury to amusement, and he laughed, and his muscles stopped cording up, and he quit wrestling, and Berry leaned backward, startled.

The cousins, the grandchildren, the relatives were laying hands on their belongings, anxious to get away from there; some of them were still lined up for that photo, twitching a little, and eyes wide. I wanted my notebooks not to be damaged, located them where my kin had scattered them about, and stacked them by the front door. Berry was backed against the sink, his eyes fixed on Richard, who calmly picked up Dobber's grocery bags and set them on top of the chair seats. It was eerie how little any other noise was being made...just the rustle of that paper and the scraping of those chairs.

"I heard you been askin' around about Alex, so whyn't you go on and say it to more people? Go on. I could use some of your part of that money. I might get it all." Richard glanced around at the shocked-silent relatives and went on, "Y'all talk about suin' him, but you don't have guts to do it, but I would."

Berry remained mute, white, trembling slightly; even from some feet away I could see that, as his eyes fixed on Richard.

"Alex just left. He took his pa's money, and he just left, started a new life for hisself somewhere else, just like you done, but you just go right ahead, make it easy for me." He glanced around at the cousins. "You go on and get in your picture, but he ain't no kin of mine; I don't want no picture with him." He turned back to his brother: "Let's get this out to the truck."

"You ain't takin' any of it," Liza told them. "I am keeping it myself."

"You can keep it all. It's nothin' but a bunch of trash anyway. I might've got a dollar or two from the whole mess." And with that, Dobber turned and left. Richard followed him, after looking back at Berry and grinning.

BERRY SAID, "I'M turning the gas off at the tank. Mama, I want you to follow me out, after you lock up. Maggie, take your mother home now yourself, okay?"

Anne handed me her little slip of paper, which I stuck into an end-flap of one of those binders.

"Will y'all be all right here?" Mother asked Liza.

"Richard is not the only one who owns a gun. You and Maggie take them chairs to Hazel. I bet she could use them when her grandchildren visit. Berry, you pack the tomatoes in your car. I'll make soup out of them," Liza instructed.

We went out onto Granny Kate's porch. —No, the porch of the old house. Berry picked up two of the chairs and set them at the edge of the yard, but there we stopped. Richard and Dobber stood beside Richard's truck, talking. They too stopped and we all stared at each other for a few minutes.

"So you gonna take 'em? Guess that was the plan all along," Dobber yelled across the yard.

Mother bristled. "If we throw 'em in the gully, how's that different from what you were goin' to do?" She grabbed one of the chairs and strode briskly toward the cars with it, and for just a minute I could see Granny Kate hopping out, walking, cane in hand, to confront the rowdies. Richard and Dobber found it funny again, made a dismissive wave at us, and got into their vehicles, pulling out in a gravel-spewing hurry. Some things never changed.

I HAD TO leave the trunk open to get the last chair in, but it wasn't more than half a mile to Hazel's, so I just drove slowly, the lid bouncing up and down, gently, as I maneuvered up Conjure Hill. But Hazel wasn't home. We walked around toward the back stoop to leave them there. "I wouldn't trust them rascals not to come up here and get 'em, if they thought we might be doing this," Mother told me. But we stopped at a startlingly menacing growl. "She has got a dog now. Well, I don't blame her."

It was a mongrel, but a big one, and it snarled and lunged inside the new hurricane fence installed around the yard and enclosing her back door. No way to put the chairs there, so we went back to the front and laid them on their sides on the porch, with Mother's note. "Harder to see 'em from the road this way," she said tersely, sighed as we drove off. "We have done the best we can," she said. "I hope Hazel gets home pretty soon."

I turned around, carefully, because I wanted to bring no more mud with me to town than was necessary. I had to ask, not really expecting an answer from her—there was a frozen, calculating hardness in her face that told me I might get no answer. I asked anyway: "What was all that about, do you know?"

"He's been sayin' Richard did away with Alex for that money. It finally got back around to him. I'm surprised you haven't heard." She gave me an assessing look to judge my truthfulness. She didn't have to tell me who she meant.

"I don't talk to most of 'em, you know."

"You talk to *him*." Again, that look, and I remembered a hot summer day and a rushing, cooling stream. "Aren't you gonna make some comment?"

"No. I don't have anything to say." That was safer.

"Well, that's a first. He hasn't told you anything about it?" She appraised my silence. "And that's another first. Just so you know, then, somebody told Richard, and after we decided we'd meet at

164

the old house, Richard put it out he'd whip Berry's ass if he showed up."

I laughed. "So of course he *had* to show up, then. Richard's kind of stupid after all, isn't he."

"Only if you think he didn't actually want him to come." She stopped at that and let me think about it, and I did, and a shiver went up me, fast. I glanced sideways at her. We were pulling into her driveway now, and the slow drizzle reflected off the windshield onto her face, painting pale, ever-changing watercolor lines and bumps down her cheeks like wrinkles. Or tears. I dropped her off, and Dad came outside to hug me before she sighed again and went through the door. And I thought it had been a long day for her.

THE RAIN GOT a little heavier later, turning from mist and drizzle into a slow liquid bead curtain that kept up until about three in the morning. By then, George had come in. I woke up just enough to realize he was dry and not cold, which puzzled me a little, but on the other hand, it was good he didn't chill the bed.

18

AND THEN CHRISTMAS was over, and the letdown of the dreary year's end arrived. You wished Christmas was the last day, and then a new year'd start the next morning, ending the old one on a high note. Or for some people, maybe. Sandra and Amy drove down for a day and a night, and left; George opened gifts, and left, apologetically for doing that on a holiday. People had got new guns for Christmas, he said, and wanted to try them out, legal seasons be damned. Since he and I hadn't had particular plans of any sort, he'd signed up for the shift. And, then, the water at the lake was about as low as they needed it to be, and would be raised soon; he was making rounds to see the eager anglers weren't doing stupid things in the rush to harvest the easy-pickings fish in the small pools. "You stayin' here the rest of the day by yourself?"

I told him I might go back up to Mother's.

He tucked one of the gifts—a pair of expensive insulated gloves, useful things, appreciated but practical—into his pockets as he left; turned back at the door: "If you get a chance, you might tell

Berry he needs to dial it back. I hear things, what he's sayin' about Richard, and it ain't gonna end well."

"How do you hear anything over there?"

He considered this a moment. "The receptionist knows Richard pretty well. We all do, I guess; he's kind of notorious. They know I have a connection to him, gave me a sort of head's-up."

"Why don't *you* text Berry?"

"He's not my kin. He might take it better from you." He gave me an odd look but didn't wait for a comment, and in a moment I heard him crank his truck and leave.

You in town? I texted. His answer was that he was at Liza's, just him, visiting for the day; Jean Ann and all her bunch had been there the evening before. I thought about that: Sandra and Amy had also driven down to have Christmas Eve with Jerry and his family and me and George and Mother and Dad, and now all the older people were alone on the holiday. And I wondered suddenly about Porter, and then about whether Granny Kate and he had spent Christmases by themselves, because I remembered *I'd* never gone up there on that day; had any of the other relatives, had everyone assumed somebody else would do that, so nobody did? Mother and Dad had Lilly today. Like me, she was a person alone, but *her* husband dead, her own children living far away. Out of pity relatives invited her over on holidays which society had decorated and tagged with familial emotions. And one of Jerry's grown kids might drop by; but I didn't want to, not today. I didn't want to accept the pity for myself.

Want to ride up country for a while? I asked.

We made the arrangements: I'd come out in my own car and we'd drive past the old house, check on things up that way. He ran that excuse past Liza while we texted, and she accepted it and offered to put out some food for us when we got back later. The streets were deserted as I left, occasional front yards occupied by children trying out new toys and bikes and skateboards. I turned my eyes away from that and ignored the speed limits when I got past the residential neighborhoods; cops wouldn't be giving tickets today, surely.

Liza's house smelled of day-old turkey roast and her fruit cake which we all knew she drenched in fine brandy when it came out of the oven. They were scents I'd inhaled in Mother's house all those Christmases past, aromas wrapping the day as much as any other gift.

But Liza and Berry were reserved; not a smile crossed her face as she said she'd have some leftovers for us later on; and he buckled his seat belt and stared out the windshield as I drove away. His silence depressed me; I wondered if he and his mother had argued about something, wanted to ask, figured I shouldn't do that.

"George says you need to back off with the stuff about Richard," I told him abruptly. "He said it before he left a while ago. Told me to make sure you knew."

A sort of scoffing noise came from him. "So we're all alone, today of all days. You, and me, and Mama, and who else, I wonder. Pathetic. So what's George heard?"

I repeated what I'd been told, waited for a comment, a curse, an exclamation, but he was silent. The roads were dry, no rain having fallen for a week now. I slowed down at the bridge, stopped, even, peering upstream, expecting a revelation I had not seen before.

Nothing. The creek wandered coldly along its way. Berry glanced out his own window, downstream.

I rounded the gentle curve and drove to the edge of the yard. A fence now stood between me and a heap of large round stones where the foundation had been; the house was not there, had not been there for I would say a little while, but Robert Beck was, stacking a few old bricks into neat piles. He straightened as I stopped, and I realized there was another man, a Black guy, with him, heaping pieces of boards into a sooty round spot on the ground. Berry softly said, "That's Sally Rowell's son Sean."

"I remember him from the funeral home. Should we stay?" I murmured. Robert Beck looked at us warily.

"Yes. Here we are, it would look stupid to leave. Anyway, he doesn't own it yet. We have the right to be here if we want to."

"Did you know about this already?"

He sighed, but didn't answer; I knew he had. It made me angry he hadn't said so, before we left Liza's. We got out and approached the fence. "I'm one of the grandchildren," I said lamely.

He nodded. "I know. You were at the signing. Glad to see you, Asberry."

"So it appears we aren't the only people not having turkey dinner right now," Berry told him with a wry laugh.

"Had all I want of turkey and dressing the past two days.

Grandkids playin' with their new stuff, wife's visitin' with 'em. I get the fidgets just sittin' around," he went on. "Called Sean to see if he had plans this afternoon, wanted to make some easy money, help out with his college bills."

Sean shook his head ruefully, chuckled a little: " 'Easy,' you said." Berry asked where he was enrolled, made a remark or two about Hazel and Sally.

I put my hands on one of the new metal fence posts and leaned my chin upon them. It was nothing like sitting on the old boards. "When did you get it down?"

Sean stopped making his stack and gave me a look. "I started as soon as the semester got done. Got a couple of friends to help at first."

"Week ago, I finished," Robert Beck added. "I talked with some of the kinfolks a while back, and it looked like it'd be better for me to go on and get rid of it. And so Miz Liza got the lawyer to write a paper and said I could. Take it down, I mean. It was a few days after youall got together here a while back. You know?"

I nodded, remembering, not wanting to talk.

"Well, somebody I guess tried to camp out in it right after that, maybe even that night, or the next one, because they started a fire in the kitchen that got out."

I gasped.

"You didn't know about that? You didn't tell her?" This, directed at Berry, who shook his head a little. "No, Miz Liza didn't want it told, did she. We hoped to find out who was squattin' here. But the rain put it out—lucky, really. No harm done, nobody was actually living in it. Just maybe used it as shelter a night or two. And it was gonna come down anyway. Edwin Bonner came with Miz Liza and they went through it, they said they figgered it was just vagrants."

In my mind I could see them glancing at each other, making the decision silently to tell nobody.

"But she signed that paper right after that, said for me to go on and start, it would be better that way."

My mind raced back to the image of Richard and Dobber standing by their trucks as we loaded those chairs into my car.

"Miz Kate didn't want anybody hanging on to it after the place was sold," he continued, defensively.

"We know. She always said, 'Let it pass,' " Berry put in.

"Yeah, she did."

It was strange how after all these weeks, it was suddenly bothering me. Maybe because it was Christmas, maybe the cool weather, the silence. Sean turned back to his work.

"I could've got one of my men to get it down." Robert Beck seemed mildly embarrassed. "Don't do much hand work anymore, though, sittin' in front of a computer all the time. Doin' it this way was really inefficient. Could've just brought in a dozer and pushed it over. I just didn't want a dozer out here. Can you understand that?" The embarrassment was bothering him, and me, too, now. "It seemed more fitting to do it myself. It was put up by hand; it ought to be taken down by hand. She was a friend of mine, you know. I enjoyed her company, too—sharp old lady. I'd drive out from town sometimes, talk with her. Get her perspective on old age. I'm headed there pretty fast myself. She'd worked it all out with me several years ago. That boy being taken care of?"

"Porter? I think so," and Berry frowned.

He picked up a couple of bricks and made his square column a little higher. "She wouldn't hear of anybody doing anything about him. I tried, you know, and so did Edwin. And his siblings didn't seem to mind. She kept saying she wanted him properly taken care of, and she figured nobody else would. It always was interesting to me how people thought he was a hindrance to her, and nothing more. None of you ever consider, him being there gave her some purpose? Everybody's got to have some reason for keeping on with their living when there don't seem to be a reason anymore. An old lady her age, managing out here the many years she did, not being put in a home or something? If they'd've took him away, somebody else would've had to do it all for her, wouldn't they."

Berry and I listened as he went on. "It always looked like none of those kinfolks had much intention of doing anything for her. They were just waiting. She would've got fired-up mad at me for saying any of this, so I didn't, not to her. She had her own reasons for keepin' that grandson around, and sometimes I wondered if she even thought she'd done the right thing by him, herself."

"You handled burying that baby last summer, didn't you?" It had been working on me, a chigger bite I'd scratched unconsciously, since the day all those papers were signed: Berry's remark afterwards, this man having all the financial details already figured out; and today I knew, and the epiphany that didn't come at the creek appeared now in these stacks of bricks and lumber.

He put his head to one side, lowered his eyes. "She asked me to do it quiet, so nobody'd bother her. So it would have a proper grave. I helped her out. I didn't think anybody knew," he added accusingly, looking at Berry.

"*I* didn't tell her."

"I figured it out myself, nobody told me. I remember Berry saying he appreciated you helping her, and I do, too. As you said, when nobody much else did."

Sean had made a fair-sized pile of old boards by now and stood back, flinging a spray of gasoline on them and then a match. They made a nice fire. It would have been fitting, as Robert Beck put it, and symbolic, to warm our hands by them, but I could not move from watching them burn. I thought about Hazel's grandson being a man whose job was to dismantle the house. Maybe I'd point that out to Berry some day.

"You came to her funeral, too."

"Like I said, I knew her a long time. Y'all knew this was coming. Hope it don't bother you too much, seeing it gone."

"It does bother me. But like she said, let it pass. You take care," I told him, and I returned to the car, crying like a fool. Berry slid behind the wheel, and I handed the keys over, and he took us back towards his mother's house; slowly.

"I HOPE THEIR hair got singed off. Richard and Dobber. You know it was probably them. One of them, or both."

He laughed just a little. Then, "It's okay. Crying's okay."

"Where'd they bury the baby?"

"You remember. It was in the paper. First Baptist Church in town, in an old section, where they buried all those babies that died in the 1800's when fever was a thing."

"They put a stone on it?"

"You know, that's what I went to the courthouse for, after she died, that day when Jean Ann pitched her fit about that Bible. I thought maybe somebody there could tell me exactly where, dropped by the coroner's office to ask him. That's how I found out about Robert Beck; the coroner just acted surprised it wasn't generally known who'd had it buried. Like, no big secret. But there's no marker for that baby. I found out what plot it was in, went and looked myself. Anyway, what would they put on it?

'Unknown'? No birth or death dates. What would be the point?"

"We never found out any of this stuff from her," I said. "No chance now. Oh, my God—I'm just like poor little Amy...."

He chose a side road to turn onto, killing time so I could get myself together—one of those ancient lanes, with the high banks where tangles of dead honeysuckle vines and rotting fence posts leaned outward over your car, seeming to want to overwhelm you. In a while he said, "So George thinks I need to take it easy on Richard. About what?"

"Thought you'd tell *me*. But probably all that about Alex White. What makes you think Richard knows anything about him?"

He surveyed the width of the road there and did a turnaround, headed back out before answering me. "Richard knows everything."

I scoffed.

"He does. He always did. Took me years to understand that. He figures out everything he can about people, and he saves it up and uses it whenever he can get the most harm out of it. He won't do it till then; he's got too much baggage himself, so it's enough for him just to know it's there, to pull it out when he can use it against you. So if you know something about *him*, he's got something on *you*, too, he's held back, and if you go after him, he'll fire his shot he's saved all that time. When you least expect it."

It came to me that he was speaking personally now, that it meant something different and weighty; and he wouldn't look at me but maneuvered the gravelly road until we neared Liza's house. And I didn't know what to ask; there was something warning me not to ask much of anything right then. He spoke at last:

"All that from years ago, when Alex and he ran around together, it came back to me after Granny Kate died. At your mother's house that day. God, the things you repress. He knows about Alex, something, at least. It's why he decided to go after me when he realized I was getting suspicious."

" 'Go after you'? Is he threatening you?"

"George seems to think so, right? Didn't you tell me he said that?"

"He didn't use those words. Maybe he meant all that big talk about suing you, when we were at the old house that day."

We'd arrived at his mother's, right there at the edge of the old country, but he sat for a matter of some seconds and then handed me my keys. "I have something to return to you, something you must keep," he told me. It was almost a legal statement, what you'd tell a lawyer or, perhaps a student you'd caught cheating: He'd do that, of course, would put it that way, his voice would sound like that. "Let's eat what Mama's set out for us, and then you can go back to your little vanilla house and tell George I'm gonna dial it back." It was a cold, miserable glance he turned on me; it sent a chill up my back that had nothing to do with the weather.

WE ATE TURKEY sandwiches and had a slice, or several, of Liza's brandy-soaked cake. He fumbled around in a bag he brought from a back bedroom, gave me two old letters. Old, and crumbly, with names I didn't recognize. "You may want to store these with your other genealogy crap," he said, and the sarcasm froze me again, and Liza turned her back on him. I said a proper goodbye to her but ignored him as I left, and resisted and didn't even glance at the letters until I was home, in my vanilla kitchen, poring over my genealogy crap.

SO I LEARNED why he and Liza weren't talking. I texted him: *On Christmas Day, on Christmas, you did this to your mother?*
And he answered immediately: *"Mother"?*
The handwriting in the old letters sent to that nephew of Granny Kate's, the other library, was spidery; they were written in that same formal language Berry'd used, the kind of words people had once put down on paper when they had significant things to say and knew the power of a pen.

I have not answered your previous inquiries until I had considered what import my responses would have on any living descendants. I have never considered any of this to be my business, as the people involved were all adults, and the arrangement suited them. Since you asked for clarification, however, I will now give it. It seems that Calvin wanted a boy or two, and as Eliza seemed unable to have any more children, he and the woman I mentioned in my previous missive to you agreed to produce several which Eliza would accept into the home and rear as her own. It appears that at some point in time one of the three parties to this agreement came to disapprove of it. From what I have been informed, after the boy arrived, the informal contract was discontinued by agreement of all three people, or perhaps by only one, it's not my place to judge or say. As the individual brought into the home was considered a full member of that household, my feeling is the matter should be left to the consciences of the people who undertook that arrangement.

The signature was strong, each letter obviously formed with care, as if it were a last will and testament. Which it was, in a way, just not by or for the person who wrote it.

And I understood everything, all of it, Cal and the barn, and Richard at the old house, standing in a line to have a last family picture made, and Berry wanting those old photographs. I waited until the next morning, the onset of that dreary week after Christmas, when the point of those last days was lost, people were taking down decorations and throwing out wrapping paper and regretting gifts ill-suited and wrongly given.

Maybe all that was before you were born, and wasn't about you anyway. I texted it without any other greeting or explanation; I knew he'd figure it out. And he did:

DNA always trumps.

19

IN YEARS LONG after that time, I wondered if I'd done right to leave Berry alone for that month, never text or call or even ask Liza on the few occasions when I saw her, not except for the first time we met after that day. She said he was just fine, thank you for asking, and smiled her usual wispy smile at me. I wondered, but maybe she didn't know I knew; or maybe she didn't care.

But I also didn't speak to him, for what would you say to someone whose orbit shifted, someone whose past and so his life was not what he'd always believed it to be?

There were other times when I remembered he may have known for many days before he told me. Maybe, like Liza, he didn't care anymore.

JANUARY WAS WET. Rain fell about every other day, which was good for the lake, George mentioned early one morning, leaving, pulling the hood of his jacket up to walk out the back door. He turned back. "I'll want to use your computer tonight, if you aren't busy with it yourself." It was a polite request, as you'd make of a colleague when your own machine was down for some reason. He'd never bought one of his own for home use.

I shrugged. "There's nothing I need to do with it right now." I hadn't told him about Cal's arrangement with the unnamed woman who gave Berry to Liza. Let Berry tell him that himself, if he wanted to, as he had the tale of Porter and the chicken coop. "I scanned in all that stuff for Berry and emailed him, and nobody's brought anything else for me to do."

"Guess they're all just waitin' for their big money to arrive," he said gravely, and winked as he left.

I DROVE TO Mother and Dad's. The streaming highway cautioned me *ssshhhhisss* as I went along; but I'd made up my mind to ask her anyway. The quilt she and Dad were working on was neutral ground I'd use for the pattern of my opening questions. For I knew not to fling all the pieces out at once, unformed, helter-skelter, in haste; she'd just snatch everything away and fold it up.

It was Grandma's Flower Garden this time, appropriate, I thought. I took a mug of hot coffee to the side table next to my chair and picked up a needle, threaded it with a long string. They'd squabbled again, I could tell from the electric silence when I walked in; but as we worked, tension eased, and I put in a piece of my pattern and asked about news, any news they might have that would be interesting. They offered some bits about Lilly and her eyes; and then a colorful story about Jean Ann and Bob's latest quarrel, and Mother's mouth sternly held a smile back and only let it turn up the edges of her lips a little; and as the rain drizzled on, we companionably sewed.

I refilled their cups and brought them a cookie, sat down, took a chance with a larger piece: "So, why didn't I ever hear about Berry's real mother and Cal?" I said it quietly, peaceably. She glanced at me over her glasses, and Dad leaned back in his chair; but the quilt gently swayed and didn't protest.

"So you found out. Well, it was long ago. None of you're

babies anymore, and nobody's thought about it these days."

"Richard does, did," I said softly, pushing my needle carefully through a petal. "He's thought about it."

She scoffed. "Richard. It's a sad world when somebody like him can sit in judgment on anybody else."

"And worse for something that's true," I offered. She looked at me again, and that time I saw another thing in her eyes; and the cooling creek going over gravel and sand returned to me, unexpectedly, blindsiding me; I sucked in a breath. "I wonder if it'll have any effect on Granny Kate's estate."

The quilt trembled. Mother's eyes were steady on me; she tapped her needle point-down into the fabric without looking at the spot. "Liza inherited her part. It'll be for her to see it gets split between him and Jean Ann. She'll take care of that."

The silence after that was fraught. I thought hard about my next question before saying it: "Did they ever actually adopt him, legally?"

"No need for it. He's family, regardless. Liza never thought of him any other way. He's always been a better son to her than many others are to their mamas."

"But in this day and age," I went on as carefully as I could, "DNA tests and all that, somebody might find out. I guess Jean Ann knows, surely? And she did that test on herself, last summer. Somebody like Richard might push it that he's not really kin. Not family. You heard what he said when we were at the old house that last time."

"But he can't do a thing to him about it."

"Why'd you leave it to Liza all these years to take care of Granny Kate? She was your mother as much as hers." There, I'd blurted out the other thing that had worried at me.

Dad was fidgeting with his needle, glancing back and forth between us; she turned briefly to him: "You're gonna have to undo all of that if you're not careful!" Then, to me: "Why're you bringing that up, right after you asked about the other?"

A really pointed query; and I went with it: "Was it because you thought she'd let Cal run over her?" And again it was what I'd figured out; I just needed for her to say it.

She leaned back a little, gave Dad's work another scornful glance. "She was the baby. She'd always let people run over her. So, Jean Ann wasn't enough for him?" She sneered. "And Liza just let him use somebody else as one of his brood cows?"

Well.

"I won't deny it, I was mad at her about it, for years I was. We weren't raised that way."

"To go out and have babies by whoever."

"No, not that! To be weak. Not to put your foot down. Not to take up for yourself. And I did my part with Mama—you know I did." It was the first time she'd turned defensive. But it was true: All those times she'd helped with garden things, took nights at the hospital, cleaned Granny Kate's own body. "She was proud of us; she told us. Proud of us two girls. But Liza wasn't as strong as she should be. It did cause some problems between us."

"So you don't think she should've taken Berry to raise? Since he wasn't family, really?"

She scowled at me. "I didn't say that atall! I said she'd let Cal just have his way. And when you figure out what 'family' is, you can tell me." It was a challenge. The look on her face said all that was going on in her mind, and that she knew what was in mind, too, as much as she used to know, when I was a teenager. "Liza said he's family. I say he's family. I never questioned that. Whether he came out of her or not. Tell me this," she went on, giving Dad a mocking glance as he hastily left his pattern, this unambiguous conversation too much for his brand of soft-focus storytelling, "tell me this: You consider Richard family? Or James? Marcus?"

I didn't answer.

"Jean Ann? Porter? You think *he's* family?" Her eyes studied my expression with that assessing look she got, and I made another tentative stitch or two to buy time.

"I guess they are. Blood's blood," I muttered.

"That's what makes it family?" She smirked. "Then I ask you again, is Berry Liza's family or not?" I added a couple more stitches, and she shook her head. "Take 'em out right now, before you make a bigger mess," and she was right, and I set to undoing the last ones.

"Are there any other big secrets I don't know about?" I laughed, shakily, conceding she'd won. "Like maybe you and Dad never really got married, or something? So all three of us are bastards, too?" I added, as he returned with more cookies.

He straightened his shoulders. "None of that. We got the license to prove it."

I'D GONE HOME right after dark, wondered idly why George didn't show up already, as he'd said he had the computer work to do; and the clock had crept on as the rain turned into misty drizzle and even the street lights seemed to dim as in a movie scene you knew was about to go bad.

At eight-thirty my phone rang. It was George. "You busy?"

He seemed not to notice that I didn't answer, but continued talking, his words somehow almost slurred in his hurry to get them out: "You gotta drive to the improved campground."

"George, you're not drinking, are you? Because if you are, you need to get sober before you—"

"If your mother or Daniel watches the late news, as soon as they see it, they're gonna call you, so you may's well know what to tell them."

"See what?"

"I want you to come out here. Somebody in the family should be here and the one that *is* here already ought not to be," and the disgust was thick in his hurried words, impatience making him rude, which told me this was big, as he was never rude: not George. "Just come on."

"The improved—"

"Yeah," he interrupted, "and don't go tell anybody else yet, all right? I don't have time to discuss it." And then he hung up. I found my keys and a jacket and pulled my own hood over my hair as he had just that morning.

I COULD SEE the glare of bright lights even before I finally chose the right road to the campground. I'd turned down the wrong way once; nothing looked the same in the utter darkness of the refuge, even my headlights fading in the mist. The floodlights' glare finally brought me in like a moth, so bright I didn't stop at the makeshift roadblock until a hand crashed palm down on the hood of my car and an angry face peered into my window.

"Maggie Williams!"

It was funny how you could be ninety years old and they'd still call you by your maiden name.

"What the hell you think you're doin'? Slow your butt down before you kill somebody."

"I'm sorry, Edwin." I grinned weakly at him. "I didn't see

you."

"What're you doin' here?"

"George called me to come."

"He wanted you here?" He hesitated, frowned, glanced backward. "We ain't lettin' folks come in right now."

"You take it up with him. I don't even know what's going on. He called and told me to drive out, that's all I know. For some reason. I won't leave until *he* does, all right? I'll stay until he goes home himself."

George materialized out of the gloom, his hair gleaming with fog condensation as he walked into the artificial daylight streaming from three big halogen lamps hung from power poles nearby, reinforced by the headlights of several utility trucks with engines running. The diesel fumes were enough to kill you. "Edwin, show her where you want her to park, and I'll keep her keys. She won't get away till you folks get it towed off and cleaned up."

"All right, but I'm not lettin' anybody else in here. Not till the fam'ly's been notified."

"Well, she's family. Not much other left *to* notify." George held his hand palm-up toward me. I dropped the keys onto his fingers.

"What's going on?"

He looked at me with a sort of stony, inscrutable expression, took my elbow, pulled me toward the edge of the lake.

"I'm wearing sneakers—!"

"They'll wash, or if they don't, throw 'em away and buy some new ones. Come on. Dim the damn lights!" he shouted, gesturing in the direction of the trucks. Erratically, one by one, the three drivers did that.

We mucked through the decayed edge where mud flats defined the margins of the lowered water level, where the glaring white lights were aimed. The truck engines rumbled ominously behind us. The lake at night seemed a strangely evil place, where you could hear small wavelets slapping the shoreline but couldn't see them, where the slight breeze rustled long-dead brush and brought thoughts to you of alligators and snakes. I couldn't imagine anybody enjoying shore fishing here at night unless they brought a radio to drown out the odd, hissing, somehow malevolent sounds; and fishing alone in a boat out in the middle would be even worse, surrounded by darkness and danger and death, floating around unconnected to any living soul. It felt like those nights sitting at the edge of the blackness at Mother's porch long ago, hearing Dad tell stories designed to scare us with fear of things we couldn't articulate.

George grabbed my elbow and pointed wordlessly. To my right a big engine roared, the way Berry's car had at the top of Conjure Hill the day after the funeral, desiring somehow to fling itself into an abyss: It was a wrecker, pulling something from the murky water, but in danger of getting mired in deep, newly-exposed mud. For some minutes there was progress; then the grinding, whining machinery stopped and we heard the loud idle of the truck engine. Men gathered at the edge of the water, making adjustments to ropes and chains trailing across the mud near the boat ramp, which now terminated far from the water because of the draw-down. The grinding commenced again, a clanking roar followed by a gritty, gravelly *shissssing* and the sound of water gushing onto— Onto what? George grasped my elbow again and jerked me closer to the gushing noise, and there arose Willis White's old once-tan Buick, a monstrous ghastly hulk pouring fluid out as it was yanked from the grave where it had lain more than thirty-five years.

CONTRARY TO WHAT he'd told Edwin he'd do, George gave me back my keys long before the grisly job was completed, but not before I watched them approach the car, the coroner with the group of men led by Edwin, and gingerly open the doors. I had jerked away from George then—"Oh, my God, why'd you make me come here and watch this?"—and retreated at a slippery run to my car, where I flung myself inside and fumbled for the keys, cursing when I remembered handing them over to him. There was careful, painstaking activity—securing the doors of the Buick after some kind of cursory scrutiny of its contents before it could be towed away—and a conversation with the managing editor of the local paper, which I listened to through my opened door.

George waited until the Buick sat on the road, still dripping brown liquid and ooze, then came to my car, holding out the keys. "Go home. I'll make it right with Edwin. I guess I shouldn't've had you here. Do me a favor. Open a can of soup and have it on the stove for me. I'll be home in a couple of hours, I imagine."

"What made you think I'd want to see this?" I hadn't intended to yell so loudly. He frowned, shut his eyes as if in pain.

"I told you: Somebody besides *him* should be here—" he

waved again toward the power-company trucks, and I realized Richard was swaggering toward the wrecker and its rusty hulk of cargo, strutting with the lights framing him into just a silhouette of black; but I knew that form. He'd worked for the power company for years; he'd have been on call, maybe.

"How'd you know it was Alex?"

"One of them durned fishermen hooked onto the car this mornin', tried to wade out to get his line loose, got in over his head, boots filled up, nearly drowned hisself...but he did at least come and tell us he thought there was a car over beside the boat launch, in the deep old creek run—over there, where they never had no business puttin' a boat launch anyway... Well, we got a diver to pull the plate off, and ran a check—wasn't any doubt after that. Just tried to keep it quiet as long's we could." He gave me a strange, speculative glance. "Somebody should tell Berry."

THE SOUP BUBBLED softly now and then on the front burner. I sat and waited, but ten o'clock came, and I turned on the television and, sure enough, there was a quick blurb about it. Still George did not come home, so at last I turned the power off under the pan and went to bed. When he got in he undressed and threw himself down. "Worn out. Not now; talk tomorrow."

"How do you conjure up the past?" I'd thought about that last night, lying next to George, unable to sleep until dawn, because sleep was not pleasant: My dreams lately were filled with images of small, dismembered corpses, little bodies washing up out of creeks and ponds. Watching Alex's Buick hauled out of the lake was like sitting behind the wheel when Berry and Edwin Bonner opened that little box in Edwin's patrol car. Or like standing on a condemned bridge on a cold November day and pondering where the box had come from in the first place. Once, I turned over carefully to gaze out the window on my side of the bed, felt George move around restlessly for a moment himself. Had he been asleep or not? I didn't turn and ask him, and he didn't say anything.

It felt as if I'd been watching dead bodies pop up for years now.

He'd already left when I finally woke up, after drifting to sleep in the thin cold air of early daybreak. I stayed home all morning and through lunch, waiting, expecting him to call and give me some more information. But it was Mother who phoned, and her severe tone enforced a non-negotiable demand: "Did you know they pulled Alexander White's corpse out of the lake last night?" Unwilling just yet to explain that I'd seen the job done, knowing she'd berate me for not calling earlier, I just told her yes, I did. "I figured that," she went on. "Figured George'd told you. So I guess you know what else they found?"

"I don't know. A girlfriend, maybe."

"Your cousin's body was dragged out of the water last night; that is not a joke. And they found a jar with some money."

"Well, he did make off with all Willis' change, you recall."

"It wasn't just a handful of pennies in the jar." I didn't ask who was giving her all this information. But George hadn't been so forthcoming with me, so I was fine with her going on.

"I guess he spent it before he went fishing."

She stopped; I could hear her breathing. "I fail to see why you're makin' jokes about this. It ain't funny. Edwin asked Richard to come in voluntarily this morning, just to answer a few things, he said. That was because of what Berry's been saying for these weeks now."

It was my turn to be quiet; this was indeed news of a sort that made my stomach tighten. The cold old house, and a stack of canned tomatoes, and some cane-bottom chairs returned to memory, pictures in my mind like a slide show. At last I said, "Well, and so…?"

It turned out that she and Liza had gathered all this intelligence through their assorted nieces and nephews as the morning passed, because since Granny Kate was gone, it seemed they'd both inherited the role of the Parvati. Everyone would go to *them* from now on with their offerings of flowers and news.

Richard didn't stay in town for long, she said, as Edwin only asked if he could remember when he'd last seen Alex, and Richard laughed and said why, just the other day he'd *thought* he saw him at the lake, fishing. Edwin didn't like that sort of smartass remark, told him he could get his ass out of there if he didn't have anything else to say, and about then James Preacher showed up with Richard's sister Linda along, "wringing her hands and acting the fool," Mother added with disgust.

"James? Why? Oh, I know: He saw a chance to read scriptures and pray everybody into a stupor to give Richard a head start."

It wrung a grudging laugh from her. Then, "He said he was Richard's spiritual adviser."

"Richard's got no spirit," I told her. "He has no soul."

"Everybody's got a soul, bad or good or what-have-you."

I had to tell her, then, and it was going to fly out of me, anyway, sometime, because I was sleep-deprived and unable to be careful of words: "He was there, too, did you know that? Running one of those big utility trucks he drives. It went out on their message board they needed some workers, overtime, emergency, and he showed up. He may not've known what he'd be doing at first. But he was there. I saw 'im myself."

"What were you doin' there last night?" The words came out slowly as if each had to be dragged out of a deep pool one at a time.

"George told me to come. He said family besides Richard should be there. That was a good point. Richard sat there in his truck, watched while they pulled out that car, pranced over in his cowboy boots and that hat. Cool as ice. Grinning."

She said nothing for a good count of fifteen; I thought the phone might've lost connection. Her voice was different, distant, and tired, when she spoke again: "Richard told Edwin it all just showed that Alex stole his pore old pa's money, like everybody'd always known, spent it on foolishness and whiskey, and drove off into the lake after he got drunk. It was a shame it happened, that's what he told Edwin, but at least everybody knew now what become of him, and it gave us some closure." She hesitated. "I believe that was about when Edwin got tired of looking at him and told him to get out."

YOU NEVER WANTED to think people, your own relatives or neighbors, could walk around and look you straight in the eye and swear they didn't do something you knew they'd done. You always wanted to believe they'd break one day, their consciences would eventually get to them. But some people, maybe even most people, could live out their whole lives and never break. They could go on and on and finally rationalize it, finally believe that, just by living productive lives and having grandkids, they'd paid whatever debt they might owe. I stayed in the house that day, thinking about it all, remembering what Berry'd said back in ancient times when we were children: Those people could go to church and mingle with others who didn't carry terrible secrets inside them; they could do it conscience-free, and you'd never know, and they'd never tell.

Alex's remains were finally buried next to those of his pa, under that previously-laid grave marker Willis'd had placed before *he* died; and Liza saw to it a stonecutter was hired to chisel his assumed death date into it: the day after he left home. That was the best guess; it may have been as right as "within this century"— what the coroner said about the baby's remains. It was, anyway, what I wrote at last in my genealogy crap.

RICHARD GOT BERRY'S address and drove to Jackson one day, after things kind of died down again. I only found out because Berry himself called and told me about it, thought it was a funny story, and then thought it wasn't, and wanted somebody else to know it had happened, *in case*. At first, he said, Richard was pious—Didn't Berry, respect nothing about the past, and even if somebody had done something they regretted, didn't them living a clean life for a long time count for nothing? And if *they* had asked the Good Lord for forgiveness, what was it to *him?*, something that happened long ago by a kid who didn't know better?

Berry said he challenged him: "You apologizing for what you did to me and Porter? Who you talking about, Richard? You confessing about something else?"

Richard got that suave, lopsided smile on his face. "That was just kid stuff; you not still mad about that, are you? I got nothing to confess. Just theoretically, referrin' to poor old Alex. Why drag up all them bad things from the past, with him dead and gone. Who'd *you* think? You ain't still accusin' *me*, are you?" He pretended to get righteously indignant, Berry said, and leaned over a little closer and spoke a little more softly: If people was able to live with theirselves, why'd he take it on hisself to get so righteous, why'd he think it was his place to say they shouldn't. Didn't *he* have things *he'd* not want out for the public to know? And so on, and ended up threatening, Berry said, some obscure brand of vengeance on him: "What goes around comes around, you know."

Berry said he stood up and laughed as cool as he could and told Richard he'd enjoyed the visit but he had work to do; and with another one of those knife-in-your-back smiles, Richard left. And Berry said he locked his door and put the chain on.

"Balance of power's shifted now," he told me. "He threw what he had, back before Christmas, he thought it was the worst he had, and now it's used up. So he's actually dangerous now. He's got nothing else on me."

I told him to buy a gun.

"Didn't you hear what Mama said that day? She wasn't talking about herself. Can you imagine her with a gun?"

He showed up about half-drunk one day after that. The house was cool and empty, and he held his head in his hands and raked fingers back and forth through his hair and yelled about Richard for a while. Then, looking around the kitchen, the living room beyond with curtains drawn and lights off, "My God, Maggie, do something about this godawful house of yours. It don't even look like anybody lives here or ever has."

"I didn't ask you to come over and critique my house!" It made me uneasy more so than angry. I set strong coffee to brewing.

"You're just a couple of acquaintances, just a house paid for together, is all. Nobody in this whole damned world responsible for anybody else. "

"Why don't you go straight to hell?"

His shoulders lurched, and I yanked him up by a fistful of shirt and dragged him through the back door where he could throw up in peace and I wouldn't have to clean it or somehow make him do it. He sagged against the wall in the chill air; it was still cool and still wet, and though it was nearly spring, I had not cleaned out the remains of my own flower bed, either, and he crushed the dead stalks.

"I'm sorry, what you found out," I said, leaning over him, my hand on his shoulder. "That's what this's all about, isn't it?"

"My mother, my mother conveniently forgets all my life to let me know what I guess everybody else did all along and laughed about, I spent years getting education to make the precious little world a good place, and then there's Richard..."

"Stop feeling sorry for yourself. You did good. You did the right thing, if he didn't. You're better than him. And anyway, I didn't know, and I bet not everybody did."

"Just forget about it all. Who cares." He rose unsteadily and wobbled inside to sip at the mug I placed in front of him.

"And we still have to go through the final closing on that will," he said in a moment. "We still have to do that. Watch how fast everybody gets nice to each other again. All that money at stake.

Nobody going to fight, all that money to lose. No, man: we *love* each other."

He gave me a look like a dog that's been beaten for no reason and doesn't understand, and staggered up and into the back part of the house, wandered into my bedroom and said, "Oh, God, no, not here," and stumbled through the door of the guest room where Amy slept when she visited. He carefully took off his shoes and motioned to me to join him, stripping off pants and his shirt, putting them fastidiously on the dresser, and lay down. I let him drift to sleep and huddled against his body, wondering what we would say to George if he came home unexpectedly, when, now, there was truly nothing to confess.

AFTER A WHILE I got up and sat alone at the table, drinking from my cup and waiting. At last I heard the noises of awakening, those I knew from years of hearing George: the slight silken crinkling of the mattress as he stood up, the shifting from one foot to another as pants were put on, a faint rasp of zipper, the slow footsteps muffled on carpet.

He came and sat at the table with me and rested his forehead against one hand; without questioning, took the travel cup I gave him, because I knew he just couldn't wait to leave. Sometimes you coveted a thing for so long, for too long, so that when it came to your hand easily, without a struggle, you found it wasn't the same thing anymore that you'd had dreams of possessing. It was still precious, in a way, but not the way you'd frozen it in time to be.

20

THE LAKE HAD to be refilled, like any other empty vessel: nature hates that vacuum, they say. George left the house as always, giving me sometimes a little peck on the cheek in the early morning hours after he silently dressed, and frequently crawling into bed after eleven and making his presence known to me only by the coldness his body exuded from having been outside. As he warmed up beneath the blanket and the quilt Mother had made me, the silent chill was replaced with a kind of exhausted, pleasant hum, and his breathing became steady and hot, and I drifted back asleep myself.

RICHARD ALWAYS WATCHED for opportunities to take vengeance for the grudges he saved up, his eyes sparkling, his mouth turning up into a grin when after a long wait he saw a chance. That had never been Dobber's style: he sighted at some fleshy spot and sent both barrels full of buckshot at that place, and the bleeding would take down his prey, even if it wasn't a clean shot or hit a vital place. Even George knew Dobber'd shoot his wad and go off sulking and that was it.

But Richard liked stalking, enjoyed having people afraid of him, and he'd take a carefully-aimed shot now and then just for fun, aiming to injure and slow you down, but not disable you just yet. Until he decided to finish you off, if he could.

Edwin kept up with him these days, driving slowly past his power truck while he perched up in the bucket working on the lines, or turning up to sit near him at the Wagonwheel Cafe where he sometimes had lunch. Richard maintained a kind of sarcastic patience as Edwin ate a sandwich at a table behind him. It was harassment, he grumbled to family, the sheriff always being where he was, like he'd done somethin' wrong; and yet he didn't threaten Berry to his face again but made sure he told the right cousins who'd get it back to Liza, who'd tell Berry, that in Edwin *he* had a bodyguard these days to protect him from a relative who'd gone about half nuts over the years and had accused him of murder. It was an exquisite sort of ironic vengeance, another carefully-targeted pot shot that left a wound not fatal but chronic, as neither Berry nor Edwin could say much about it, a denial only raising more questions in the minds of Richard's cronies. So far as I knew, it was a game he and Edwin played for many years after Granny Kate died.

GEORGE TRAMPED THROUGH the refuge at day and sometimes at night, coming home with hands that grew more reddened daily from exposure. I awoke from dreamless sleep sometimes to find him huddled against my back for warmth, those cold hands of his shoved under my ribs like slabs of frozen meat, and I lay still, forcing a shallow, regular breathing upon myself in case he should discover me awake. —As if trying to disguise my awareness from a cat burglar who'd broken in and was creeping about to find stuff to steal from me. After his own quiet snoring began, I stared out the window as I used to during those times when it was my turn to sit with Granny Kate at the hospital. You cannot be dishonest with yourself when you are awake in the dead of night in a room with a person connected to you and yet at that moment oblivious to your presence, and the things you see about yourself you can't really tell anybody, ever. Straining to make out the shapes of the bare tree limbs, the scratchy junipers near the window sill, the mailbox at the edge of the street, I wondered whether Berry ever had nights like these, wondered whether he was alone.

The house was empty most of the time now and felt it when I came in from a day spent at the library; there was a scent of unused air, a coolness from scarcity of human habitation. It didn't really feel like my house those days, but someone else's into which I was intruding.

I bought yellow paint.

It wasn't so hard, once I got started. The paint flowed from the roller in wide, slurpy swatches. I'd forgotten you were supposed to prep the molding and such before you started. I stopped and rummaged around in the junk drawer for masking tape. None there. Perhaps George had some in the garage.

Leaving the roller in a plastic bag, I crept into the cold, humid building, feeling even more of an intruder, a grave robber entering a tomb. I seldom messed around with George's tools and hunting equipment, sometimes giving it at most a glance before getting into my car. He kept his stuff neat, the screwdrivers arranged largest to smallest, tape measures and assorted levels all stacked on one shelf, nails sorted by size in old butter containers. Gently I pushed things aside to search for the masking tape, making sure I replaced everything where it had been before moving on.

Shoved behind a Sears toolbox was a photo of him when he was a kid, delivering his newspapers. He'd once been *our* paper boy, I remembered with a shock.

And on a high shelf, an ancient hammer with his initials scratched into the handle. I'd never seen it before.

The masking tape lay beside an assortment of sockets and a couple of wrenches. I picked it up and stood for a moment with the photograph in my other hand. Strange, what things a person kept as symbols of himself in simpler times. I couldn't think what mine might be. I'd even had Berry haul off those old articles.

A chill up my back reminded me it was cold. I laid the picture down, thought better of it and tried to put it back where it had been. I'd never seen it before, and I wouldn't embarrass him with my knowledge of his having it.

The kitchen shone brightly by afternoon. I decided to run to the store and buy fabric for new curtains. I would pick sunflowers—a large sunflower print would be cheerful, no matter what the season.

The curtains were hanging crisply when George came in that night. I had sat up later than I usually did, watching TV in the living room, planning what I would do there. His footsteps halted after he shut the door behind him. I could imagine him slowly taking in the golden walls, the sunflower curtains, then hearing the television—another change—and the footsteps picked back up and he appeared in the doorway. I pretended to be interested in the TV.

"You've been busy today."

"Mmm," I agreed.

"Looks good." He always took off muddy boots before coming into the house and padded now in his bulky thick socks to the sofa, tentatively, awkwardly patted my shoulder. "You going to do something in here?"

"Maybe."

"Need any help?"

"I can manage. Don't have anything else to do."

You can sense when someone's watching you. Even if he's not facing you. But at last he shuffled on into the bathroom, and in a few minutes I heard the shower. That noise continued for a while; the various bumps and squeaks I knew by heart—he would be soaping his hair, turning around with his back to the water to rinse, setting the bottle on the shelf. Then, the hair dryer, and cabinets opening and shutting, and the bathroom door swung wide and banged against the wall opposite, and I flinched: I'd asked him so many times through the years to stop doing that. He came to the living room entrance again, stood just out of my line of vision. The towel flopped around, and I could imagine him swinging it idly back and forth before taking it to the washing machine, as he always did after bathing.

"What's Berry up to? I guess he doesn't feel welcome here these days; even over at the office we hear about Richard's shit all along."

I took a slow breath. "I imagine he's busy. And he probably does try to stay away now. Maybe the two of you oughta go fishing sometime. You should ask. You liked to fish together."

"He didn't come over to fish. You know that. Or, at least, not that sort of fishing."

It was like clues in a board game whose rules only allowed you to give one at a time. "I don't know what you mean. 'That sort of fishing.' "

I waited for him to say something else about that, or to come and sit by me the way he used to long ago. But there was a silence then, not the comfortable sort. Something was different in this one. I turned to look at him, standing there in flannel pajama pants and no shirt.

"There's an opening at that refuge out West," he said. "That one they sent me to for that fire-fighting workshop last year. I've applied for it, that was why I needed the computer."

"I forgot about that; it was when they found Alex, wasn't it. Do you still—"

"Oh, no," he interrupted, "I did it from the office the next day. And they've offered me the job if I want it." Another silence. "And I do. I'll go on over there and rent some sort of little place, if you don't mind trying to sell this house, and then if or when it does sell, you could—" He stopped and shrugged again. I could do what—go out West and join him, stay here? What did he suspect I'd decide to do?

"Your choice," he said.

"My choice? What do *you* want me to do?"

His face registered a little surprise; not much. "Either's fine."

"Really, 'either's fine'? You don't care?"

The sides of his mouth turned up slightly; he just looked tired, not angry, not resentful. "Not like I oughta. And not you either. And we're too young for this. It's not healthy for people to just be livin' together, passing the time while they wait to…to die, I guess. It's not how people should live. If it sells, you can decide." He hesitated. "Your mother and dad're leaving their house to you. I guess you know that."

The room went blurry for a moment. "They told *you* and not me?"

"Your mother did. When you were up at the old house the day after that funeral, you know, when I got Drew to bring me out there to visit."

"I didn't know who brought you. You were just there when—" And then *I* hesitated.

"When you and Berry got back." There were too many pauses, too many unsaid things, and whatever was in his mind he kept there. "Your mother said you might need it some day. For me not to worry about you not having anything, if."

"I'll never live there again."

"I got that, I wouldn't either. But you tell *her*. Anyway, sell or stay, whichever, one day. You decide."

"Okay," I said. "I'll think about it." We looked at each other for a moment before he turned and went into the bedroom without saying another word. I sat up very very late and decided I'd wait a while before painting the living room any time soon. Some old houses you just couldn't do much with, no matter what, when they'd deteriorated for so long.

BERRY EMAILED ME; I could imagine him deciding what he said was too significant just to text.

I've been thinking. Before I came back, Granny clearly told Mama she wanted you to get the old family Bible. I think it was a spur-of-the-moment thing that day last summer, when she gave it to me. She wanted me to think about something, she wanted me to get back some sense of—I don't know. Something. 'The essence of what I am.' Isn't that what I wrote in that first piece I did about everybody, that goofy thing after her birthday party that time? So I think maybe you ought to be the one to have the Bible. I'll Fed-Ex it to you one day before long. Maybe it shouldn't have come to me. Jean Ann's got a point. Who'll find it in my stuff when they clean out my house one day?

Who'd find it in mine? I picked up my phone and sent the text right then. And I told him: **You should come over and go fishing with George or something. Do it soon. He's taking a transfer to a refuge out West.**

In half a minute he answered: **Really.**

He plans to get some little hole in the wall to live in until I can get this house sold.

And then what?

I composed and backspaced and composed again before

sending it: *I don't know.*

You should go with him.

I thought a while before sending the last message: *I know.*

HE SENT THE Bible to me, an accompanying note tucked inside in his cramped, self-conscious script that looked almost like the handwriting in the letter about Cal: "I truly believe this is yours. Old Bibles are for people who can forgive."

Now, *that* made no sense to me. *"You've forgiven a lot more than I would've,"* I wanted to tell him. *"If that's your criterion, then you should be the one to keep it."*

I fanned the pages back and forth a couple of times and, like Granny Kate, put it up on a shelf.

HE WROTE A wistful elegy about links to other generations disappearing and the funeral of his old grandmother, almost redeeming himself in everybody's eyes. I left two voice mails asking how he connected old Bibles with forgiveness. He didn't answer either message, but I knew what he'd say about that, anyway: that keeping relics of that sort for generations embodied tenacity and continuity, and those things were the products of forgiveness.

George packed his clothes, his biology books, personal documents, basic kitchen stuff, but not the picture in the garage; I went and looked, later, and it was still there. But he'd taken his Sears toolbox, and the photo lay alone on the bare shelf, neatly square to the edges, and maybe he'd arranged it that way, a final monument in the cemetery. We spoke words to each other while we put the things into his truck and the little U-Haul attached, words that could've been random syllables in another language for all they meant. I reminded him to let me and his mother know when he got there, and he said he would, and he leaned over and gently pecked me on the mouth, one-arm hugged me and was gone.

I told Mother he'd taken a better job, might change his mind but was checking into it for a while. There were too many words in all that, and she watched me, trying to pick out the lie as she always used to be able to. "When are you going?" she asked.

"Lots of stuff to do, decide whether to sell the house or rent it out, all that."

The stare bored into me. At last she said, "If you get to wantin' company, you know you are always welcome. We'll just make up the bed, fresh."

This failure of mine was too much to bear along with the other one. I left the house during the day to sit in the library, reading, and stayed up late long nights watching old movies, seeing the actors and hearing the words of dialogue and thought occasionally of November, standing on Conjure Hill, looking downward to the old house.

21

"I DO NOT believe all these people have any reason to be here. They did not come because it was a party for me."

It was almost like long ago, Porter and I leaning against a wall now instead of sitting on a fence; and he was right: The relatives doing their slow dance around in Larry's den and kitchen weren't there for his sake. It was the official justification for the gathering. But after enough of them had arrived, and their spirits lifted at being together for something other than a funeral, Linda let it slip, with a sparkly-eyed giggle: "This is like a pre-game party!" Then another giggle and, "Oops, shouldn't have said that, should I?"

For the grandchildren and Liza had been informed that their presence was required tomorrow, at last, in the conference room of an office with high ceilings and tall windows. But Alicia'd already paid the caterer for food; and the lawyers had decided not to negotiate with a multitude of heirs, but to set a date themselves; and fate had thus arranged that this celebration ostensibly for Porter would be the warmup for the distribution of money the next day.

Larry let everybody chatter and laugh for a while; things seemed calm, normal, even, which had to be a relief for all of us, except perhaps the few who enjoyed uproar. And that included Richard and Dobber, and I found it hard to believe Larry'd invited them; maybe they'd heard about it and just crashed in. Richard had, after all, said, "I'll go where there's food."

I was stuck there until Mother and Liza decided they'd had enough of it: They'd importuned me to bring them, as Berry had declined his own invite.

Porter's doctors had tried this and that drug, modern stuff as opposed to what Pauline had been dosed with, and something or other had calmed the obsessiveness and made him pleasant in a social way, though it removed the depth in his eyes as if he carried along now a constant weariness in his soul. But whatever he was taking turned him into a more typical good old boy, so Larry bought him another little trailer, one with electric heat and stove this time. Now he was afraid to cook, though; but since he had the new, quieter personality, Larry's family had him eat meals with them whenever it seemed he hadn't been getting proper food by himself. Larry was in a born-again, fresh-from-the-revival mood after the vacation from being his brother's keeper, and decided to throw the party for him and invite cousins who lived nearby. It was the work of malicious fate that they'd all be seeing each other again the next day.

Porter held the wall up beside me and mournfully gazed at the throng at the trough. Larry glanced our way, nodded his head at Alicia, and on cue she whirled around and laid a cake on the kitchen island, a sheet cake decorated with the words "Welcome Home!" Then Larry beckoned to Porter. "They want you there," I told him. "You should probably go on so it'll be over with fast."

"I could make it be faster," he said, looking straight at me.

Larry praised the cake: "It's a welcome-home cake, and a birthday cake, too, his birthday was earlier this year. It's strawberry inside; everybody loves strawberry, I hope." It went on like that a little bit too long, and finally Porter made it be faster by scooping up a dollop of the frosting:

"Like he said, it's not my birthday, though," and he licked his forefinger clean and went in for another taste.

The smiles froze. Richard snickered softly.

"Let's cut it so everybody can enjoy!" Alicia grabbed a serving utensil and gently elbowed Porter to one side.

"Let me just say, I thank you, I thank you all for the welcome-back sentiments, and you can come and visit me whenever you want. It's a little different from back in November, ain't it. Now we're all gonna be good cousins!"

Nobody moved, but stared at him. Alicia kept cutting slices, cutting them frenziedly, laying them on little paper plates, pushing the paper plates forward. "Come on, y'all, don't be shy," she urged.

"So you're all welcome to visit, but let me know before you come, so I can get back in, if I should happen to be outside."

Alicia glanced around desperately, shoved a plate and plastic fork into his hand. "You first!" she told him.

He balanced that piece and picked up another one: "Please put a fork on it, too," he asked, and she did; and he began to amble back towards me, and there was unspoken relief in the room when they realized he wasn't going to eat both pieces himself. Alicia kept her eyes on her process, and I noticed her hand shook a little bit. A sort of buffet line formed, people's nerves settling down now with something they could physically do. "Looks really good," "I love strawberry cakes," things like that—it was background music accompanying the rustle of feet and clothing; they were all happy to put their attention on the food and away from the honoree, who stood beside me, just holding his cake, watching the throng at the trough. I knew something was about to happen when he silently passed me the little paper plate and strolled back to the island.

"Let me move that stool out of your way. It might trip you, and you might fall and hit your head," he told Richard, who'd got to the front of the line now and stood there haggling with Alicia for a larger piece.

IN ALL MY life I'd never seen a more exquisite, better-executed takedown, a more stunning reveal of intellect and discernment, a more awesome retribution for things done. It made me jealous. I wished Berry could've seen it. Richard stared at Porter as he gently eased the stool out from under the island and brought it tenderly to me, and I sat down and said, "Thank you," and gave his cake to him; and he turned to face me and at last began eating. A second or two; and then James laughed, a deeply appreciative, long laugh that came from the depths of his gut. "Good one, Porter!" he said.

And others chuckled, and Alicia smiled; and there was a tense grin on Richard's face, even; but his eyes narrowed. He ate his cake, glancing our way from time to time, and left early. Mother watched him; if she'd been quilting, the fabric would've shaken with fear at her gaze.

"MOTHER, I WANT to go to the lawyers' office with you tomorrow."

"All right," she said. "I think you should. You're the historian."

She told me when to come by the house to get her.

In the evening I sat in the living room, holding Granny Kate's old Bible on my lap. Superstitiously, I'd laid it there, spread my knees a little, and ordered it to open up where it *should*, where it was *meant* to open, wanting a revelation to appear for me; and it had fallen at Psalm 23, possibly something she'd read a lot, which was why the spine buckled there. But it brought no peace to me. I'd been at a table in the presence of my enemies; no rod and no staff gave me comfort, and I did fear evil. Inside me instead a tenseness grew. It was near the end of February. The days were still short, and cool; I wondered if George was out somewhere tramping around, cold. I could call him; but, no. It was too late for ICU, and a post-mortem wouldn't accomplish anything. I could call Berry; but, no. I'd see him tomorrow, and best not for *both* of us to have to conceal something in a roomful of watchful, analyzing eyes.

22

MOTHER REACHED OUT a claw hand to me from time to time as the lawyers took turns explaining. One of them was there for the closing of the estate; one, for Robert Beck and his purchase, long awaited by these eager people around the oval table.

The claw was for the purpose of clutching at my forearm in much the same way Granny Kate had grabbed Berry's knee that day that seemed so very long ago. It was no more for support now than it had been then.

I tried to stay above it all, removed from the wide, avid eyes as documents passed around. I tried to busy myself with wondering about other things; for instance, how these people, my family if you counted DNA and blood, or not if you didn't, were going to spend their money.

So there we were.

And yet, not all of us. Smith, the estate lawyer, said several cousins had decided to sign their papers in absentia, fax or email them in. I didn't blame them; that would've been my wish.

Mother and Liza found it disrespectful. In their minds this was one duty not to be shirked, the coming forward and facing the relatives as what remained of the matriarch's life was redistributed, the final thing you did for a person who'd passed—just as necessary as spading that dirt in. If you took what was left, you looked each other in the eye as you did it, recognizing you'd done nothing to earn it yourself.

Richard had come in shifting his gaze around, taking in the whole room the way you'd look for the closest exit in a dicey beer joint as he'd sat down heavily next to his brother. I stared straight at him, hoping he'd look away first—you always thought people would, if something shamed them somehow; but he didn't, and, instead, looked right back and let his lips lift at the corners in a sarcastic smile. And I was the one who turned away.

James kept his chin down and his eyes closed: probably praying. Rhonda's head was lowered, too, as if she were joining him in supplication. But I noticed she was either deep in REM sleep or was peeping under her lids to match her physical movement to his; I guessed it was that instead of a nap. June sat next to Richard, scribbling what must've been funny things on a note pad; from time to time they'd snicker a little. Maybe James was praying for his sister to behave herself in this solemn undertaking. His prayers went unanswered.

June would have a boob job, I thought.

Jean Ann wasn't there, not having a stake, yet; but Berry sat on the other side of Liza, intently contemplating a pattern in the wood grain of the table, passing the documents on to Liza, occasionally indicating where she was to sign something.

One of those not here was Porter, nor were his siblings, all of them having taken care of their part of the proceedings earlier in the week, Smith said. They had obligations, Robert Beck's lawyer added, preventing their attendance; but as it was anyway a formality, the being present, none of us need have come, ourselves, although he appreciated those who had.

The matter of Granny Kate's estate was to be quickly dealt with, her documents having been meticulously prepared long ago, Smith told everyone. The papers passed around so that everybody could have a copy if they wished, since they *were* named in the will. It was just a ritual to be completed, Smith said; and we all understood that. Without glancing at them, Mother passed her pages to me. Idly, I flipped through them.

Hamilton, Robert Beck's lawyer, adjured us that the more

important issue was for everyone to sign on the instruments regarding the sale of the property, and everybody's head lifted then.

Dobber would spend all of his on another truck and in six months would wreck it.

Rhonda signed onto the sale documents, passed them to James; he took the pen and laboriously began to add his name where sticky arrows had been affixed. And then Richard turned to a page in his copy of the will.

"It may not be the time to bring this up, but I been thinkin' about these stipulations here."

Berry's head swiveled upward. Liza and James both closed eyes again, almost involuntarily; I didn't think they had time to pray right now. June, sitting between James and Richard, let a sort of amused, scoffing noise blow out through her nose, but she kept her eyes down. And now—why now?—Richard wouldn't look at anybody but the lawyers sitting at the head of the conference table, the two men whose body language showed not a sign of surprise or concern or, really, any emotion at all.

"Which page are you on?" Smith asked calmly.

Richard flipped back to the first one, then turned that, and jabbed at the middle of the next one. "These conditions right here. Once and for all I wanna know if it's legal to say somebody has to do something like that, or they don't get a share of proceeds." He nodded his head at June; I was glad to see she wasn't looking at any of us. She would've been a pile of ashes if she had been, right then.

"James's sis June here knows about the law, works with a lawyer right here in town, and she's told all of us it may not be legal. Like a man sayin' his wife can't marry if she wants to inherit his money when he's gone. Y'all all remember her sayin' it, after our grandma's funeral. You know she did."

Berry seemed to be trying to sand the table down with his forefinger. It was the only part of him that moved. Liza stared at her lap, shaking her head back and forth a little.

"We decided all this that day," James spoke softly.

"No, y'all decided. I said all along we needed to take it to court. Or to find out for sure. But no, you were hellbent on pushin' it along, greedy for the sale and the money. But Dobber and me, we said all along it oughta be thought out more."

Smith and Hamilton were immobile and impassive. "Don't you work in Will Talley's office?" Hamilton asked June. "I believe we've spoken once or twice. I wasn't aware you were a paralegal."

It pleased me that she turned red, got flustered. She didn't answer right away, either.

"She's the receptionist there," Mother said in a flat tone. I could see the needle going through the fabric.

Hamilton seemed to scribble a note on a piece of paper; possibly it was just idle doodling, but it got June's attention: "I don't have a legal degree, but I've helped out from time to time at work."

This time it was Smith scrutinizing her. "I see."

"With copying and things like that. Not with writin' stuff. I don't have a legal degree," she reiterated.

Richard wrote a word or two on the little note pad between him and June; she read, turned it face-down. I lifted the first page of Mother's copy of the will, scanned the next until I found what must've been Richard's focus, where dispositions had been made.

Why hadn't we had a copy of it before today, I wondered. There it was, what Richard referred to: Other than what the two surviving children received, proceeds from the sale of her property would go to the grandchildren; she didn't name them all. Then, three parts were to be held aside for the care and wellbeing of Porter White, the interest off which would be remitted to his conservator who would step forward from the aforementioned grandchildren of his or her own volition; barring that, proceeds from the sale of Katherine White's land would go to said Porter White in entirety, with each remaining grandchild to receive $100 and an item of personal interest from her household.

And she'd suggested one of those items for each person, and the Bible wasn't in the list.

Mother and Liza would receive each one-sixth of the money, or if one or both didn't survive the testator the said Katherine White, their portions would be split—in the case of Jane White Williams—among her heirs; and between Jean Ann Tanner Clark and Calvin Asberry Tanner, in the instance of Eliza White Tanner.

I'd never known he had Cal's name, too. He'd never used it.

Another strong-woman story: She named him and Jean Ann specifically, not as she'd named us, Mother's "heirs"—not as grandchildren, but in plain bequests. She'd taken care of him, in case Jean Ann ever decided not to do that herself; and I bet she'd made sure Liza'd done the same. But there was something about all that page that began making me anxious, made my head swim and my heart race. I couldn't think at the moment, right then, in that room with lawyers and cousins and family not-family, but something wasn't just right; and I didn't think it was what Richard was objecting to as he continued, his voice becoming more belligerent: "This's the part I mean. What would it take to contest that part? Why's three portions going to be held away from the rest of us?"

Smith cleared his throat and didn't flinch from Richard's glare. "It's my understanding that his brother Larry White's agreed to be his conservator. That's an appropriate disposition."

"We just about forced 'im to do it!" Dobber cut in. "Just about had to hold his feet to a fire! Now *he's* the one gettin' all the interest."

"Again, he *is* immediate family, and he—"

"She said 'grandchildren'," Richard interrupted, jabbing at the page. "Says here it's to be left to the grandchildren."

Smith and Hamilton exchanged cool glances. "With the stipulation she added," Smith corrected.

"So what'll keep that goddamned brother from reneging after the money's distributed?"

James moaned softly, shook his head, but Richard plowed on: "That's what I wanna know. If he decides not to take care of 'im anymore, who's gonna collect that interest back? Who'll it go to then? Will the rest of us have to pay back our parts? That ain't right! And I don't think it's legal, neither!"

The table adequately sanded down in front of him, Berry had curled his hand into a fist, and Liza laid her own over it, gently, kind of patting it as Mother had mine on the day of the funeral. I noticed that, kept it in my mind, but the something about that page worried at me, and I knew my breath was coming fast, and people could tell, if they looked. Maybe they'd just think I was mad.

The lawyer Smith raised his eyebrows, looked over his reading glasses. "Do you understand the process of contesting a will, where property of no more than this amount is at stake, do you understand the length of time it might take, and the fees involved? There'd probably have to be consideration also of the testator's, that is your grandmother's competency, her mental state, you know—"

"I know what that is. You don't have to talk down to me."

"My mother was old, but she was in her right mind," Liza whispered, but in the quiet room you could hear it plainly.

"And so I'd testify myself," Smith agreed, "as to her competence, having known her, having helped draw up her will; but it would be another lengthy court matter."

Robert Beck leaned across the table into Richard's face, shook his finger. "And there'll be a breach of contract suit, too!" Hamilton held out a hand in a calm-down manner.

"You tryin' to threaten me?" Richard bellowed. "I ain't afraid of people that's got more money than me! I got as many rights as you do! I'm willin' to push this to get the right thing done! Why should some dim-witted man get it all, ahead of her other family?"

"This's is just like that money goin' to them Rowells up the road," Dobber railed, "you don't know about that, but she let them colored people up the road take property off *her* place and sell it, and it was considerable money, and none of us had any say-so about it, and it was Porter's doin', mostly, he set the whole thing up with 'em, plotted it to cut us out and make us look bad! I've heard of people takin' advantage of their old folks, misusin' their money, abusin' 'em..."

"That's what them dim-witted people do, they scheme and figure out diabolical plans. Amazing they can do that, dim-witted as they are." Berry said it coldly, and I admired his boldness but feared suddenly, for everybody knew Richard always had a gun on him, though possibly these lawyers didn't know it. Richard leaned across the table, and James reached a long, gangly arm behind June and grabbed a handful of Richard's shirt to drag him back.

Smith smiled a little. He picked up the phone on a handsome walnut console behind him. "Tiffany, would you find my file on competency hearing procedures, and I know you're busy, so would you have Ben bring it in here; I didn't see much on his schedule this morning."

"Yes sir," Tiffany said.

Richard was telling Berry how little he cared for him, just not in those words, when the door opened and the file was laid gently in front of Smith; and then James stood up, smiling and holding out his hand, and so did Berry and Rhonda; and Liza wept a little, Mother folded her claw hands together in front of her on the table, her piece completed now, and I couldn't help it—I turned away and reached for the box of Kleenexes I guessed the lawyers always had handy on that console. Ben Rowell spoke to all of us, asked how we'd been, and a good fifteen minutes of lawyers' fees were wasted catching up on old times.

23

I CAUGHT BERRY'S sleeve and told him, quietly, after the papers had been returned to Hamilton, and Smith was also satisfied, "I need you to come by my house after you take your mother home. Please drop mine off, too. Maybe they'll visit together a while, calm each other down. I'm serious. This's important."

After just a few seconds of staring at Ben, Richard had conjured up all the oily unctuousness he could, and grinned, his eyes sparkling, and so did June; but Dobber held back, keeping his mouth in a grim scowl. I respected him for that, for he was consistent, and not so much wicked, like the other two, as merely dim-witted himself. But it was over with, then, whether because Richard knew Ben had something on him from long ago, or even more recently, or because he'd had a chance to do some of his figgering and calculated on losing a great deal of that money if he kept up his objections. In a few moments he'd turned back to the table and scrawled his name on those pages; so did the other two—Dobber after a grimace and a low-voiced curse. Berry gathered Liza and Mother quickly, leaving everybody else to straggle out as they would; it was then that I grabbed his sleeve.

There'd been a final half-hearted suggestion of everybody's meeting at a coffeehouse somewhere, later, a laugh about whether the old-friend-now-lawyer would charge for that. We'd all been happy to run out, away.

I had time to arrange scenery before he arrived, the Bible on the kitchen table so that it would be there, open to those family pages, like the Ark of the Covenant, like the big Bible always open at the Presbyterian church in town...legal testimony, irrefutable; and that will with the first page folded behind, the second on top. I brewed coffee, which I needed.

"Today's not my birthday, though."

Granny Kate would surely have remembered the birth date of the grandson who'd lived with her fifty-something years: That was my hypothesis when I'd come home from Porter's Welcome-Back party last night. So I pulled the Bible down off that shelf and I looked.

It was your standard, dog-eared old Bible with loud-colored illustrations and a family record section situated appropriately enough between the Old and New Testaments. But even in death, Granny Kate surprised me; for a woman who'd gone to such lengths to settle her estate before she died, she'd been sloppy recording family members' birth and marriage dates. "June 9" would be crossed out and rewritten "June 10", and that crossed out, changed back, almost always in ink. Maybe half the birth and marriage records had been corrected somehow. Even Porter's date of birth had been changed once or twice, a day or two different.

Had Porter filled things in for her? But, no: The handwriting was consistent throughout, and, besides, Porter didn't write this way. I'd seen grocery lists he'd made.

I'd turned pages back and forth, hoping for something to spring up, wishing to see revelations penciled in between the lines, family secrets revealed in the end papers. But nobody ever really wrote anything revelatory in a family Bible. It was meant for the stodgy stuff—my genealogy crap, as Berry would say. The sagas and dramas and scandals were told through letters and wills, whispered behind hands.

Not having regular visitors or family that called her very often, maybe Granny Kate had sometimes written what she'd thought was right, only to find out later she'd been off a day or two.

But on the death page, embellished with dignified dark ribbons and drooping lilies, nothing was crossed-out and corrected; everything neatly printed. I knew why: You lived the good news in the moment, soaked it in, savored it with people nearby, heedless of a person out of sight; but we'd been quick to let her know about the bad news, the deaths, expected her presence even, as reassurance of a continuity in a cold world. Others died, and we hastened to the All-Mother to tell her, to be certain she was still alive.

She'd stuffed the printed obituaries in the end pages as receipts: The death dates were all accurate.

I heard his car, and poured two mugs of coffee, unlocked the door. He let himself in, picked up his mug, gestured at the Bible. "So, we having prayer meeting?"

"We need it. We just escaped a catastrophe. One could still happen."

"It *was* pretty awful. But it's over. No catastrophe in the near future. I see you've decided to do something to the house at last. Trying to blind me with godawful gaudiness now. I like it."

"Yeah..." I glanced around at the horrible yellow walls, the stiff artificial sunflowers plastered up as curtains.

"This why George left? Don't blame him."

That was mildly funny; I offered him a short laugh to show my appreciation, but no witty riposte came to me, and I just motioned for him to sit down at the table, which he did, shrugging. At Smith's office he'd seemed to try to erase the table with his forefinger—now, gently, as if reading Braille, as if finding words I couldn't see, he ran that finger over the page I had open, the old family records. Partaking of the elements of the last supper.

"I missed you at Porter's soiree yesterday. You'd have loved it. Many laughs."

"I just bet. Yeah, that would've been the last straw, though. Didn't have to do that; did have to be there for my mother today."

I stood with my back to the sink and drank from my mug, waiting for what I didn't know, for him to figure it out on his own, and then come up with a brilliant solution? The coffee was doing neither of us any good. It seemed unless I said something, we'd just hold our warming stones in our hands and hunch over like old people pondering our past. Which we were: We were old people pondering our past.

"So what's Liza going to spend her money on?" It was meant to be funny, but he raised his brows as if I'd insulted him. "Look, I tried to take my mind off everything this morning by wondering how everybody'd spend their inheritance."

"Mama told me long ago she had no need for anything—she has a good enough car, enough money to live on, her house is basically where she wants to live the rest of her life. She's probably gonna let that money sit for me and Jean Ann. And before you ask: She's got that fixed up already. She did tell me that part on Christmas Day." He grimaced. "I didn't ask. She just felt obligated to tell me, I guess. In light of the other."

"Did you, did you actually have a DNA test?" I hadn't meant to ask that, but I wanted to know.

"Yep. I did. It'll give you a list of near relatives if you want 'em. Go on and have a laugh about that if you like. But it was all those letters you gave me that made me do it. I'd've never even considered, never thought… So all that genealogy crap of yours was important, after all." He finished off the coffee in a long guzzle, handed me the mug for more. "DNA. That wasn't how I found out about Katelyn, either, by the way. My daughter." He looked up at me suddenly, shook his head. "Not my daughter, but I thought for a while she was. Couple of months. Then Leigh told me she wanted to be somewhere else, that Katelyn wasn't connected to me, anyway, so that part'd be easy. Easy. And that was it. Your mother ever tell you?"

"No. Not all that. And you didn't have to. It's not my business."

He scoffed. "Yeah. We're not family, either, not that close. Look…about that time I was here, before Christmas…"

"Forget it. I knew what it was, then. It's okay."

Mother threw things around when she didn't want to face me, when she was afraid I'd see she wasn't being a strong woman right then—spoons clattering into my sink here not too long ago; potato salad splattered around when Aunt Sabrina got snarky with her. I turned away to slosh the remaining dregs of my coffee down the drain, twisted the spigot so that a torrent washed everything out. So that he couldn't see I wasn't a strong woman right then. He left me alone for half a minute.

"Would you please look over that part right there," I said, facing him again, wiping the counter top with a paper towel. "See what you think. It's why I asked you to stop by."

He had no luck, because he hadn't been to the party yesterday, because he was maybe thinking of too many other things right now; so like Mother I made a scornful noise and stalked to the table, took one page and pointed, and another and pointed. All he said, softly, was, "Holy shit."

LATER HE WAS more eloquent: "So there are other little bastards running around here, to use Richard's way of putting it."

When he left for his own home, I fidgeted with the Bible, swishing the pages back and forth like a deck of cards in the somber stillness. They made the sound of leaves falling from a

sweetgum tree in the dead of fall, a heavy breeze, cold, wet air. I
turned them all and then closed the thick book.

We devised a strategy, texted and emailed back and forth about
it. It gave me something to do while the early spring storms and
tornado watches blew through the county, something to do as I
learned the art of being alone, as if I hadn't already known.

I wanted to be the one who talked to Hazel Rowell. I knew the
methods by which Mother laid her war plans and all the levers of
power she pulled, and I would use those on Hazel, I plotted. She'd
be able to say for sure what I needed to know. She'd helped
Granny Kate with Porter, when he'd been a sickly baby with colic
and childhood measles and other things. I would take Mother and
go see her under false pretenses, I told Berry, trying to quell the
feeling of nausea that thought inflicted on my stomach.

"You look forward to bullying her?" Berry asked me.

No, I did not. "Do you?"

"Here's the thing: Your mother won't ever go with you up
there, because she's sharp, she'll know right off what you're doing.
But Liza'll go with *me*, out of duty to me. You know I'm right." I
noticed he didn't call her "Mama" today.

"You know I'm right," he insisted again when I didn't say
anything. "By yourself, you'll never be mean enough to find out
anything from her, and your mother'll haul your ass out of there if
you even try. But Liza'll go with me, and the two of 'em'll end up
letting it slip, if I ask the right stuff."

"You believe she knows, already?"

He turned cynical eyes on me. "You doubt they both know how
to keep secrets?"

We argued for a while about it, and eventually he said, as if he
were a hit man doing a paid-for execution, "I'll do Hazel. You try
seeing what your mother'll tell you. Mine came clean when I
showed her those letters and my test results. If you just tell your
mother now, she might fold. Don't know till you try."

I USED THE key they'd given me some years back, the one I was
to keep just *in case*, and unlocked and opened the front door,
determined to catch her off guard, to use *her* tactics. She'd been
quilting again; Dad was watching TV. I caught the tail-end of a
comment about the unacceptable length of her stitches as I swung
the door inward. They stiffened, they took the posture of people

who expected to be given bad news and had to buck up for it.

"Nothing's wrong," I said. "Just here for a visit."

It had rained on me again on the way out, the smooth asphalt hissing again, warning me; it always seemed to have rained or to be about to rain when I drove up country. I draped my coat over a kitchen chair and put a towel on the floor under it. Mother sat assessing me once again, and I thought maybe I shouldn't have flung that door wide; it was an unnecessary show of force too early. The thread was taut, tense from her needle down to the fabric. Suddenly she stabbed the pattern and removed her thimbles.

"I don't believe you. I know you better than that. So what is it this time?"

I'd only fired a shot across the bow, but she'd just answered with a barrage straight at me.

Obviously distressed at this turn of conversation, Dad hurried out of the room through the swinging door, alarm on his face, saying he'd get us something to drink. So the victory was hers: I knew I'd better find out while he was still in the kitchen.

"I know about Porter. I know he's not Everett's son."

She pursed her lips for a moment. "You have to forget that."

So Berry was right, and the feint had been successful. Families held so many secrets, so much you might never discover unless you got lucky with the right question, or you asked a person who took truthfulness seriously. So that afternoon I found out a great many things. "When your Aunt Sabrina had to be dried out and was in the asylum for a while—didn't you know that?" she asked when my jaw dropped—"didn't you figure it out, when she claimed to go on that bus tour up to New England, she was really down at Hattiesburg in the asylum? Everybody else knew it. I went with your daddy to see about her a few times. Those folks that worked there would let me see Pauline, too. She didn't know me from Adam anymore. So she'd just tell me whatever came to her head. Including about Porter. It was a sad thing."

"Did you ever talk to Granny Kate about it?"

"Why would I do that? Havin' to worry about it gettin' out and who else might know. She probably knew anyway. I didn't ask her. If she wanted to claim him all this time as a grandson, I don't figger it's any business of ours. It don't bother me. She felt guilty about not watching over Pauline better. And it helped him and give him a normal life. He might not've had one otherwise."

"He might've been helped more if he *hadn't* lived with her."

"Maybe, maybe not. They didn't use to know how to help people like him, like they do now."

We heard ice cubes falling into glasses.

"You know it," I said, "and Hazel knows. Berry thinks Liza knows."

"Of course she does. We had to get things figured out—" She stopped there, pursed her lips, something held tightly inside that mouth.

"And you didn't want your mama to have to take care of any of them, in the first place—am I right?"

It spilled out through her tight mouth the way a ventriloquist speaks—she didn't want to say it, didn't want the words to be hers, but there they were: "She'd raised us, she'd already had enough hard times."

Another thing that "came between" you and Liza, I thought— *Liza saw need, you saw it as unasked-for obligation.* But I wouldn't say it. She'd probably had to reconcile all that in her own conscience before now.

Instead, I went on: "Well, anyway, you know, and Liza, and Hazel. Others might. Everybody might. Anne and Marcus and Larry. Larry's the oldest. He might've figured it out; would he've told the others sometime?" I'd always viewed Porter separately, as if he were unconnected from his siblings, somehow. "It would mean he'd put it together with the date of when Everett died." I stopped, but she gave me a sharp look and went on with my thought:

"...And wondering if they were still livin' together as man and wife."

That phrase again, instead of just saying, "sleeping together." I asked: "So were they? Doing that?"

"No." Firm. And don't ask me again.

"How do you know?"

"She'd been put back into the place there. She had an episode. And he was in his death bed."

The glasses clinked on the countertop in the kitchen. "Any one of the other three could've said something that day."

"But they didn't. And that ought to make you think better of them. They know their mama'd want him treated right, if she could have a say. So if they do know, it looks to me like they've made their peace with it."

Dad burst back into the room with the tea.

She got up carefully from her chair—I remembered suddenly that cold aggravated her arthritis. Strange how you'd just forget some things when you didn't really want to think about them. She wore a thick robe over that old purple sweat suit, though the heater was on. The robe swirled around as she moved, and I remembered her yanking me up and patting out hot flames, wrapping her arms around me, ornery and uptight and protective. Or had that been a dream?

She didn't quilt placidly, but resentfully, impatiently, as if it had been assigned to her; how she sat and did it all the time was beyond me...mindless work just to pass the moments, as far as I could see.

I thanked Dad for the iced tea and yanked on a quilt corner, trying to find the name, twisting the heavy piece about in the frame. "Who's this one for?"

She jerked it back and gave me a defiant look. "Let it be. You'll tear the stitches."

"Couldn't do anything but help 'em," Dad snickered.

She made a soft scornful sound at that. "I haven't made up my mind yet. Who doesn't have one? You think Berry could use it?"

BERRY: HIS JOB was more abominable. He strong-armed Liza into going with him as he said he would. "Confirmation," he'd told me. "There's gotta be confirmation. I'll convince her we're just there to visit. She'll realize that if Mama's with me, she already knows. I'll just ask her the way you did your mother."

And so it happened.

He emailed me about the whole visit—it was like that letter, more formal than just a text, with more care put into choosing the words. Liza was nervous as he drove, he said, gave him reasons why they shouldn't impose on Hazel—"She suspected, I'm sure"—and, when they got there, took a soft recliner and picked at the fabric on the arms, plucking at it as if she saw things crawling. Hazel offered them home-baked apple tart, which he took but Liza turned down. Hazel put him in one of the cane-bottom chairs because, she said, she knew he'd be glad to see them being used. It was the opening he'd waited for: "You know we had to keep it a secret that day, about where these chairs ended up," he said to her.

"The Lord will do the judging," she answered, and so he went on:

"Keeping secrets's fine and dandy, but some of 'em could end up a problem." Liza fidgeted. Hazel stared at her a long moment, he said; and he waited it out; and, still watching Liza, Hazel must've decided he knew, and shook her head sadly, and told him, just like that: Porter's cord hadn't even healed when Granny Kate got him. Hazel knew he wasn't any three-month-old baby; he *was* a newborn. He'd arrived a good half-year after Everett died.

I read that email and felt the nauseating drop in my stomach again, grasped for any bits of explanatory flotsam that might lift me out of the deep water I'd fallen into: That meant he could still have been Everett's child, I emailed. We'd both been told through the years that Pauline had sometimes shared a bed with Everett even after being institutionalized. It was the sort of family lore you were shocked about but loved running through your mind, like reading over and over parts of a racy novel, just the idea that, even in the depths of fatal disease and insanity, you could still be a slave to lust—that would be how Mother would've phrased it: a slave to lust.

But in just a few seconds my phone buzzed with his response, a text: ***Mama said Everett was bedridden the last two or so months he lived,*** and I couldn't argue with that. I'd heard that all my life. Eventually, he sent me the one question I couldn't answer: ***So you think we should make him get a DNA, too, find out for sure?*** I knew it wasn't a true question, though; it was a challenge, and not one I wanted to answer.

Delete all these texts and emails, he said, at last. It would've been better if you'd just burned those other letters and pictures last year, too.

SO THE TALE of Porter's genealogy was affirmed; it was our burden now. While the others looked over their checking account deposits and considered what to spend their inheritance on, Berry and I decided how to conceal a secret we didn't even know for sure *was* a secret to anybody.

We talked on the phone about it, no texts or emails, and compared the dreadful possibilities that came to us in dreams as we tried to sleep.

Granny Kate, knowingly or otherwise, had fixed it so we had to decide the same damned things the others had had to, in a way: whether to redistribute the money, and who was responsible for Porter. It was one of those problems in ethics, Berry told me in one phone call, character-building shit that schools used to do: five people in a four-man lifeboat, one an old lady, one disabled, and who do you throw out to save the rest? and at the end you frustrated the kids by telling them there was no right answer. There were all bad answers, answers nobody wanted to be responsible for.

He'd once even had his classroom teachers do it at the last-chance school he'd helmed; and it turned into a *Lord of the Flies* thing, with some kids metamorphosing into Richards, eyes agleam as they cast lots to decide who was least valuable and could be tossed overboard. Berry'd ordered the exercise abandoned after the one time.

I told him about that panic attack at Smith's office, where he'd been so busy trying to rub out the wood grain that he hadn't even seen my struggle. The will said the money was to go "to the grandchildren." We wondered if there was a case that since she didn't make a special bequest to Porter, naming him as she did Jean Ann and Berry, he might not have a right to more than just one part, or maybe even anything, if the wrong person learned about Pauline. But wouldn't it count that she *considered* him a grandchild, even though he wasn't, really? His name *was* mentioned in the will as a person whose life was to be administered, and conditions imposed on how one of them might qualify for the job. But anyway, the checks were cashed, and what was that old thing: possession being nine-tenths of the law?

We talked about asking a lawyer. Was Smith aware of Porter's circumstances? Robert Beck had been deep in Granny Kate's confidences; but perhaps he was someone who'd tell the wrong person, accidentally, maybe, and it would get out and everybody else would know.... And Porter's money was in a conservatorship. *Could* it be handed back over?

And why'd she give him that very Biblical portion James admired? We agonized over that through the rest of March. Had she *made* Porter stay with her so she could remain independent herself? Had she felt guilt huge enough so she thought he deserved restitution after she passed? It was an awful thing to contemplate about the grandmother you'd made a graven image of.

He drove over one afternoon while I was repainting the kitchen. It had felt indecent to leave it yellow, a reminder of the final failure; and was I really going to stay in it myself, now? And if I wasn't, then it would be better to make it bland again, for a sale...so my thoughts went. Yet the truth was there, and I must accept it—that it hadn't been home, really, all those years, anyway, and neither yellow nor vanilla paint would have made it one.

I finished as he watched, understanding, not commenting. Then we rehashed all the arguments and legal theories and suspicions, and then there was nothing else to say. We were tired of it. We'd always be looking over our shoulders, for we could never tell anything about any of it. As Berry said, maybe everybody knew anyway and was content to keep the matter quiet. Maybe their better angels had swooped down and beat the shit out of them along with the greed. We laughed, grimly, saying that, both remembering the last time we'd spoken those particular words..."better angels." We sat and inhaled paint fumes; we were used up, spent, our energy poured out on the sand.

"I got another story in mind, working on it; you gave me the idea the day the will was wrapped up. 'How They Spent the Money.' I'll be doing research for a while. How long you think it'll take them to go through thirty-five grand? Couple of months, at least? And when I drop it, think they'll be mad at me again?"

"Mother says you wouldn't have anything to write about if you weren't who you are, after all these years, if you hadn't been raised here."

He laughed, his eyes wide. "By God, she's right! So you see I'll always be going back to Conjure Hill one way or another, whether I actually, physically, go or not."

"Berry, who was the baby?" —There it was, the question he'd bought that map for, hoping it would deliver an answer, like things written in invisible ink slowly materializing in the sunlight at the top of a hill, or in a golden haze glancing off quiet ripples of a creek with an ancient bridge over it. I wanted an answer now. Or maybe I believed I did.

He gazed at the renewed vanilla walls. "I don't know. Doubt we ever will know. Hazel changed the subject when I mentioned that, and Mama was already about to strangle me, so I stopped. I don't think Robert Beck knows, nor Edwin. I think he believes what she said...you remember what she said: She had no idea why it was there. That's what she told him." He shook his head in admiration. "And it was the truth, exactly. She had no idea why it was *there*—at the creek. And nobody asked anything else. And if Edwin does have doubts about that, well, he'll keep them to himself.

"But here's my theory: I think Pauline may've had another baby at that place, after Porter came to Granny Kate. God knows somebody took advantage of her there for him to be in this world; it could've still been happening. Maybe whoever did it figured they'd got by with it once, that being Porter, and nobody'd done anything. Maybe they figured she was just another discarded person, a woman nobody was going to worry too much about."

"A thrown-away paper sack," I muttered, remembering the man waiting on Mother's back porch, watching dead leaves flap around in a cold damp breeze.

Berry turned to regard me solemnly. "I said we'd probably never know. But if we looked hard enough, I bet we'd find a record of a stillbirth. I bet it would say the body was released to Granny Kate's custody."

"Can they do that?"

"Don't know about now. They used to be able to. Didn't have to embalm a body if you buried it quick, in twenty-four hours. You could even get permission to bury it on private land."

"I know she couldn't say anything about Porter, obviously, but she could've told about *that* baby, it being Pauline's, so when it washed up last year, nobody would've been surprised."

He scoffed. "Eventually they'd wonder, well, she had one there, what about Porter, earlier. Nope. She couldn't let 'em know about the other one. But she could see it didn't happen again. And everybody knew Pauline got better treatment at some point. Granny Kate probably threw a fit, threatened to sue." He took his coffee cup to the sink. "You want to look it up?" His eyes were sad.

"No."

"Me neither. At least that baby's where it won't be bothered again." He took his phone, pulled up a photo. At first I couldn't understand what it was—just a square, flat thing surrounded by dirt. He zoomed the picture, and I could make out the words: "Gone, Not Forgotten," carved into a plain sheet of inexpensive marble.

"That was nice of you," I said.

"Yeah, it would've been, right? I didn't do it. I should've. It says much about me, I think, that though I knew, I didn't do it." His own words had gone formal again. I raised my brows.

"Larry," he said quietly. "He didn't tell me. I asked the right people and found out. He did better than we did. Exactly the proper thing to put on it."

In a moment I said it, what I'd been thinking the whole time: "Do we get rid of the Bible?"

He leaned into my face, his nose almost touching mine. "What Bible? Oh, you mean the one you brought to the old house to show everybody last time we were there, with your notebooks and albums; but you left it, accidentally, in all the uproar. You mean the one that got burned up when somebody set a fire that night."

"What? No. You gave it to me later, I didn't have—"

"Yes, you did," he interrupted. "I sent it to you way back after her funeral. You know. I took Jean Ann's advice about it not belonging to me, and I overnighted it to you, and you brought it to the old house that day Richard and I fought, and it burned up. And nobody can say otherwise, because how would they know it *wasn't* there unless they went back after everybody else left. And why would they do *that* unless they were up to no good. See, I've learned from Richard to hold some ammunition back." And he waited a little while, and so did I, considering the right answer.

"That Bible. Yes."

"Good thing it's already gone, huh."

He left, and it was the last time we spoke about it. It was as if the baby had passed through the world, and nobody knew; gone, and nobody remembered.

24

LARRY DECIDED IT was time for Porter to drive, now that he seemed so calm—and *was*, at least in a way—and since he already knew the basics, had been driving Granny Kate to Liza's or Hazel's or to church for some years. Larry took him out on the four-lane, and he learned very quickly. But Larry wouldn't let him drive by himself, and it must have been frustrating for a man that age to be treated so.

Porter wanted to go to the quick stop one day, out on the big highway; and so of course he was to be chaperoned—it was a given. When he cranked the old car Larry had picked out for him, and which he insisted Porter keep in Larry's new garage so he always knew where it was, and started to back it out (this part Alicia told—she'd just glanced out the window), Porter looked past him all of a sudden with a flash of the old secret grin and kind of jerked the wheel to one side and tore down half the far wall, bricks and all. They fell over Larry's side of the car, and there he sat, Alicia said, screaming like a banshee while Porter put the transmission back into drive and did the same thing again, with the same results.

Was it an accident? Did he remember about Jean Ann and Bob, and plan it out ahead of time?

He calmly suggested that, as he had plenty of money, albeit in a trusteeship, he could pay for the damage. He apologized, said maybe Larry should just let him take his own risks and drive alone so he didn't endanger anybody else. The whole thing ate up several thousand dollars, not counting the damage to the car, but, after all, it was his car, and he sold it for scrap and found another pretty good used one.

After he got his money, Richard seemed relaxed for a while, showing up at the Wagonwheel, sometimes paying for Edwin's meal, waving as he left the place; although through time he developed a little twitch at his shoulders, a tic, if you will, as if he'd toted something heavy a long time that kept his muscles aching. Arthritis, he said. It ran in the family.

Whatever Dobber did with his share of the money, it never showed. But Berry even told *that*, eventually, as he said he would, and to the delight of several hundred thousand readers. Dobber, he wrote, just let the left side of his hair grow out longer and longer to cover the spreading bald spot on top, and kept skidding around the roads in his old truck with the rebel flag decal that covered the back window and a bumper-sticker that swore somebody'd have to pry his cold dead fingers off his gun, and we were sure somebody eventually would.

June spent most of her part as a down-payment on a used Mercedes-Benz. She said legal people were expected to have nice cars to show off, prove their prosperity and full client list; and then she began wearing startlingly filled-out, low-cut blouses, so I figured I'd been right, that day the will was settled.

James Preacher invested his money promoting himself as the lead singer of a gospel-music group he organized and named the Doves of Peace. They made a couple of CDs. The local deejays play them once in a while.

Jean Ann had always fought with Berry, and was too proud of it to quit now, still nagging him about the story he'd written about her and her car. But if anybody disparaged him in her presence, she'd just stare them down and pat her purse; she carried a gun around, too.

SOMETIMES I LIKE to drive by what is now indisputably Robert Beck's land—no longer Granny Kate's, as the house and the chicken coop and the privy are all gone and seedling pines thriving in the soil near the road, those pines being his statement of ownership and existence in the world as the weathered gray siding had been hers.

In my mind I try to see her carrying under one arm a small stout box, not heavy, the contents of which shift a bit now and then, crocheted edging disarranging itself on the dress that clothes a small thing inside, as she moves awkwardly through the woods with a spade under the other arm and goes about completing a distasteful task. It might be night, or it might be day, but Porter would be left in Miss Hazel's care, along with Anne and Larry and Marcus. "I have to properly take care of this myself," she would've told Hazel, and Hazel would've understood and agreed. Granny Kate finds some spot, not a previously-planned one, but one that seems convenient at the moment, because maybe the soil is soft there; and she sets the box down neither gently nor roughly, but dispassionately, because in it is carbon and protein, and begins to shovel dirt aside. And she stops when the cavity seems deep enough or when she's too exhausted to continue alone, a tired older woman doing something somebody else should've properly took care of. And she turns at last when the box is however deep she manages to inter it, and she cleans the spade by knocking it against a nearby tree and goes home, not with the self-indulgently sentimental emotions Berry or I could afford but with relief that nobody but Hazel, her best friend, knew what she's had to do.

In my mind I see her doing this; I envision it the way I

would've, sitting on a front stoop in summer near-dark, as my father embroidered the story.

IN A SUDDEN burst of energy, it being an election year, the county supervisors got around to paving all the remaining dirt roads they could find, ironing a nice, flat little veneer of asphalt over the old ruts, making journeys easy and quick and clean and unemotional. When it was time to do the old road by Granny Kate's place, they straightened out the half-C at the hill a little, so you didn't even have to slow down as you descended, and you forgot eventually how difficult a passage it was, once. I drive by the houseplace and fly up the hill now and wave at Miss Hazel if she's outside.

Or I did, until one day when, like the sweeping lady, she was no longer there to wave back. Berry and I went, together, to her funeral, noting that June and Dobber didn't attend—although Richard did—but of course Liza and Mother and Dad were there, and Edwin, and some of our cousins; Sandra even brought Amy. But now Amy was eighteen and had outgrown those visits with me, having her own car, able to take herself wherever she wanted to go when she needed to get away from home. And as we were leaving the cemetery, there was Joe Miles, white-haired like Liza, his face covered with a full beard; and I wouldn't have recognized him at all if it hadn't been for Mother calling his name. He shook Edwin Bonner's hand like any other old friend, walked over and explained to Mother's questions that he'd been in Milwaukee all those years, and she turned and actually cackled, eerily like Granny Kate, I thought, and took Berry's arm in one of those strong pinches she could immobilize you with. Joe laughed, too, though it was right there in the graveyard, and said, "So, Asberry, they tell me you used to think I was thrown down a well, or something! It just looks to me like the two of us both left these parts, yet here you are, back, after all!"

I asked Mother one day why it was Conjure Hill—was it something mystical, a name bequeathed by an itinerant poet or a departing Choctaw, or was it just that there were people living here sometime by that name or a similar name misspelled, people who decided in human arrogance that they owned it, a hill? and she gave me the same kind of look she did that night after the funeral and finally said she couldn't remember; what did I think, I could try to find out some day if I really wanted to.

Berry will not let me drive us together anywhere lest I take him past the old place as a captive passenger; he will never go back, he says, and I don't know if he ever goes alone, when I'm not with him. He likes to remember it from the day we stood at the top of Conjure Hill and looked down upon the homestead in its desolation. But I keep the Bible on one of our end tables to remind me of the money he or I—one of us—could have made on a good story we never wrote.

ABOUT THE AUTHOR

SJ Alawine is a musician and artist, writer and mother of four of the smartest women she knows. All the things she learned in her life were informed by the reality that they came through her tough carpenter grandmother; and her stronger-than-steel mother who had the grit to give her a name not common in the Deep South at the time she was born; and all other women who stepped into the middle of family disasters and fistfights and griefs and gave succor.